T0030777

Praise for the novels of C. ___ ___ C. Higgins

"Triumphantly Black, queer and contemporary. Magic...the dialogue snaps and shimmers."

—*New York Times Book Review*
on *D'Vaughn and Kris Plan a Wedding*

"In a romance featuring Black joy, plus-sized beauty, and Mexican pride, the conflicts are entirely believable, and not overly dramatic, and make for a thoroughly enjoyable read. It is fake dating at its best."

—*Library Journal*, starred review,
on *D'Vaughn and Kris Plan a Wedding*

"A beautiful distillation of the ways love can come if you simply open your heart, your arms, and fall, trusting the other person to hold on while they fall alongside you."

—*Entertainment Weekly* on *D'Vaughn and Kris Plan a Wedding*

"Funny, angsty, and sexy—the fake-dating-trope trifecta."

—*Self* on *D'Vaughn and Kris Plan a Wedding*

"The story strikes the perfect balance for its subgenre, reflecting queer people's authentic experiences while keeping the mood light and frothy. Higgins gives world-weary readers looking for an inclusive and thoroughly enjoyable escape exactly what they need."

—*Publishers Weekly* on *D'Vaughn and Kris Plan a Wedding*

Also available from Chencia C. Higgins and Carina Press

D'Vaughn and Kris Plan a Wedding

Also by Chencia C. Higgins

Her & Them, An Illicit Seduction
To Buy a Vow
To Build a Vow
To Break a Vow
Things Hoped For
Janine: His True Alpha
Lenora: His Omega Mate
Alicia: His Troublesome Fate
Benefriends
Beyond Benefriends

A LITTLE KISSING BETWEEN FRIENDS

CHENCIA C. HIGGINS

If you purchased this book without a cover you should be aware that this book is stolen property. It was reported as "unsold and destroyed" to the publisher, and neither the author nor the publisher has received any payment for this "stripped book."

carina press®

ISBN-13: 978-1-335-50821-8

A Little Kissing Between Friends

Copyright © 2024 by Chencia C. Higgins

All rights reserved. No part of this book may be used or reproduced in any manner whatsoever without written permission.

Without limiting the author's and publisher's exclusive rights, any unauthorized use of this publication to train generative artificial intelligence (AI) technologies is expressly prohibited.

This is a work of fiction. Names, characters, places and incidents are either the product of the author's imagination or are used fictitiously. Any resemblance to actual persons, living or dead, businesses, companies, events or locales is entirely coincidental.

For questions and comments about the quality of this book, please contact us at CustomerService@Harlequin.com.

® is a trademark of Harlequin Enterprises ULC.

Carina Press
22 Adelaide St. West, 41st Floor
Toronto, Ontario M5H 4E3, Canada
www.CarinaPress.com

Printed in U.S.A.

Recycling programs
for this product may
not exist in your area.

To my bisexy and pansexy babies.
Your identity isn't determined
by how your relationship presents.

Chapter One

Cyn

Board Bully

Let my daddy tell it, I came out the womb with rhythm, and if you really get him to talking about it, he'll tell you that my first cry was the sweetest staccato his ears had ever been blessed to witness. He'll say that he knew—even then—that I was destined to be a musician, and that it was no surprise to him when I began showing a propensity for recognizing notes and immediately playing them back on the various instruments crowded in the front room of our home from his years in a band way back before he met my mama. While other babies and toddlers were banging on pots in the middle of the kitchen, Marvin Thomas had me mashing on the pedal of a bass drum and plucking at the strings on an electric guitar. Although both of my brothers were musically inclined, the art of making music was only shared between me and my daddy. It was *our* thing. He instilled in me a deep respect for composing and gave me room to allow music to just…be.

And then, on my tenth birthday, he presented me with a drum machine, and that's when everything changed for me.

Creating became an integral part of my day. It became a part of me, making up the foundation of who I was. Being a musician was who I was just as much as being a lesbian was, though I knew music sooner than I realized my sexuality. With music at the heart of our bond, it came as no surprise to any-one, let alone my mama, that I was a daddy's girl. And because my daddy and I were so close, he was the first person to know the most important revelation. I was nine when I came home from a long, draining day of being a fourth grader and rushed through my homework to meet him in the front room.

That was our routine. Before I could lay hands on a single instrument, I had to finish my tasks and check with my mama to see if she needed help with dinner. The rules were the same for my brothers, and oftentimes I would check in with my mama to find that Caleb was already chopping vegetables or sifting flour.

We were tuning the guitars when I spoke up.

"Daddy," I said.

"What is it, Star Shine?"

Star Shine was the nickname he'd given me at my infancy. He always said that my mama was the sun in his solar system and I was the brightest star. It was the only way he addressed me, and it brought a smile to my face whenever I heard him say it.

"I got in a fight at recess today."

In my peripheral, I watched as he stopped twisting a tuner and looked at me.

"Who did you fight?"

Sighing, I stared at the guitar across my lap. I didn't want to look at him because I could already hear the disappointment in his tone.

"Britney Berry. She's a girl in my class."

"Why were you fighting?"

"Because she's stupid," I muttered, kicking my foot against the carpet.

"*Excuse me?*"

When he infused bass into his voice, I knew he wasn't accepting any nonsense from me. In the Thomas household, using the word *stupid* was a capital offense. I should've known better, but I wasn't thinking.

Eyebrow quirked, he gave me a firm stare. "Do you want to try that again, little girl?"

Nodding, I lifted the guitar from my lap and placed it on its stand. Then I went to stand in front of my father as I explained everything.

"Today is Britney Berry's birthday and she wore a really pretty dress to school. I told her that her dress was really pretty and she said thank you. And her hair was in these braids with beads on the ends that were the same color as her dress, so I told her that her hair was pretty too."

"Did she say thank you that time?"

I nodded. My daddy was always big on manners. "She did! So then we were in line to get on the monkey bars and she was in front of me, but then she turned around and asked me if I want to be her girlfriend! And I said no!"

"You said no?!" His eyebrows had shot up and he looked perplexed.

I offered another vigorous nod. "I said no, Daddy! Because Reina from Mr. Williams's class had already asked me to be her girlfriend at recess on Monday, and remember when you told Caleb that he could only have one girlfriend at a time, Daddy? Well, I told Britney Berry that you said that and that's why I couldn't be her girlfriend."

Daddy sat back on his stool and stroked his chin. "Well, what did she say when you told her that?"

I took a deep breath. "She said I was lying!"

"She what?" His voice rose, the show of outrage fueling me.

"*She said I was lying, Daddy!* But I wasn't, so I told her that she could ask Reina herself, so we went and found Reina on the jungle gym. She was hanging upside down and her braids looked like the beaded curtain at Nana's house. So then Britney Berry asked her if I was her girlfriend and Reina dropped down from the top, and it was really cool because she did a back flip, and when she stood up, she flipped her hair back over her head and she told Britney Berry that I was her girlfriend. And then she kissed my cheek."

"She *kissed* you?"

"Yeah, Daddy. On the cheek." Tapping my cheek, I took another breath and got to the point. "*So then*, Britney Berry got mad and pushed Reina down and then told me I wasn't invited to her birthday party anymore. And that made *me* mad because she was having it at Celebration Station and Mommy had already sent the r-s-v-p that I was going, *and* we bought her a gift and everything! Actually, it was *two* gifts, because we bought her a Barbie *and* a Ken!"

Daddy tilted his head to the side. "And what did you do when you got mad, Star Shine?"

"Well…" I rubbed my hands against my thighs, using the denim to dry the sudden dampness on my palms. Shrugging, I bounced my eyes around the room as I stated, "I pushed her."

The room was quiet for a moment, long enough for me to realize that it was serious. The front room was never quiet. There was always some sort of noise emitting from one of the instruments, or the metronome, or the hum of the amp. But this time, everything had gone silent, as if every particle in that room had bated breath while we waited for my daddy's reaction. Marvin Thomas was a lot of things, but a violent man was not one of them. He was the epitome of being a lover, not a fighter, and because of that, he'd always tried to impress upon me and my brothers the importance of problem solving without raising our fists.

Unfortunately, the other half of our DNA derived from a woman who was known as Killa Carissa around her neighborhood. Carissa Thomas née Woodson would whoop a trick just for staring at her too long, and me, Caleb, and Cody definitely took after her in that vein, fighting like cats and dogs throughout our childhood and teenage years.

"What happened then?" asked my daddy.

"*Well*, after I pushed Britney Berry, she pushed me back and then we started wrestling. Then Reina ran to get Mr. Williams and he put us in time out for the rest of recess."

"I didn't get any calls from the school today," he mused, rubbing at his chin thoughtfully.

"I think Mr. Williams gave Mommy a paper about it when she came to pick me up, because she asked me why me and Britney Berry were fighting and I told her that Britney Berry had uninvited me to her birthday party, but I didn't tell her why. That's when she said she didn't know what to do with me."

"So she sent you to me."

I nodded, even though it wasn't a question.

"You know what I'm going to tell you, don't you?"

"Yes, sir."

"Good. So, tell me all of the things you could have done with that anger instead of pushing Britney."

"Britney Berry, Daddy. We have four Britneys in our class, so you have to say her whole name so everyone can know who we're talking about."

"Okay, Star Shine. What could you have done with that anger instead of pushing Britney Berry?"

Releasing a long-suffering sigh, I dropped back down onto my stool. "I could've gone for a walk or run."

Nodding, he pointed across the room. "Mmhm. Pick up that guitar and finish tuning it while you talk."

Doing as he said, I cradled the heavy instrument in my lap and rattled off a list of ways I could have managed my emotions. It was a list Daddy had ran down for me and my brothers countless times. He always said that he made us recite the list to him so that when we were in situations with heightened emotions, at least one alternative reaction would likely pop into our head and we could make better choices. It didn't occur to me then, but years later, I realized that in that moment—my *coming out*—my father had chosen to focus on my bad behavior instead of the possibly jarring news that his only daughter had a girlfriend in the fourth grade. He normalized it by not spotlighting it, and when I was old enough to learn how that usually went for many people, the memory of that moment stuck with me forever.

I hadn't even questioned whether or not to tell him the whole story. Where Mommy might've fussed at me, I knew that my daddy would hear me out first and tell me what I did wrong without making me feel bad. It was the way he was with everything, especially music. Whenever I made something new, he was the first person I went to, my stomach knotted in anticipation as I watched his face intently while he absorbed my creation.

Twenty-three years after receiving that drum machine, I still experienced butterflies in my belly when I got ready to play new music for someone. It wasn't nerves, not really. That's just how deep the love that I had for what I did was. It was excitement. Pure, unfettered exhilaration fluttered around inside of me ahead of the aural perfection that I was preparing to unleash unto some unsuspecting being. I wouldn't classify Xeno in that way, but even though we'd been rockin' since my senior year of high school, and she knew better than anyone—other than my daddy—of my capabilities, she was never not impressed when I presented my latest creation.

I hadn't seen her in a minute—hadn't seen *anyone* in a minute, for that matter—because I'd spent the last six weeks in L.A. working with Naima and other legendary songwriters to complete a full concept album for a popstar who was ready to try a different sound. I'd had to sign an NDA before even receiving the information about the album camp, and I still wasn't informed who I was making music for until I arrived to the mini mansion in Beverly Hills. Due to the secretive nature of the artist, none of us were able to use our phones the entire trip. While the experience was unmatched and priceless, going no contact with my loved ones had been hard.

Less than a week since I'd been home, and Xeno and I had slipped right back into our routine like only a weekend had passed. We were three songs into our weekly listening session when I queued up the only track that already had vocals laid down. While rap tracks were my bread and butter, the lovey-dovey R&B stuff had my heart. Seemingly sweet songs with melodies that wrapped around you like a warm blanket—just before the sexy undertone snuck up on you like a double shot of Hennessy mixed into a tall glass of lemonade—were some of my favorite projects to create. Maybe I was lowkey a lover rather than a fighter like my daddy after all.

Silently, I watched Xeno bob her head as she stared at the soundboard, waiting patiently for her to give me something. As long as I'd known her, I understood that she needed a moment to process the music, so I gave her that because her opinion was on the short list of those that mattered to me. When the song ended, she pointed at the board.

"Aye, run that back."

Grinning, I pressed the button that would replay the song. Her desire to give it a second listen was a great sign. I mean, I knew the song was good—the beat was immaculate and Ray's vocals were on point—but it always felt good to get that confirmation from outside sources. When the song faded out for a second time, Xeno turned her pleased expression my way.

"Yo, you know that was dope, right?"

I nodded. "Thanks, bro."

She blew out a breath as if she were winded and shook her head. "Who is that singing?"

"A lil shorty named WundaGirl Ray. I found her on You-Tube." As I talked, I fiddled with the knobs on the board to queue up the next track. "Well, actually, she found me. She commented on a video of me creating a track from start to finish and said she'd love to work with me and lay some vocals down. And you know me."

Tossing her head back, Xeno laughed. "Yeah, I know you. Extra friendly ass." She cut me a knowing look. "She pretty?"

"Yeah, man," I chuckled. "She cute or whatever."

"Mmhm. Or whatever. Right."

Her tone and the way she dragged that "right" were clear evidence that she thought I was downplaying it, and I got it. I had a firm rule about not sleeping with anyone who came into the studio to work with me, but I had eyes. There were so many fine-ass women in the music industry that I could kick it with a different one every day for a year and still never touch one of the dozens I'd worked with over the years. But this situation wasn't like those others.

"Nah, it really is whatever. Baby girl is straight."

Xeno lifted an eyebrow. "How you know that? I know damn well your mum's-the-word ass ain't discuss sexuality with a woman you'd just met! Hell, you barely discuss it with the women you hook up with. Got these women out here just goin' off vibes and that lil backpack you be carrying."

Dragging a hand down over my head, all I could do was

laugh at the facts she was spittin'. Since the moment I realized that I was a lesbian—long after having that first conversation with my father—I pointedly did everything I could to avoid having "the talk." The way I saw it, if the straights didn't have to announce themselves, then why the fuck did I?

The simple answer was that I didn't. I mean, I got why so many queer people chose to do so but, personally, I was good on all of that. I also had the benefit of *looking gay*, so it wasn't too hard to go off "vibes," as Xeno put it. And the *lil backpack* was a bonus as far as I was concerned. When people saw me, a five-foot-ten, dark-skinned, three-hundred-pound, masculine-presenting woman with a taper-fade and a bottom grill, the assumption was almost always that I was a carpet-muncher and not just a fat tomboy. And the assumption was one hundred percent correct. I mean...genetics made me fat, but I did indeed love to eat.

Turning to Xeno, I shook my head.

"Nah, I didn't have to say a word. Shorty showed up with her dude in tow, but I wasn't trippin' 'cause he was mad cool. He kept quiet while me and Ray worked, and when we took a break he would talk music. The problem is that when he went to the bathroom, Ray got super flirty with me, talmbout she ain't never been with a girl before but had always wondered what it was like." I rolled my eyes and shot Xeno a look. Her lips were pursed and she looked disgusted. Thankfully, she got the point.

"So, ole girl was—"

I nodded. "Yup. Bicurious George."

"Damn," muttered my friend, echoing my sentiments. "And not just that, but a fucking cheater."

"Hmph. I can tell you right now that she def thinks it doesn't count 'cause I'm a woman."

Xeno groaned. "That's that bullshit!"

"That's what I'm saying, man. So, yeah."

Nodding, Xeno shrugged. "Or *whatever*."

There was nothing left to say on the matter. This was unfortunately something I'd experienced multiple times over the course of my life. Apparently, hooking up with a lesbian—especially a stud—was like a bucket list item for many a straight woman, and that was a lesson I learned the hard way. One too many times had I thought I was dealing with a bisexual woman, only to get burned by a het shorty who "don't really do that" when it was time to Uno reverse some head or pop out for a little date situation in public.

"So, what you doing with this?" she asked, swiftly changing the subject and thankfully keeping me from going down a long mental road that led to a painful memory. "You sending it to the radio stations or throwing it up on streaming sites?"

"Eventually. My daddy already said it was impressive, so now I wanna see how it goes over at Sanity. I sent it to Jucee a couple of days ago, and she's gonna dance to it tonight, which will give me the opportunity to watch the crowd."

Xeno grinned, swiveling around in her chair to face me. I could already tell from the mirth in her eyes that some nonsense was about to spew forth from her mouth.

"Ah, I shoulda known you'd send it to your *bestie* first."

And there went the nonsense. Groaning, I rubbed my forehead.

"Technically, I sent it to my——"

Xeno waved her hand. "Aht aht! That don't count. Sending it to your pops is like sending it to an extension of yourself. That's basically a part of your creation process. *This though?* That's different and you know that." Her grin was silly as fuck and mildly annoying.

"You gotta chill, man. It's not even like that." It was pointless to explain why I needed to see first-time reactions to the song, because Xeno knew better than anyone. *This* moment was simply about her giving me a hard time.

"Nah," Xeno teased, shaking her head, her pencil-thin locs swaying from left to right. "That's exactly what it's like. But it's all good. I'm not offended."

Xeno and Jucee were my homies and I regarded them both as my best friend, but that didn't go over well with either of them. They claimed it was all in good fun, but neither of them missed an opportunity to tease me about my "other best friend." The two were my closest friends for completely different reasons. Xeno was my day one. I'd known her since before I even knew what it meant to be a stud and I just thought I was tomboy.

Back when I was making beats in high school for whoever was willing to drop a few Benjamins into my hand. Back when Cyn Tha Starr was thought up as homage to my dearest daddy and attached to an AOL email. Back when the only fight I had in high school was when a boy called me a "fat bull dagger" during our grade level lunch because I declined to give him a free beat after his sob story about having his money stolen on the walk to school that morning. That time, my daddy *did* get a call from the teacher, but when we sat in the principal's office and he heard what had been said, he grabbed me by the arm, carted me out of that school, and just before we got in the car, he called my name.

"Cyndi," he said, breaking my heart and instantly bringing tears to my eyes. I looked across the roof of the car at him, lip trembling with shame at having disappointed him. "You did the right thing," was all he said before opening the driver's side door and climbing behind the wheel.

I stood there, crying like a baby, because my daddy the pacifist had shown me understanding, and while that wasn't un-common of him, he tended to be more strict when it came to physical altercations. He was, once again, showing me what mattered.

At that time, Xeno and I hadn't met in person but were already pretty close after connecting on Tumblr and talking damn near every day. I remember detailing the incident to her that night, and even back then she was always cool-headed and mellow. She was also incredibly goofy, then and now.

"Am I even still invited to the barbecue on Sunday," Xeno asked laughingly, "or is it a one-best-friend limit this time around? Let me know now before I get my hopes up."

Laughing, I pushed back in my chair, shaking my head in amusement. "Does Trisha know you got this mean jealous streak?"

Trisha was Xeno's girlfriend and I was curious to know if this was something I needed to share with her asap. A half-empty water bottle flew through the air, aimed right for my head. I ducked, cracking up as the bottle hit the wall and fell to the floor.

"Whatever, man!" she laughed. "Just tell me what you're about to do with this track, 'cause it's too good to sit on."

"Uh huh," I muttered, cool to let it go if she was. "I'm thinking of just uploading it to the streaming sites and letting radio catch wind of it organically." I had a large enough following on social media to get a buzz going without paying for a spot in the rotation during peak hours on the radio. If enough people liked it, they'd call the stations and tag them online enough that it'd be in rotation without me having to do a thing.

That was also where Jucee came in. Her sets were damn near legendary among the city's club scene, and someone was bound to post a clip of it online. The song was guaranteed to go viral if that happened. And even if I discouraged her, Jucee was bound to help it along. It was one of the things I loved about her. I'd met her three years ago, just when I was starting to get national recognition for my work behind the sound-board. I already had a name for me in Houston, and the work I did with local artists was enough for me to live comfortably and never have to ask my parents for money. It wasn't until a clip of Xeno performing went viral that so many eyes turned onto her, and by extension, as her producer, onto me as well.

Houston has a vibrant strip club culture—something that I loved about my city—and the women I encountered there showed me love because they recognized my name. Jucee never tried to get at me after finding out who I was. Before we'd even officially met, she would make videos with my music playing in the background, tag me, and never ask for anything in return. Her support was because she respected the music, and that fueled me to meet her in person. Even when I reached out in her DMs, she was never on no flirting shit, and she stayed that way when we met up for lunch. It was unexpected but refreshing, and I knew from the moment she first hugged me and kissed my cheek that she would be the homie.

And a year later when my daddy suffered a heart attack, she was right by my side, along with Xeno, giving me support and helping me take care of myself when I felt like I couldn't do anything. After that, we became attached at the hip. When she broke up with her boyfriend, I extended her that same care she had shown me, pulling her and her son into my family to offer them community since the only blood relatives she had were back in Dallas.

With my two best friends, my family, and my music, my life was fantastic, and I wouldn't change it for the world.

Chapter Two

Jucee

Go BesFren, Das My BesFren

No less than forty-five minutes after giving birth, a memo is sent out informing the life-bringer that their time as a bad bitch has expired and they are henceforth *Somebody's Mama* and must act accordingly. It comes with a pamphlet that spells out, in no uncertain terms, what all "act accordingly" entails. Wardrobe, career, relationships, extracurriculars. All of that shit is supposed to change. And although the memo is sent directly to *Somebody's Mama*, the rest of the world also, somehow, has received the list of rules, memorized them, and pledged to be a constant reminder for when *Somebody's Mama* has forgotten her role.

I'd been Amani Jones's mama for five years, and had been proudly bucking the system from day one. It's not that I missed that memo; I simply ignored that shit. There was no way in hell I was going to trade in my crop tops and short shorts for the latest Amish fashions just because I moaned "Yesssss!" when Samir asked if he could nut in me one Wednesday night after hot yoga had me feeling all limber and horny. Aht aht! I was going to live a life that I loved *now* so that I didn't have an overgrown man–child puffing up his chest because I informed him that *"Mama gotta have a life too, Jody."*

I was younger than my son when I took up dancing, and after years spent contorting my body in ballet, I joined a contemporary dance troupe shortly after my eighteenth birthday. All I'd done was trade in one group of judgmental assholes for another. And here I'd thought contemporary had also meant progressive. The thing about change that never failed to piss me off is just how slow it was to make a difference in the everyday life of the average person. While the ideal type of woman in music videos and on every social media platform is the hypersexualized version of the ultra-voluptuous BBW, fat women with less desirable shapes—those of us with family-sized chicken dinner bodies full of thighs and breasts and wings and rolls—were still getting harassed because fatphobia ran rampant in the streets like crack in the eighties.

Which is why Sanity had been the goal before I'd even set foot in Houston. The move for me was a no-brainer, since the only thing in Dallas worth caring about was my granny's gravesite. Samir came to me with a job offer he'd received that was too good to pass up—as the assistant director for a dance team at an HBCU in Houston—and that was all I needed to hear. I'd had enough of being passed over for roles where I was over-qualified, and I was ready to do something different. Within the next week, I'd scoured the review websites for the highest-rated clubs that were queer-friendly, Black-owned, *and* Black-operated. That left me with Sanity. I contacted the club and inquired if they were hiring for new dancers. After I received confirmation that they were, I scheduled my audition and headed down to Houston.

There were three people present for my audition: the owner of the club, Mal, her assistant, Josey, and the choreographer and dance mother, Milly. Although I was unfamiliar with pole, Josey had assured me over the phone that they would teach me that skill if I was hired. Thanks to Samir quickly helping me put together a routine, I gave a damn good performance. Keeping my limitations at the forefront of my mind, I didn't try anything advanced on the pole, but I did include it in my routine, pretending it was a stern Samir watching to make sure I didn't fuck up his moves as I grooved to the beat of Xeno's "Drown Me."

When the song came to an end, I smiled in satisfaction. I could tell from the expression on everyone's face that I'd killed that shit. I'd done enough auditions to know how that looked.

In Sanity, I'd surprisingly found not only some bomb-ass coworkers, but also a group of people I grew to love fiercely, who cherished me just as much as I did them. They became my family, and Mal was like the older sibling that I never knew I needed. She wasn't just my boss, but she was a mentor, a consultant, and confidante when I truly needed one.

My phone chimed and I reached over my laptop where I was working on my quarterly budget to pluck the noisemaker off of the coffee table. The movement brought the screen to life. Mercedes had texted me. Opening the message, I gasped at the high-definition photo of a plate of loaded French fries that took up the entire screen. Immediately, I typed out a response.

Me: Oh my Goooood!

Cedes: These fries are so damn good. Nobody else would appreciate it like you.

I looked at the picture again and whimpered a little bit. The golden potatoes were overflowing with cubed brisket, crispy bacon, melted cheddar, chives, and barbecue sauce. I loved when the brisket was chopped instead of shredded and I could still see the smoke ring. Dropping my head back, I groaned. Had it only been a couple of hours since I'd had a bowl of cereal, buttered Texas toast, and an iced caramel latte? Yes. Was I being greedy and already thinking about my next meal? Yes! But was I ashamed? Absolutely not!

Me: Save me some! ◊◊

Another picture came through, this one of a second container with my name scrolled across the top in black marker.

Cedes: I had them put the toppings on the side since I won't see you until later.

Me: You love me! 😵

Cedes: You know it. 😌

Mercedes was one of the women I'd immediately clicked with when I started dancing at Sanity. She was a fellow single mother, with a background in dance, and two boys who were close in age to Amani. With so many similarities between us, it was no question why we got on the way that we did. We'd become so close that she was like an auntie to my baby. I'd gone from having just my granny, to losing her right before Amani was born and only having Samir, to now having a live and in the flesh sisterfriend.

And then of course there was Poppa. My bestie boo. *Speaking of Poppa…*

I navigated back to my text messages and selected our ongoing thread.

Me: What did you eat today?

Poppa: …

Poppa: I had a cheeseburger before I made it to the studio.

Twisting my lips to the side, I shook my head. If I didn't know that girl as well as I did, I might've been satisfied with that answer. I mean…it sounded good enough and kinda sorta answered my question, if I tilted my head to the side and squinted. The thing is…I wasn't about to do all of that. It wasn't even necessary. I was willing to bet that even though she'd only been back in town for a few days, Poppa had been at Rhythm & Rainbows since the night before, which meant she hadn't eaten a thing today. It was only eleven in the morning and she likely had no intentions of leaving the studio anytime soon.

Closing my laptop, I sat it on the coffee table where my phone had just been. Grabbing my keys from a hook on the wall and my purse from the coat rack by the door, I left my condo and headed toward one of my favorite food markets.

Briggs Food Hall was essentially a mall food court without the haggard families doing school shopping, or the groups of emo teenagers drinking bubble tea and wearing studded belts from Hot Topic with thumb holes cut in the shirt sleeves. It was the anchor business in a small commercial strip, tucked into the heart of Third Ward, minutes from 288. The parking lot held eight cars, max, and most everyone parked on the streets surrounding the building. I lucked out and caught someone pulling out near the door just as I took my chances with the lot. The moment I stepped inside of the building, I stopped and took a deep breath, inhaling all of the delicious aromas from the different booths.

There were six restaurants located in Briggs Food Hall, all

of them creative endeavors by local masterminds, but I was there for one place only. Yee-Raw was a Tex-Mex sushi fusion restaurant owned by a married lesbian couple who decided to merge their Japanese American and African American heritages with their Texan roots. What emerged was a surprising roster of dishes that became immediate favorites. Me and some of the girls from the club stumbled onto Briggs one day after a workout and I'd been the only one willing to give Yee-Raw a try. The moment that brisket temaki touched my lips I decided that Tessa and Anna would never have to pay for another lap dance as long as I lived. They'd yet to visit Sanity, but the moment they did, it would be five-star treatment for them all night!

Six months later, and I had Poppa hooked as well, and since I was sure her ass probably hadn't eaten anything more than a couple of cold toaster pastries all day, I knew just what to get her.

"Hey, girl, hey!" Tessa Kimura-Brown called out to me as I neared, waving from her post behind the counter of the stand she owned with her wife. Her ginger-dyed halo of kinky coils was in a massive puff at the crown of her head, her edges secured by a red bandana printed with the Yee-Raw logo tied around her temple.

Lifting my hand, I offered her a huge wave as I sped up my steps, practically skipping past the cafeteria-style seating. The relationship I had with food was very, *very* serious—we were madly in love—and as a culinarian, Tessa was one of my favorite people on the planet. On top of that, not only was she a sweetheart, but she was gorgeous, with her smooth, chestnut hue, round face, and bow-shaped lips that were always spread in a toothy grin.

"Hey, boo!" I got in line behind a woman giving Tessa her order, and looked up at the menu over Tessa's head as if I didn't already know what I was going to get.

Once the woman ahead of me accepted her receipt, she turned around to sit at one of the nearby tables, allowing me to step up to the register. Before I could speak, Tessa held up a finger.

"Hold on a sec." Twisting her neck, she called over her shoulder, "Babe, Juleesa's here!"

My eyebrows shot up in excitement. *Was I a VIP now?* I stopped by Yee-Raw at least once a week, and both Tessa and Anna recognized both my face and my name, which came in handy when I placed mobile orders, so it made sense, but it was still surprising. Shifting my gaze behind Tessa, I peered through the wide rectangular opening in the wall that separated the front of their stall from the kitchen area. Anna stood on the other side of the wall behind a prep table, her jet-black hair up in a tight bun at the top of her head, a black mask over her mouth and nose, and the same red bandana that Tessa wore tied around her temples. She waved at me, her eyes crinkling as she smiled behind her mask, and gave her wife a thumbs-up.

Tessa nodded and turned back to me.

"The usual?" she asked, her eyebrows up near the bandana as she waited for the answer she already knew was coming.

Laughing, I nodded. I'd tried everything on the Yee-Raw menu and while each item could get ate at any moment, there were certified bangers in my eyes.

Tessa's grin widened and she echoed my nod. "Mmhm. So, two brisket temaki, elote tempura, and seaweed salad?"

"Yes, ma'am." As I pulled my card out of my bag I eyed her. "What was up with the fanfare?" I tilted my chin toward the back kitchen. "What are you and Anna up to?"

Smile widening, Tessa winked and took my card. "It's a surprise."

"Ooh," I breathed, bouncing on my toes. "I love surprises." Tessa swiped my card and spun the screen toward me so that

I could sign. As she handed me my receipt, my phone buzzed in my purse. I chose a tip and scrawled some chicken scratch when it prompted for my signature before I pulled the device out and stepped away from the counter. I stood over to the side, out of the way of traffic but not as far away as the tables either.

"Juleesa!"

I looked up from the Sanity dancers' group text about the workout session at Thick n' Fit that afternoon to see Tessa waving me over. Glancing around, I noted that the woman who'd been ahead of me in line was no longer sitting at the table, but pushing through the exit. That meant my order was ready. Tucking my phone away, I approached the counter just as Anna stepped through the swinging door holding a covered container in her hands. My cheeks bloomed as an excited smile came across my face.

There was a bag on the counter in front of Tessa that was already filled with containers of assorted sizes. She added napkins, chopsticks, and condiments while Anna placed the container in her hand on the counter and smiled at me.

"We made something for you."

A little squeal might've slipped from my lips. I brought my fists up to my cheeks and peered at the container. Laughing, Anna peeled off the top.

"Baked beans gyoza."

I gasped.

"Whatchu say?!" The pan-fried dumplings smelled amazing. Tessa smiled. "It's a small token of our appreciation of you. You're not only one of our favorite regulars, but you spread the word about our little business and it shows."

Nodding, Anna added, "We aren't yet able to fit marketing into our budget, but as soon as we can, you can expect to be put on payroll."

"Y'all are so sweet. I'm not doing this for any money, so

don't even worry about that right now. I do love getting to try new dishes though!"

They laughed and handed over the bag, with a promise to see me later. They absolutely would. Not only was the food amazing, but they were good people, and that went a long way with me.

Food secured, I navigated onto the highway and headed southwest to Rhythm & Rainbows, the studio Cyn co-owned with the rapper Xeno. Xeno was Poppa's *other* best friend. They'd known each other since they were teenagers and essentially built their careers together. While Poppa did all of her work behind the soundboard, Xeno was an incredibly talented and *incredibly fine* rapper. She'd been major in the city for nearly a decade, but started blowing up on a national level a few years ago after being name-dropped by a heavy hitter in the rap game, which catapulted her and Poppa's careers from small stages at local festivals, to requests for tracks from major labels, to nominations at prominent award shows.

The center where the studio was located was surprisingly crowded for a Thursday evening. I texted Poppa that I was outside, and by the time I reached the door, she was already there, holding it open for me. I expected her to make a joke about the food I carried, or stand back and let me enter the building, but she did neither of those things. Pulling a wide grin out of me, she stepped onto the sidewalk and spread her arms wide. We'd spoken on the phone briefly when she landed at Hobby before meeting Carissa in the pickup line, and we talked when she told me about the latest song she'd finished, but I hadn't seen her in person in so damn long. It felt like forever, and a hug from my bestie boo was an invitation that I'd never decline.

I skipped into her embrace and propped my chin on her shoulder, cheesing from ear to ear as she squeezed me tight around my back. She was warm and soft and felt like home.

It didn't hit me until just then, but ordinarily we were at-tached at the hip so I'd been missing home in her absence.

"I missed you, Marie."

Throwing my head back, I cackled at her use of my middle name.

"I missed you too, Poppa."

While it wasn't a rare occurrence for her to lock herself in the studio while she hyperfocused on bringing a project to completion, the nearly two months without seeing each other was a length of time I wasn't accustomed to.

After a final squeeze and lil rock from side to side, I stepped back and pressed a kiss to her cheek. She shook her arms out as if I'd been the one holding on too tight instead of the other way around, took one look at the bag of food in my hand, and shook her head.

"I should've known."

I smirked at her dry tone. "You absolutely should've."

Pursing my lips, I ignored the rolling of her eyes and stepped around her to the lobby area of the studio. While I waited for her to lock the door, I observed her. For someone who'd been sitting in a dark room all day, she looked good. Her purple basketball shorts and gold t-shirt were only slightly wrinkled, giving her the look of a co-ed from her alma mater, Prairie View A&M University, who was on the way to class. A match-ing logo baseball cap covered her head, the bill off-center and tilted down, as if she'd been tugging on it while she worked. The two gold chains hanging from her neck completed the relatively simple look.

Door locked, Poppa turned to me, those deep-set, hooded eyes that reminded me of the late Christopher Wallace eyeing the plastic sack expectantly, a slow grin lifting her round cheeks.

Her eyes swept up to my face. "What'd you bring?"

"Your favorite from Yee-Raw."

"Hell yeah," she moaned, bringing her fist to her mouth.

"You always lookin' out. Come on to the back."

Taking the bag from me, she grabbed my hand and led me through the lobby and down a short hallway toward the larger of the three recording rooms. Rhythm & Rainbows had a simple layout, much like an old shotgun house. There was a studio on either side of the hallway and one at the back of the unit, and all three were named after famous women in music. Missy was the one at the back, slightly larger than the others, and was Poppa's personal studio that she and Xeno used exclusively. The other two rooms, Foxy and Queen La, held much of the same equipment, according to Poppa, but her heart was in her boards.

A quick peek into the window of one of the rooms showed a trio of women standing around the room, bobbing their heads as a fourth woman fiddled with dials on the soundboard.

Inside of Missy, two women sat on the small couch against the wall, and a man sat on a stool inside of the recording booth.

"How y'all doin'?" I greeted, offering a nod to the women before taking the bag back from Poppa and bringing it over to the small, two-seat table near the door. They returned the greeting, polite smiles on their faces as they nodded my way. One of the women quickly turned her attention back to her phone, but the other kept her gaze on me, her expression pinched with overt curiosity.

Crossing the room, Poppa leaned over the soundboard and pressed a button, her eyes on the man on the other side of the window.

"Say, Hitta. Gimme five right quick."

The man in the booth gave the "OK" signal and pulled the headphones from around his neck, hooking them on a stand next to the stool before coming out of the booth.

"We good?" he asked Poppa as soon as he was on our side of the booth.

"Yeah, man." Poppa pointed to me. "Hitta, this is my ace boon, Jucee. Jucee, this is Hitta."

"Nice to meet you," I responded, dipping my head in acknowledgement.

"You too." Squinting, he eyed me. "Say, do I know you from somewhere?"

Furrowing my brows, I looked from him to Poppa, but she only shrugged. Taking a step back, I looked him up and down. Hitta was a rapper whose music I'd heard in the club before, but as far as I knew, we'd never met. His light brown eyes and tawny skin didn't ring any bells in my memory, and I didn't fuck enough men to get them confused, so it definitely wasn't that.

Echoing Poppa's movement, I shrugged. "I don't know, do you?"

"Wait!" His jaw dropped, eyes lighting with recognition. "You dance at Sanity?"

A proud smile came across my face. I nodded. "Yeah, I do." His eyes widened in shock as if he didn't expect me to say yes, even though he clearly recognized me. He brought his fist to his mouth.

"Oh, snap! Bae!"

I watched as he stepped over to the sofa and grabbed the hand of one of the sitting women who'd been watching our interaction—or maybe just me—closely. Pulling the woman to her feet, he turned back to me.

"This is my wife, Sigie, and her sister, Sheri. Sigie is a huge fan of yours. We've been in the city for two days, but all she can talk about is getting to see you dance. I tried to take her last night but…" He trailed off with another shrug.

"Jucee doesn't usually dance on the weekends," Poppa offered.

Sigie's caramel skin flushed red as she elbowed Hitta in the ribs. She gave me a sheepish grin.

"I told him that you only danced nights the last weekend of the month, but he don't listen unless you're talking music."

Hitta gave his wife a scandalized look. "I listen well enough to know she's ya bestie in ya head."

When Sigie gasped and shoved him away from her, I laughed. "Oh, please! I showed you a picture from her Instagram. You saw ass and agreed to whatever I asked."

Another shrug from Hitta. "Shit..." He met eyes with Poppa and grinned. "What can I say?"

Poppa cracked up. "I get it."

I nodded. "I do have a great ass."

Sigie eyed me. "Among other things."

Poppa's eyebrows shot up. I met her gaze and tried not to bust out laughing at the silly look on her face. I was very familiar with the tone Sigie's voice had taken on. At least once a week, it came from a woman who thought she was straight and had come to the club with her boyfriend or husband, got handsy and adventurous, fueled by the dark lights and an abundance of liquor. I'd been propositioned by too many women to count with their men sitting right next to them.

Hitta just shook his head and laughed, clearly unfazed by his wife's suggestive tone. He took one look at the containers I'd begun removing from the bag and grinned at Poppa.

"Oh, you finally 'bout to eat?" Turning to me, he pressed his palms together and held them up by his chest. "Aye, thank you so much! I tried to get her to take a break and eat with us when my wife brought in some pizza a couple of hours ago, but she wasn't going."

Swiveling my head toward my friend, I narrowed my eyes at Poppa, who released an exasperated groan and shook her head. "Oh," I drawled. "So you didn't *forget* to eat, you just chose *not* to? That's how we livin' now?"

Rolling her lips into her mouth, she stifled a laugh and wrapped her arms around me, pressing her face into my shoulder.

"*Man.* You know how it is when I'm in the zone."

Nodding, I turned back to the table to finish unbagging the food, studiously ignoring the way my stomach started twisting in knots the moment she grabbed me. It was only because I was hungry, and it was just pure coincidence that it happened when it did.

I did know how Poppa got when she was in the zone, which was why I got on her like I did. It was one thing to be so wrapped up in your work that you barely remembered to check your phone, let alone remembered to eat. But being reminded and opting out was another thing completely. This was exactly the reason I had to bring her hard-headed ass lunch.

"Mmhm," I hummed once I finished emptying the bag. "Sit down and eat. You're gonna need more than five minutes though." I added the last part, remembering her asking the rapper for a small break.

Her eyes lifted toward the ceiling, but she nodded. "*Yes, Mom.* Anything else?"

"No, smart ass." Laughing, I tilted my head toward the food.

To her credit, she didn't say another word, just sat down and lifted her chin at Hitta. Both hands lifted in the air, he shook his head before she could speak.

"Aye, I heard her loud and clear. You gotta eat and I won't be the one to argue." He motioned to the folks on the sofa. "We're gonna go for a little walk and stretch our legs." Then he turned to me. "Twenty okay?"

I smiled. "That's perfect. Thank you."

They left and Poppa shook her head. "You really think you run the show, huh?"

Sitting down, I lifted the lid on the gyoza. "Girl, shut up."

Laughing, she pulled the temaki out of the container I'd

pushed toward her, and the aroma of the smoked meat and vinegared rice hit the air. Poppa bounced her shoulders and my stomach rumbled.

"This smells amazing."

I snapped apart the pair of wooden chopsticks Tessa had tossed in the bag and used them to divvy up the gyoza and tempura between the two of us before digging in. Although it sounded odd, I had no hesitations about the gyoza. I completely trusted Tessa and Anna, and when I took a bite of one of the dumplings, I was reminded why. The tangy sweetness of the beans immediately transported me to my youth, when my family would gather together at the park on a holiday and have a cookout. As usual, I was in awe at how Tessa and Anna managed to take two things that I would've bet cold hard cash did not go together and marry them in a way that just made so much sense.

We fell into a comfortable silence as we ate, with only murmurs sounding every now and then. I'd missed our mundane moments like this while she'd been away.

"What are you about to do?" Poppa asked once we finished eating. We'd put all of the empty containers back into the bag it had come in and stood up from the table. She'd lifted the bag of trash from our meal off of the table, but I took it out of her hands.

"I'm heading to Sanity for a little bit. I have a meeting with Glenda and then I'm going to try and catch Mercedes's set."

Poppa nodded. "You coming by the house after?"

I turned to her, eyebrow lifted. "You asking?"

Her lips spread into a slow grin as she looked toward the booth, shaking her head.

"Man..."

Tilting my head to the side, I propped my hands on my hips

and faced her. She always tried to pull this on Thursdays, knowing good and well that I had a standing date with my television.

"No, let's talk about it, because you know that I'm binging *Instant I Do* reruns before season four drops next week, and I don't want to hear your mouth. The reruns started before you left and I'm not giving that up just because you're back."

Just as she busted out laughing, the door opened and Hitta reentered with his wife and her sister. Catching my eye, Hitta gave me an expectant look.

"We good?"

Poppa sucked her teeth and dropped down into the executive chair in front of the soundboard.

"Aye man, say man! Don't be asking her like she the one running shit in here."

Hitta raised his hands in surrender as me and the other women busted out laughing.

"No offense, Cyn, but shorty definitely give off Big Boss energy." He shrugged, a sly grin coming across his handsome face. "I mean...she said eat and you sat your ass down and ate, amiright?"

Tossing her head back, Poppa gripped the bill of her cap and cracked up. Watching her laugh made me laugh even harder. It took a minute for her to sober up enough to point toward the booth.

"Man, get yo ass in the booth!"

Chuckling, Hitta did as instructed. As he headed to the center of the room and the microphone he'd abandoned, I shifted the bag of trash to my left hand and hugged Poppa from behind with my right, pressing a kiss to her temple.

"Thanks for taking a break to eat. I'mma head out."

Nodding, Poppa swiveled around in her chair to face me.

"I'mma see you later, right?"

I busted out laughing and pulled open the door. "Bye, girl!"

Ignoring the call of my name, I walked out and pulled the door shut behind me. There was a ding that indicated I'd received a text message before I even exited the building, and it didn't take a genius for me to guess that Poppa had sent it. She didn't need me to respond; of course I was going to go by her house. Her TV was bigger than mine, and reality shows undeniably looked fantastic in 4K.

Chapter Three

Cyn

Very Important Person

If I'd had any doubt that WundaGirl Ray's sultry voice paired with the bass–heavy track I'd laid out was a winning combination, the Saturday night crowd at Sanity cleared that up within the first fifteen seconds of the song. "The Rest of You" opened with Ray humming a melody in C–minor just before the beat came in, and I heard a few whispers inquiring about the song near the back of the room where I sat while the stage that held everyone's attention was still darkened. Forty-five seconds in, and folks were on their feet, rocking from side to side as Jucee squatted in front of the pole center stage, her back to the crowd as she isolated her ass cheeks to the rhythm. Two minutes in and folks had handfuls of cash in the air as they rubbed their hands down their bodies and whined to the song about friends becoming lovers and the desire for mind-blowing sex. Three minutes and twenty seconds into the song, the temperature in the room had ratcheted up to the eighties as the scene on the stage had everyone captivated.

Jucee had climbed to the top of the pole, which was at least two stories high. Using only her arms, she twisted her hands and spun her body while sticking her legs out at a forty-five-degree angle as she mimed walking around the pole in exaggerated steps. After making a complete turn, she brought her body flush with the pole and spread her legs into a wide split in the air. She held the pose for a full ten seconds, letting the final crescendo build along with the anticipation as everyone became silent, all eyes riveted to her—magnetized. And when the piano and horn came in, along with Ray's harmonizing, the beat dropping at the perfect moment, so did Jucee, sliding down the pole effortlessly, as if she had no grip on the chrome at all. It was amazing to witness.

And when she reached the bottom, Jucee wrapped both hands around the pole, tightening her grip, slowing at a nerve-wracking pace just before reaching the ground, where she spread her legs and landed in a full split. The moment she touched the floor of the stage, the entire building erupted into a cacophony of cheers that drowned out the end of the song, but I didn't care. Showers of bills flew into the air, raining down on the stage like confetti from a piñata. Cody and I probably tossed out a cool five thousand between us, and we were small potatoes next to the rappers and athletes who took up residence near the stage.

This was why Jucee made sure to dance one weekend out of each month. She earned a year's worth of expenses in just four total hours over two nights. It made the money she earned by dancing during the week look like pennies, although two to three thousand for a collective twenty hours of work was nothing to sneeze at.

Turning to my younger brother, I cracked up at the awe on his face. He'd come with me to Sanity several times over the past couple of years, but it never failed to amaze him when Jucee took the stage. Everybody knew he had a little crush on her, but as long as he didn't act on it, I was cool with it. Cody wasn't allowed to fuck with my friends, and that had been a rule since we were teenagers and he transitioned from simply liking girls to wanting to hump them like a puppy. I learned the hard way that some of those same girls would shamelessly go through me to get to either of my brothers. Caleb had always been a hard nut to crack, but Cody's extra-horny self never turned down no pussy—and I mean…I couldn't really blame him since I was the same way—though once I put him up on game, he became more discerning when chicks would get to smiling in his face after he saw them hanging around me first.

As Jucee finished her set and exited the stage, four women wearing uniforms of shiny, pink hot pants and cropped purple t-shirts came out with large canvas bags and began to collect the money that covered the floor like a carpet. Each of them wore black latex gloves and black masks over their mouths. Two used push brooms to gather the money in the center of the stage while the other two stuffed the bills in the bags. DJ High-Fee turned up the music and jumped on the mic, addressing the crowd as additional servers flooded the room, the two working in tandem to keep the cleaning of the stage from crushing the vibe. The crew at Sanity was a well-oiled machine, and the process took less than five minutes before the lights were dimming again and two women were on the stage circling the pole and each other.

After about ten minutes, Jucee sauntered over to us wearing a different outfit than she'd had on stage, her hips swaying to a rhythm all their own with each step she took in those sky-high-ass platform booties. Even in the darkened room, I could see how folks stopped talking midsentence as their attention gravitated toward her as if they were magnetized. And I completely understood.

Jucee was a sight to behold. Five feet and seven inches of pure confidence and sex appeal. Her aura commanded the attention of every room she stepped in, and that was before you stepped back to admire the body she was blessed with. And what a body it was. With the kind of curves that required a caution sign and a smile that could make you lose your train of thought.

She reached us and I stared up at her, momentarily lost in the way she beamed, skin shiny and glittery in the afterglow of another successful set. Bending at the waist, she kissed my cheek, and the contact snatched me out of my thoughts.

"Hey, Poppa."

She turned to give Cody the same treatment, patting his cheek afterward before she turned back to me. Cody's ass was cheesing hard, and those stars in his eyes flashed brighter. Chuckling, I shook my head and regarded Jucee.

"Whassup, baby girl. You killed it, as usual."

"Thank you, baby," she responded in a demure tone that would've sounded shockingly genuine to anyone who didn't know her the way that I did.

Her humility never failed to blow me away, even after three years of knowing her. Although she was the baddest and best dancer at Sanity, she never let it go to her head. Her ego stayed in check and it just made her that much more loveable.

"That song had the whole place in a state of euphoria, Poppa!" she gushed, sliding onto my lap and draping an arm over my shoulder. "I thought an orgy was about to break out, the way everyone's eyes were glazed over."

Laughing, I lightly squeezed her waist out of reflex and then moved my hand back to the arm of my chair. It didn't matter how well we knew each other, the policy at Sanity was that patrons kept their hands to themselves at all times. I might've missed the fuck out of her these past few weeks and felt like I needed to touch her, but I respected the rule and I respected Jucee, and because of that respect, I kept it cute.

"Nah, girl," I deflected, not sure why I suddenly was having trouble adhering to a rule that I'd followed for longer than I'd known my friend. "That look was all you. Everyone was mesmerized by what *Jucee* was doing up there."

She grinned and shook her head. In the low light I watched her roll her eyes, her thick lashes fluttering playfully.

"Whatever" was all she said, easing off of me. She knew better than to argue with me about her talent. Of course, I'd seen the crowd appreciate the song, but that euphoria she'd mentioned was absolutely because of her. The song helped, sure, but watching my girl kill it up on that stage was the culprit.

Standing to her feet and towering over both me and my brother in her six-inch heels, Jucee shot me a wink as she turned to head off. I knew the deal; if she wasn't making money, there was no reason for her to sit still. Before she could walk off, Cody grabbed her hand. I shot him a questioning look but he ignored me, staring up at Jucee pleadingly.

"What's up, baby boy?" she asked him, amusement clear on her heavily made-up features.

"Can I get a lap dance, please? Just this once? It's my birthday."

"It ain't your damn birthday, fool," I growled, slapping his hand to make him release her.

Keeping his eyes on Jucee, Cody shot me the bird. "It'll feel like my birthday if she gives me a dance. Hell, it'll feel like my birthday, Christmas, and Valentine's Day all rolled into one."

Giggling, Jucee turned to me, her eyebrow quirked in question. Immediately, I shook my head.

"Hell naw! It's thirty other women in here," I exclaimed, waving a hand around the packed room. "Pick one of them and leave mine alone!"

My little brother shot me a surprised look and then tossed his head back and laughed. "Yours?! You own her now?"

Pursing my lips, I glared at him. He was tryna make it something that it wasn't. He got that shit from his mama. Hell, *and* his daddy. I could—and regularly did—acknowledge how damn fine Jucee was, and how big of a heart she had, and how funny she could be, especially when she was fussing because she needed attention, but I needed her in my life like I needed my music, and I would never jeopardize that by going for anything other than what we had. That also meant fielding everybody's insinuations that we were anything other than friends.

"You know what I mean, fool. My *best friend.*"

"Yeah. Sure," he smirked. Giving Jucee wide, puppy-dog eyes, he whimpered. "You gon' miss out on this $200 because Cyn cockblocking?"

Sucking my teeth, I dug a few bills out of my pocket, folded them, and slipped them into one of the garters strapped around Jucee's thick-ass thigh over her glittery fishnets. It was possible that my fingers lingered on her for a couple of seconds longer than necessary, but that was just a brain fart—a momentary short in my synapses—nothing more. "There. That's $400 to ignore this idiot."

Cody frowned and Jucee cracked up, moving out of the circle of chairs we were in.

"Y'all are too funny."

I shook my head. "Nah, *he* funny 'cause he know damn well I don't play about you. Now, g'on somewhere 'fore I have to knock his head in for trying me."

Laughing, Jucee shot a wink at Cody and walked off, stopping a few tables down when a group of women wearing bridal veils waved her over. One woman stood to her feet and waved a stack of hundreds as incentive. Once it was clear that she was occupied, I turned to my brother, expecting to find him sulking. To my surprise, he was studying me, a shrewd expression on his face. I frowned.

"You buggin'."

A wide smile erupted on his face. "Nah, bruh. I'm chillin'."

His easy demeanor was suspicious as hell. As the baby, Cody was known to hold a grudge and pout when he didn't get his way. Narrowing my eyes, I stared a hole into his face. Noticing my gape, he cracked up.

"Since you big money tonight, go ahead and order a platter of wings. Ya boy is starvin' like Marvin."

"*I'm* big money? You the one fuckin' up commas. I'm just tryna get like you, baby bro." He'd recently secured a position as a senior cloud practitioner at NexTech making six figures, and this stop at Sanity was doing double duty as part of his new-job celebration.

He laughed. "Man, kill all that."

I joined in on his laughter but went ahead and signaled to one of the servers who was walking by wearing neon-pink fishnets, hot pants with *Sanity* across the booty, and a low-cut, sleeveless, deep-purple body suit with *Sanity* across the chest area.

"Hey, Cyn," she greeted with a smile. "What can I get for you?"

"Let me get a platter of wings." I turned to my brother. "What flavors?"

"Pshh. Lemon pepper, of course!" Cody gave me a dumb look as if I should've already known the answer.

The server, who I recognized as a young woman named Nini, giggled. "One thirty-wing platter, lemon pepper flavor." She wrote it down on a little notepad that she pulled out of her fanny pack. "You want waffle fries too?"

I nodded. "Yeah, that'll be dope."

Nini nodded and tucked her notepad away. "Extra blue cheese, right?"

Grinning, I nodded again. "That's right. You know me so well, Nini."

Even in the low lights, I could see a blush rise to Nini's car amel cheeks as she returned my grin and pushed a lock of her blonde bob behind her ear.

"I just pay attention, is all."

I shot her a wink. "Well, you do a damn good job of it."

"Thanks, Cyn." She beamed, backing away a few steps before spinning on her heel and swishing her hips from left to right as she headed to the kitchen to put in my order.

Lifting my glass of water, I watched her disappear through a set of double doors beside the bar. Nini was a cute lil thing, but she was young as hell. I had no idea her exact age, but if she were born before 2000, I'd be surprised.

"Amazing," muttered Cody loud enough for me to hear. I glanced his way and saw him shake his head as he sipped from his glass of cranberry juice and lemon–lime soda.

"Who?" I asked incredulously. "Nini?" Don't get me wrong, Nini was a sight to see, with her wide brown eyes and cherubic smile, but she was so far from Cody's type that she might as well have been in Austin.

"What's amazing is that I'm by far the best looking of all of us and yet I gotta sit here and watch stunners—veritable brick houses, tens across the board!—fall over themselves to cater to you. On some Destiny's Child type of shit."

I hollered with laughter. "The only thing amazing is that you think you're the best looking." Waving a hand in the air as if his wrong opinion was the thick smoke from a hookah, I corrected him. "It's Caleb, then me, Dougie, *and then you*."

He sputtered, spilling a little of his drink, the red liquid dribbling down his chin. "Dougie?! The fucking dog?"

Tears sprang to my eyes at the hilarity in his reaction. That goldendoodle was the love of our parents' lives. They'd even turned Caleb's old room into a playroom for him, complete with obstacle course and a miniature dog house that resembled the structure of my childhood home.

"You ain't shit, bruh," Cody declared, chuckling as he used a bar napkin to dab at his shirt. "If there is a word to describe how ain't shit a person is, I bet money your picture is next to it in the dictionary."

Clutching my stomach, I leaned to the side, wheezing. I fought to catch my breath, ready to hit him with a comeback, when a familiar figure stepped into my peripheral, breaching the circle of chairs and heading my way.

"Cyn Tha Starr," uttered a silken voice. "It's an honor for you to grace us with your presence once again."

Standing to my feet, I slapped the proffered hand of the owner of Sanity, shaking my head as I did so. While the sentiment sounded completely genuine, I still didn't want to hear that shit.

"C'mon, Mal," I laughed. "Don't do that."

Malinda Maverick snickered and squeezed my shoulder. Dressed in a purple silk shirt that was tucked into pressed pink trousers that had to be custom, Mal was as smooth and stylish as always. Her thick, long hair was brushed into a slick ponytail—made possible by Lord only knew how much EcoStyler gel—at the nape of her neck and then braided into a single plait that draped over her shoulder, the end secured by a couple of thick, pink rubber bands that matched her trousers and dangling just above the pocket on her shirt. The suave look was finished with a single—but not simple—golden rope chain that hung around her neck and deep purple brogues on her feet.

At least ten years older than me, Mal was an inspiration. Not just because of the way she'd built Sanity from nothing into a powerhouse—no, a paragon—in the Houston LGBT scene, but also because of the way she wasn't afraid to be a woman. She was masculine presenting but never let society tell her what she couldn't do as a result. She wore acrylics, kept her eyebrows threaded, got regular waxes, and, according to Jucee, wore sexy-ass lace bras with matching panties. I wanted to be like her when I grew up.

Shifting her left foot back a few inches, Mal pursed her lips. "I know you're not this humble."

Cody, who had also stood to his feet, snorted. "Not at all. This is a front."

Rolling my eyes, I laughed. "Ignore him."

Mal nodded, mirth dancing in her deep brown eyes. "Your girl did great tonight."

She was talking about none other than Jucee. My chest swelled with pride as if I had taught my boo that routine myself.

"As always," I quipped.

"I understand the song she danced to was a new track of yours."

"Yessir. Just finished it a couple of nights ago. Literally hot off the presses."

Mal dipped her chin in acknowledgment and held her hand out to shake. "I appreciate you bringing fresh tunes to the club. Your music always gets the crowd hype and they open their wallets in response. As a thank-you, your tab tonight is on me."

I'd already grabbed her hand and started to shake my head. "You don't have to do that."

"I don't have to do anything but stay Black and die. This is something I want to do, and you oughta know you can't stop me."

Defeated, I laughed. "Understood. Thank you."

Mal released my hand and clapped Cody on the shoulder. "You two enjoy the rest of your night, and you—" she eyed me pointedly. "—keep bringing the heat up in here."

With a final wink, she nodded at both of us and walked off, two cockdiesel women wearing all black following close behind her. I turned back to my brother to see him giving me a look that said, "I told you so."

"Destiny's Child type of shit" was all he said before returning to his seat.

As soon as he sat down, Nini walked up holding a silver platter with a mountain of wings, waffle fries, and several one-ounce cups of blue cheese dressing. She slid everything onto the table and then moved to the side, revealing a server I hadn't noticed. The second woman placed a basket of cheesy garlic bread next to the wings.

"What's this?" I asked as my stomach grumbled in anticipation.

Nini smiled. "I know you didn't ask for it, but I remembered you ordered it a few times so I decided to bring you some. Don't worry about the cost though. I put this on my tab."

She fluttered her long lashes at me and swished away. I didn't even need to look at Cody to know what he was thinking. He started humming the melody of "Cater 2 U," and all I could do was laugh as I dug into the wings.

Chapter Four

Jucee

Baby Mama

"Where's my baby?" I called out as soon as I stepped into Samir and Morgan's backyard. No one had answered the door after I'd rung the bell twice, but before I could pull out my phone to call someone, joyous screams of laughter led me around the side of the house.

Morgan's two girls, LeeLee and Pooh, along with Amani, wore soaked swimsuits and were screaming their heads off as Samir chased them around the yard, shooting jetted streams of likely cold water out of a bulky water gun as the kids jumped in and out of the spray of the sprinklers in the center of the yard. It was obvious that none of them had heard my question, so I turned toward the house to go look for Morgan. Chilling on a lounger under the awning attached to the house, Morgan used her free arm to wave a hand and catch my attention. I headed straight for her, dropping my keys onto the wicker patio table and immediately reaching for the sleeping infant in her arms. She gave her up without a fight, shaking out her arm as she sat up and reached for the canned margarita on the table, taking a long drink before sighing and sitting back.

"Hey, Leese," she murmured, removing the burp cloth from her shoulder and placing it on the table near her drink.

"Hey girl, hey," I chirped, shooting her a quick grin before allowing my gaze to naturally return to the cherub in my arms.

Sanai was the newest addition to Samir and Morgan's household, bringing their combined brood to four. Although she wasn't who I'd been referring to when I'd asked about "my baby," I never hesitated to scoop her into my arms whenever I came by to drop off or pick up Amani. At three months, she was a juicy, sepia-toned bundle of sweet-smelling love, and shockingly an exact replica of Amani when he was her age. She looked so much like my son that I'd fallen in love with her the moment I saw her wrinkled face at the hospital. Thankfully, Morgan wasn't put off by my attachment to Sanai, and let me love on her as often as I wanted.

"Girl!" Morgan suddenly exclaimed, startling me enough that Sanai twitched in my arms. When I glared at her, she gave me a sheepish grin. "My bad. I just wanted to tell you that you killed your set last night!"

I gave her a surprised look. That was interesting. It wasn't unusual for Morgan to visit Sanity, but no matter how many times I told her it wasn't necessary, she usually let me know when she'd be there.

"You finally listened to me?!" I teased.

Laughing, she rolled her eyes. "Nah, girl. I went out with some girlfriends last night, and one of them suggested we go there on a whim. You know I'm not rolling through without announcing myself."

"Which I still don't understand," I chuckled, bending my neck to nuzzle Sanai's neck.

Instead of acknowledging what I'd said, she waved a hand

at me. "Anyways, we're talking about your set. That song! Oh my god!" Dropping her head back, she made a pained face. "It was sexy as hell. I was so wet."

Widening my eyes, I turned to look at Samir, who wasn't paying us any mind.

"Uh..."

Morgan snapped her head forward, eyes wide as they focused on me. "Was that too much information?"

Immediately, I nodded. No matter how close we'd grown in the two years since she and Samir had made things official, I did *not* need to know about my ex's girlfriend getting aroused as I danced semi-naked on stage.

Bursting into laughter, Morgan covered her face. "I'm sorry, Leese."

I loved Morgan.

I really, really did.

But *Lord* did she make my head hurt sometimes.

The line between being good friends and simply being two women who'd sat on the same dick at different times wasn't thin in the least, but Morgan seemed to have made it one of her life goals to long-jump over it as often as I would allow. For the most part, I let it fly. Morgan was a few years older than Samir and I, and cool as hell. At thirty-five, she was well into her career as a registered nurse, spending ten years at Texas Children's before trading in the twelve-hour shifts for a less demanding, but just as fulfilling, position as a school nurse for a newly built elementary school.

The two met six months after Samir and I decided that we were better off as friends, and spent the next six months pretending that they weren't falling in love with each other. Morgan was a divorced mother of two beautiful little girls, nine-year-old Lillian, who everyone called LeeLee, and Patience, also known as Pooh, who was five just like Amani, but a few months older. I saw with my own eyes how well the kids got along. LeeLee and Pooh treated Amani like he was the little brother they'd always wanted, and that plus the way Morgan loved on my baby and never treated him different than her girls was enough for me to mark them as okay in my mind. And it was nothing to give my blessing when Samir came to me and said he and Morgan wanted to move in together. I trusted him to protect our son, and Morgan hadn't given me anything to be concerned about.

When it came to describing the co-parenting relationship I shared with Samir, *blessed* was putting it mildly. Samir was one of my dearest friends, and everything we did together just... worked. We met as teenagers, when we both joined the same dance company in Dallas, and became fast friends.

Okay, so maybe not *everything* we did together worked. After years of being told we were perfect for one another, we tried the relationship thing. It was cool in the beginning because we already shared so many interests as friends that it seemed like a natural progression for us to become romantic. For a while, it felt effortless. That while lasted a good two years before we realized that we were phoning it in. Our romantic partnership was draining the life out of our friendship, and when we sat down and discussed which relationship we'd rather salvage, friendship was the unanimous decision. That was after I'd moved to Houston with him, and although I was in a new city with almost no one of my own, I didn't want to leave.

I'd made great friends and loved my job at Sanity, not to mention, I made a ridiculous amount of money for the number of hours I clocked. It wasn't easy work, but it was satisfying, and it pulled on the years of training that I had. It was what some would call a win-win.

Except, the thing about sex work is that it made it difficult to find meaningful romantic relationships. So while Samir had met and fallen in love with Morgan, I had gone on a string of unsuccessful dates with stupid men who projected their fetishes onto me, and ignorant women who assumed that, because I was fresh out of a loving relationship with a man, I was only into girls as an extended performance. As if I was incapable of separating my job from my personal life. As if I couldn't in any way be a bisexual woman. Tired of that bullshit, I removed myself from the dating pool and stuck to surface-level hook ups every now and then when my toys weren't enough.

"Hey," Morgan whispered, touching my arm and breaking me out of my thoughts. "I'm going to go put Sanai in her crib and I'll be right back to help wrangle the three musketeers." Slipping her hands underneath the slumbering baby, she lifted Sanai out of my arms and went into the house.

As soon as the screen door clicked shut, Samir came running over, a giggling Amani tucked under one arm like a sack of potatoes, Pooh hanging limply from his other arm, and LeeLee clinging to his back with her arms wrapped tightly around his neck. Stopping in the grass, he shook his body from side to side, causing the kids to shriek with laughter. Pooh and Amani began to twist and kick, trying to free themselves, while LeeLee dropped her hands from Samir's neck to his torso, digging her fingers into his sides and tickling him mercilessly.

Samir, who was the most ticklish person that I knew, fell to his knees, allowing the two youngest to slip out of his grasp and join in with the tickling. When he started screeching as he twisted and writhed on the grass, I laughed so hard I almost peed myself. I couldn't even offer him any assistance because I was physically weak with laughter.

"Uncle!" screamed Samir. "Uncle!"

The three giggling terrors ignored his cries of defeat and continued attacking him.

"Hey!"

Everyone froze at the sound of Morgan's stern voice. I hadn't even noticed that she'd reentered the backyard, but she stood in front of the sliding door, sans Sanai, hands on her hips as she faced the cluster of tiny ticklers. Her eyes were narrowed as she moved closer to the group.

"I know y'all heard him say Uncle. Come up off of him!"

She lunged, and the kids shrieked and jumped back before taking off into the yard, heading for the sprinklers. Morgan crouched over Samir, taking in his heavy breathing.

"Did you pee on yourself?"

Bending forward, I hollered.

Samir frowned up at her.

"What?! Hell no! Why would you ask me that?"

She gestured at his wet shorts.

He sucked his teeth. "Why you tryna play me, man?"

Morgan cracked up and reached for his hand to help him to his feet. Once he was righted, she turned to reclaim her seat, only to be pulled back when he refused to release her hand. He tugged her toward him, placed a hand at her neck, and kissed her. It was so damn sweet.

"Awww," I cooed, hugging myself. "Y'all are so cute."

Morgan's smile was wide when she finally dropped down into her chair.

"You got here just in time," Samir informed me, picking up Morgan's drink and gulping it down. "I've been trying to get them in the house for an hour."

"More like two hours," Morgan corrected. "Sanai done woke up from her nap, had a bottle, and went right back to sleep in the amount of time you've been 'trying' to corral them."

"You're losing your touch?" I asked, tilting my head back to look up at Samir, who rolled his eyes at my question.

Chuckling, he shook his head. "Nah, man. I really thought I had them this time. I didn't expect LeeLee to start tickling me though. That threw a wrench in my plans." He gestured at me. "But now that you're here, they have no excuses. Bath time for everyone!"

"You're welcome," I offered with a gracious dip of my chin.

"Mmhm, go ahead and grab one of those towels," Samir pointed to the colorful stack of fluffy bath towels in the center of the round table. "You know the drill."

Laughing, I nodded and did as I was told. I did, indeed, know the drill. Standing to my feet, I stepped off of the stone patio and shook out the towel, grabbing an end in each hand and stretching the towel lengthwise as I spread my arms wide. Morgan and Samir did the same, and we all stood in a line while Samir whistled to get the kids' attention. Pooh glanced our way first and immediately began to run our way, followed by Amani and then LeeLee. Pooh launched at Morgan, who immediately wrapped the giggling girl in the towel, sweeping her off of her feet in a dramatic fashion that had peals of laughter bursting out of Pooh's lips.

LeeLee headed right for Samir, jumping into the air only to be caught and swung in a circle as Samir wrapped her up like a burrito with only her head and feet exposed. The smallest of the three, Amani, reached me last, jumping at me with his arms spread open just like mine. As he clung to me, I draped the towel across his body like a toga and rubbed vigorously as we all headed into the house. After being in the yard for however long, my baby smelled like a puppy and had blades of grass all over his legs and in his hair. He needed a bath before we could go anywhere, but Samir spoke without me having to say a word.

"Let's go, Amani. It's bath time, baby boy."

"Okay." Amani wriggled in my arms. "I gotta go take a bath, Mommy."

As soon as I knelt to set him down, he took off running toward his father. Samir scooped him up and carried Amani and

LeeLee toward the stairs with Morgan right behind them, still holding Pooh.

"We'll be right back," Samir tossed over his shoulder before disappearing up the second flight of stairs.

We'd done some variation of this routine enough times that I knew I had around thirty minutes to chill before my son would be ready to leave with me. I didn't even mind the wait. Amani loved the time he spent with his father so much that he used to have full-on tantrums if Samir tried to get him ready before my arrival. We learned early on that Amani needed to lay eyes on me to accept that it was time for him to leave his father's side. It saved us plenty of headaches—and tears—to just build an extra half hour into our exchange times, and it had actually benefited our relationship as parents. Seeing Samir and me spend time together as a family, but not as a couple, had been so healthy for all of the kids.

As a child of two people who could never agree on anything but abandoning their only child to be raised by her grandmother, I never would have believed in my wildest dreams things could be so...amiable between non-coupled parents. Add to that Morgan's determination to help us in any way, and just imagine Big Sean's "Blessings" playing on a steady loop in the soundtrack of my life. I sat on the couch, picked up the remote from the coffee table, and turned on the latest episode of *Abbott Elementary*. Just as the show came to an end, my exuberant baby boy came barreling down the stairs, headed for me at full speed. Bracing myself for impact, I scooted to the edge of the sofa and spread my arms as I had with the towel outside. To my surprise, Amani screeched to a halt at my knees and climbed in my lap, wrapping his arms around my shoulders as he kissed my cheek.

"Hi, Mommy."

Looping my arms around his tiny body, I hugged him to me and rocked him from side to side. "Hey, my baby. I missed you."

Amani leaned back, bringing his hands to my face as he gazed at me; his warm brown eyes that were so much like his father's were dipped low, making his expression appear almost studious. His normally tawny skin had taken on a light caramel hue from the sun, and his thick brown hair was damp and smelled like cocoa butter.

"I'm hungry," he stated, his tone matter-of-fact.

That was so far from what I expected to come out of his mouth that I cracked up laughing.

"I'm gonna feed you, greedy boy. We're going to a barbecue."

Gasping, he jumped out of my arms and ran across the living room to grab his sneakers. He was sitting on the floor in front of me, one foot planted on the ground, the other in the air, waiting for me to lace his shoe, when Samir came down the stairs.

"You heading out?"

"Yep. There's a barbecue at the Thomas residence and we've been invited."

"Aww, man," Samir whined. "I know Mr. Thomas put his foot in that! I'd tell you to bring me a plate but…" He trailed off with a sigh.

Finishing Amani's shoe, I stood to my feet and stretched.

"But what?" It was almost dinner time and there was nary a pot to be found on the stove in the kitchen. There was a question on the tip of my tongue, but Samir had already anticipated it.

"One of Morgan's old coworkers from Texas Children's is having a birthday dinner, and it's kid friendly." He made a sour face that made me laugh.

"I take it you don't want to go."

"Hell no! This is one of her bougie friends. Her husband is cool, so I know I'll have someone to talk to, but the food is about to be nasty as hell. I'm considering making a sandwich before we leave."

Laughing, I waited for Amani to give his father a hug and kiss before reaching for my hand.

"Good luck with that," I offered. "I'll be sure to eat an extra rib in your honor."

Samir walked us to the front door, shaking his head. "That's cold-blooded, man."

"It is what it is," I laughed. "See you later."

Outside I opened the backdoor of my compact sedan and stood on watch as my baby climbed into his booster seat and buckled himself in without my help. Closing the door, I slid behind the wheel and backed out of Samir and Morgan's driveway. I was barely out of the neighborhood when my phone rang and Mercedes's name flashed across my dashboard screen.

Glancing in my rearview mirror, I met eyes with Amani, who grinned toothily and waved at me.

"Hi, Mommy!" he shouted, as if a playground separated us instead of merely two feet.

"Hey, my baby."

I pressed a button on my steering wheel to answer it and quickly spoke before she had an opportunity to.

"You're on Bluetooth and my baby can hear you."

The sound of my friend sucking her teeth confirmed that my warning was well placed. Clearly she was about to say something that little ears need not hear.

"Hey, Tee Tee baby!"

"Tee Tee 'Cedes!"

Another glance at the rearview and I watched Amani's eyes light up. A grin took over my face as I let them talk. There was something about people having genuine love for your child that just brought so much peace to your soul.

"Mommy!"

Pulled out of my thoughts, I quickly glanced at Amani through the mirror before making a left turn at the light.

"Yes, baby?"

"Can I go spinnanight at Tee Tee 'Cedes's when Malik comes from break?"

"When he what?" I asked chuckling. I'd clearly missed some key information in their little chat.

Mercedes laughed. "The boys will be with their dad this week, but they get back Friday and 'Mani can come spend the weekend with us. Or just one night, if you or Samir have plans."

"Please, Mommy?" Amani asked, giving me puppy-dog eyes and a poked-out lip like a true master manipulator, aka a seasoned toddler.

I thought about it as I navigated onto the highway.

"You don't work next weekend?"

"Nope. I'm off and was thinking about taking the boys up to Six Flags on Saturday with my sister and her kids. 'Mani can just go with us."

Mercedes's sister had five kids under ten, and the thought of all those kids at the big theme park had me skeptical. "Which one?" Referring to which park location she was thinking of.

"San Antonio, chile," Mercedes said with a quickness. "I'm not traipsing all over Arlington with eight babies. Even if three other adults will be there too."

I laughed at the fact that we were on the same page.

"That's fine with me. Put his season pass to good use so that I'm not paying all this money for nothing."

"Exactly!" Mercedes agreed.

We laughed together before I called out to my son.

"You can go, baby."

He cheered, pumping his little fist into the air as if he'd just finished first place in a 10k marathon.

"Is that what you called for?" I asked after the line fell silent for more than a minute.

"Yep!" she exclaimed. "Now that that's out the way, what y'all about to get into?"

"We're heading to the Thomases' for a barbecue."

"*Oh*," Mercedes drawled suggestively. "Going to kick with the in-laws, huh?"

"Girl, fu—" I caught myself and laughed. "I almost cussed you out. You can go right to Lucifer's lair. Quickly and with haste."

Her amused cackling exploded in my ear, causing me to roll my eyes in response.

"Yeah, okay."

The jokes I got behind my friendship with Poppa were no different than the ones I'd received for me and Samir. What was it that made people think two adults couldn't be *just friends*? Never mind the fact that Samir and I did eventually get into a relationship. Before that, we were strictly friends and nothing else, and honestly, I think the constant inquiries from everyone around us were what made the idea seem plausible to us.

This time around, I knew better. All opinions from outsiders were simply ignored.

Chapter Five

Jucee

Summatime Fine

The Thomases had a modest home on the southwest side of the city, in the Mission Bend area. Their particular neighborhood was full of older homes with two-car garages on larger-than-average lots. As cliché as it sounded, the grass over there was, without-a-doubt, greener. The air also smelled a little sweeter, cleaner. Maybe it was the mature trees that dotted the community, their lush canopies naturally shading the wide streets and providing a home to a bevy of raucous birds and skittering squirrels. It was beautiful to experience in the spring and fall months, but it was especially captivating in the winter, when the entire neighborhood came together to decorate each street with lights and displays for the full month of December.

I shifted the car into Park and twisted in my seat to find Amani already pulling his arms through the straps of his booster seat. Laughing, I turned off the car and stepped onto the street, using my hip to close my door before opening his and finishing the job of disconnecting his buckles before he got stuck.

"Wait, baby!" I urged when he began to lurch against the straps.

"Hurry, Mommy! Nana Cherry's in there!"

The moment that the last buckle across his chest was released, he slid out of his seat and pushed past me to jump out of the car. As soon as his sneakered feet touched the grass on the embankment, he took off running, heading right for the Texas-shaped pavers that formed a path from the sidewalk to the front door.

"Careful!" I called out, knowing even as the word left my mouth that my determined baby would do no such thing.

He kept on, pace undisturbed, little arms pumping as he crossed the large lawn. The door flung open and Poppa's septuagenarian grandmother crouched on one knee, her arms spread wide.

"My 'Mani!"

"Nana Cherry!" Amani shouted, somehow speeding up out of nowhere with no extra traction immediately visible.

My first instinct was to grab him or, once again, call out to him, this time with instructions to slow down. The last thing I wanted was for him to unintentionally harm the nearly eighty-year-old woman, but after Nana Cherry fussed me out good one similarly beautiful Sunday afternoon for attempting to "stifle his expression of joy," I now just stood back and watched the marvel that was the bond they shared. Seven decades separated them, but Nana Cherry caught my baby and lifted him into the air as if he weighed four pounds instead of forty. The urge to tell Amani to get down was strong, but my good sense was stronger. There was no way I was about to argue with a woman who'd not only helped bring several babies into the world with her own hands as a midwife, but who also played a major part in the upbringing of one of my favorite people on the planet.

"Hey, Nana Cherry," I murmured, bending slightly to press a kiss to the woman's paper-thin cheek. Her eyes were glued to my giggling son, but I wasn't offended that she wasn't paying me much mind. The way she doted on him was healing for the part of me that still mourned my grandmother, who'd passed right after my eighteenth birthday.

"Hay is for horses, Juleesa," she quipped. Though she hadn't looked up at me, I could see her sharp cheekbones lifted in amusement.

"Yeah, Mommy!" Amani instigated, peering at me upside down from his perch in Nana Cherry's arms. "You have to say 'Good afternoon' because it's after twelve o'clock p.m.!"

Expelling an exaggerated gasp, I snapped. "You're right, 'Mani! I completely forgot the time!"

Tilting my head so that I was in Nana Cherry's peripheral, I smiled. Without a doubt, I knew that was something that she had taught him. Poppa's grandmother kept Amani for me three days out of the week when his four-hour kindergarten class let out before I finished work, and also on Fridays since he didn't have school and both Samir and I had to work. What she did for me was more than just babysitting.

Every day with Nana Cherry was essentially homeschooling for Amani. Just by nature of keeping him, she taught him so many things that they weren't even concerned with at his school. While the other kids were identifying shapes and colors, my baby knew the difference between root and cruciferous vegetables from working alongside her in her garden, he knew that you couldn't take certain medications with juice because it would nullify their effect, and he also knew what Victor Newman did for a living and how his trifling children could never do right. That last little tidbit had sent me into a wheezing fit of giggles when it had come out of his mouth.

Nana Cherry reminded me so much of my own grandmother that it made my heart ache. Mommie would've been a couple of years younger than Nana Cherry but just as animated and active.

"Good afternoon, Nana Cherry."

This time, she looked up at me, watery blue-brown eyes full of mischief. Puckering her lips, she waited until I offered her my cheek to kiss before speaking. "Afternoon, Juleesa. Thank you for bringing my favorite great-grand to me. Cyndi's been looking for you."

As if cued by someone offstage, Poppa entered the foyer just as her name was called, looking good as hell in a yellow linen short set with the top unbuttoned showing off a white tank top with low lemon drop Dunks on her feet. My brows furrowed for a second because that yellow on her deep-brown skin was sexy as fuck—and that was a thought I shouldn't have about my best friend.

Lips twisted to the side, Poppa gave her grandmother a side-eye.

"How you gon' call 'Mani your favorite like Dougie ain't get that Pomeranian down the street pregnant?"

Nana Cherry shrieked with laughter and shifted Amani to her hip as she swung out at Poppa, who jumped back before the slap could land.

"Hush up, you!"

Hands lifted in surrender, Poppa shook her head. "I'm just saying. Dougie is a part of this family—don't ignore his children."

Pursing her lips, the older woman flicked her fingers at her only granddaughter. "How about you worry less about what I said and worry more about feeding Juleesa. She looks hungry."

With that, she spun on her heels and left the foyer, my baby on her hip, grin big and wide as he waved me goodbye.

Grateful to have something to focus on other than my unruly thoughts, I turned to Poppa and frowned.

"I look hungry?"

Instead of immediately answering me, Poppa laughed and

pulled me into a hug, both of her arms wrapping around my lower back as she squeezed, stealing my breath for more than one reason as she lifted me a couple of inches off of the ground. I felt and heard something crack in my back and yelped, pushing her away.

"What the hell, Poppa?! You tryna break my damn back?"

Laughing, she pulled me back toward her, looping an arm over my shoulder and dropping a kiss onto my cheek. "You can take it."

The double entendre made me burst out laughing. I shook my head, leaving her arm in place and allowing her to lead me through her parents' house and to the sliding door that opened out to the backyard.

"That don't make it right, you perv."

Chuckling, she slid the door closed behind us. "Why I gotta be a pervert just because you like it rough? Make that make sense."

Unable to contain my grin, I shook my head again. "I'm not about to play with you today."

"Yeah, yeah," she muttered, "tell me anything."

She started heading for the food table, but I made a left and walked toward the group of people line-dancing in the grass. As hungry as I was, there was no way I was going to sit down and grub without speaking first. I didn't recognize everyone in the yard, but I still smiled and waved when I made eye contact. It wasn't hard to spot Poppa's father in the throng of people doing the Electric Slide. Not only because Poppa was his spitting image, but because his hulking frame towered over most everyone else. Mr. Marvin was the definition of a teddy bear, big, loving, and gentle, and Poppa took after him in many ways.

Just observing him brought a smile to my face. His shiny, uncovered, bald head glistened under the bright sun, his white teeth gleaming as he grinned. And he was clearly having a good time, his eyes on Mrs. Carissa, who had her hands on her knees as she freestyled the cha-cha part in front of him, tooting her butt in the air with her tongue between her teeth as she looked back at it.

"Okay!" I cheered, stopping on the side of their makeshift dance floor and rocking to the beat.

The song came to an end and immediately transitioned into "K-Wang." I expected them both to jump into the steps, but they surprised me by simultaneously heading right for me. Mr. Marvin used a yellow hand towel that matched his polo to wipe his face and head while Mrs. Carissa threw her arms around me.

"Juleesa!" she exclaimed, rocking me from side to side as if it had been ages since she'd seen me. Her exuberance each and every time I saw her was one of the things I loved about her.

Mr. Marvin tossed his towel over his shoulder before bending down to hug me to his side as his wife stepped aside.

"Good to see you, baby girl. Did you eat?"

I shook my head. "Not yet. I wanted to come speak first."

Nodding, he squeezed my shoulder and stood back. "Well, I'm glad you made it. Star Shine has been watching the door for at least an hour."

Beside me, Poppa sucked her teeth. "Why is everybody acting like I've been pacing a hospital waiting room while I wait for the surgeon to come out and give me results?"

Her parents met eyes, sharing twin smirks that made Poppa roll her eyes.

"Man, whatever! Y'all not gon' make me feel bad for waiting on my friend to eat."

Mr. Marvin lifted his hands in surrender and ducked his head. "We wouldn't dream of it." Looping an around his wife's waist, he tucked Mrs. Carissa under his arm. "I also wait on my best friend to arrive before I eat and have been doing so for thirty-five years."

"Chill out, Daddy," Poppa chuckled, grabbing my arm and leading me to the other side of the yard.

Laughing, I waved goodbye.

"Don't do them like that," I scolded teasingly. "They're innocent."

"Nah," she denied. "They buggin'. One of my cousins had a baby a few weeks ago and since then, they've been throwing hints here and there about grandkids. This is just another level of that."

That stopped me in my tracks. Hinting that me and Poppa should get together was one thing, but wanting us to get together and produce a baby was a flavor of déjà vu that left a sour taste in my mouth. Part of me and Samir hooking up was due to pressure from his parents to produce grandchildren before they were "too old to spoil them." I loved my baby, but I refused to be pushed down that road again. I just wanted to have a best friend that everyone respected as my best friend, who remained my best friend without any fanfare.

Poppa had released me to walk alongside her, our arms occasionally bumping as we squeezed past people in the semi-full yard. After stopping by the table where Nana Cherry and some of her girlfriends sat fawning over Amani as he ate, we continued on. My stomach grumbled loudly, causing Poppa to stop in her tracks and swing widened eyes onto me.

"That was your belly howling like that?"

Laughing, I clutched my stomach and nodded.

"Yeah, man. I'm starving."

"What a coincidence," chimed Cody, popping up on my right with a plate of ribs and sides in his hands. "These have your name written all over them."

My eyes lit up at the sight of perfectly smoked meat, seasoned baked beans, grilled corn, and dirty rice. I lifted my hands, palms upward and ready to receive my blessing.

"Thank you, Cody!" I cooed once the plate was securely in my hands. I didn't hesitate to raise a rib to my mouth and take a bite.

"Seriously?" scoffed Poppa. "I waited on you and you gon' take food from this fool?" The look in her eyes gave me pause. It wasn't the normal exasperation that I saw when her and Cody went back and forth, but I didn't quite know how to catego- rize it. It was almost something like jealousy, but that didn't make sense.

"Sowwy," I murmured with a full mouth, finding it hard to be truly apologetic with the succulent meat still on my tongue. "You heard my stomach." Sliding my gaze to Cody, I dipped my head.

His cheeks bloomed as he bit his lip, giving him a boyish ap- pearance. Quicker than I could blink, he hugged me to his side and planted a kiss on my temple before stepping back. Ignoring Poppa's glare, he shoved his hands in his pockets.

"You should let me take you out sometime. Let me show you how many more of your needs I can anticipate and meet without you asking——" licking his lips, he winked at me "——or having to point me in the right direction."

Cody was nothing if not persistent, but I couldn't deny that he was also smooth as hell. If I was another woman, that line might've had my panties in hand, ready to transfer ownership. Another thing I couldn't deny was his attractiveness. Despite being the baby of the Thomas bunch, Cody was both the tallest at over six feet, and the biggest with years of playing football through high school and college working with genetics from his father to make him broad and solid. Where Poppa looked like their father and Caleb taking after their mother, Cody was a perfect mix of Mr. Marvin's mahogany skin and sleepy, deep brown eyes and Mrs. Carissa's thick black hair and dimples.

To put things simply, Cody was a problem in the best of ways. But someone *else's* problem.

Several someone elses', actually. He didn't lack for female attention, which is why I was certain his fixation on me was solely his attempt at needling Poppa. She'd made it clear that he'd ruined friendships for her when they were teenagers, and she refused to let him do that to her as an adult. I thought the whole thing—his constant flirting *and* her reactions—was funny as hell.

Huffing, Poppa walked off, traversing the final few feet to the table where food was in buffet trays over lit butane cans. Shaking my head, I headed after her, chuckling when Cody fell into step with me.

"You need to leave her alone," I stated before biting into the perfectly buttered ear of corn from my plate.

"Now where's the fun in that?"

Not having an answer for him, I just shook my head again and went to sit at one of the picnic tables. I learned early on that this was about *and* between them and didn't really have much to do with me at all, so I did my best to stay out of it. Once I settled down and started to eat, Poppa slid an overloaded plate on my right and climbed onto the bench seat, accidentally on purpose bumping my elbow as she got situated.

Smirking, I waited for her to finish before grabbing my last rib.

"You done flirting with my knucklehead brother?"

Dropping the rib, I threw my head back and hollered.

"Who's buggin' now?" I asked.

Her face was to her plate, but I saw her cheeks lift as she grinned, indicating that she wasn't really upset.

"Definitely still my parents."

All I could do was laugh. Poppa knew damn well that I wasn't checking for Cody, and she likely knew he felt the same way. I was an only child so I didn't understand it, but this was probably just a way they played with each other. As long as no one was genuinely mad at me, I didn't mind it.

The companionable silence that we'd fallen into as we ate was interrupted when Amani ran up to me, hope and excitement all over his face.

"What is it, baby?" I asked, wiping my fingers on a napkin and turning to straddle the bench so that I could pull him up to sit between my legs.

"Mommy, can I spend the night?"

My eyebrows rose. "You just spent the week at your daddy's house, baby boy. Aren't you ready to come home with Mommy?"

Jumping off of the bench, he took off across the yard, running up to Nana Cherry. I stood to my feet and followed his path. When he spun on his heel, preparing to run back to me, I caught him around the waist and lifted him into the air, tickling his sides as I cradled him in my arms and approached the circle of elderly women.

"Whose idea was this?" I asked, my lips curved into a smile. There was really no telling when it came to those two.

Nana Cherry raised a hand. "Guilty. I know you just got him back, but Mary was telling me how they're playing the latest animal cartoon movie at Discovery Green in about an hour, and I thought 'Mani might like to go since Mary is meeting her grands up there who are about his same age. We might do ice cream afterward, and I didn't want you to have to wait up for him, so I told him to ask you if he could just stay the night."

Pursing my lips, I thought it over. I had just gotten Amani back. He'd spent the previous week with Samir and I'd missed him, but one more day wouldn't hurt. Kissing my baby's cheek, I set him on his feet.

"I trust you not to have him up too late, and to make sure he doesn't have too much sugar."

Nana Cherry cringed, and I huffed a light laugh. Clearly my rules were cutting into their plans.

"I'll make sure he gets the right amount of sleep," Nana Cherry assured me, pulling my son toward her. Grinning triumphantly, Amani nodded.

"Yeah, Mommy."

It didn't miss me how she didn't address the sugar intake, and all I could do was shake my head. The decision was made, whether I knew it or not, and all I was left to do was pretend like it was up to me despite me knowing otherwise. When those two came up with a plan, there wasn't much I could do to sway them. Luckily, it was never anything that I ever felt the need to put my foot down on.

Heading back to the picnic table I'd been sitting at, I gathered up my empty plate and went to toss it in the trash. When I sat back down, Poppa nudged me with her elbow.

"So, I take it you're kid-free for one more night."

Sighing, I nodded. "Indeed."

Sucking barbecue sauce off her thumb, Poppa echoed my nod. "Cool. I have to head into the studio for a couple hours, but Xeno wants to pop out to VR for a lil bit so, since your schedule is open, come with."

As much as I teased Poppa about Xeno and I sharing a title, I didn't hold any animosity toward the other woman. In fact, I loved hanging out with the two of them, which often included Xeno's girlfriend, Trisha, who was funny and reminded me of some of the girls I grew up with back in Dallas.

"What time are you thinking?"

Poppa pulled her phone out of the pocket of her shorts and tapped at the screen a few times.

"Around eleven," she finally answered.

I nodded. That gave me a couple of hours to go home and catch a nap.

"Count me in."

Chapter Six

Jucee

Real Friend Girl Shit

Amani and Nana Cherry left for the park about half an hour later, but I didn't say my goodbye until after seven. As soon as I got in the car, I called Mercedes and told her the plan, inviting her to join us. She usually danced on Sundays, so I was prepared for her to decline, but she said she'd meet us at the club since she had an earlier set.

Thirty-five minutes later I was in my condo in Midtown, scarf and bonnet secured and timer set as I slid beneath the cool sheets. Even though I danced during the day, I was no stranger to impromptu naps and found myself asleep in less than ten minutes. When I woke up, there was a strange sort of buzzing in my gut as I rifled through my closet, and I realized that I was excited about going out. Poppa and I hadn't had many opportunities to hang out over the past few weeks because she'd been busy in the studio. I understood, but I also missed my friend. Daily calls and texts were great, but they weren't enough.

I was used to us meeting each other for breakfast and video

chatting regularly. I was used to sending memes back and forth on several different platforms and immediately making plans to watch it together that night. When Poppa was in grind-mode, her phone was off and she rarely left the studio. She sequestered herself and whichever artist she was working with inside that room and made magic come alive out of thin air. Now that she'd resurfaced, I wanted to spend as much time with her as possible.

The club we were heading to was more on the upscale side, so I dressed in a black tube-top bodysuit with a sheer, knee-length bodycon dress over it. For a pop of color, I chose golden stiletto sandals with straps that wound around my calves and tied into a bow behind my knee and a matching golden clutch.

After scooting my seat back to make driving easier in my heels, I headed to Poppa's ranch-style house in Memorial. When she opened the door looking scrumdiddlyumptious, I grinned. She wore a black dress shirt with the top buttons undone, giving a peek at the valley of her hiked-up titties, gray slacks, black suede loafers, and her signature gold jewelry. I followed her into the house as she grabbed her wallet and keys off of the leather couch.

"Oh, you must be tryna catch some pussy tonight," I mused, "looking all fine and shit like this."

Just like Cody didn't want for female attention, neither did Poppa. And neither did Caleb, for that matter, but he tended to date men more than women and was also more the relationship type than his playboy younger siblings.

Poppa's grin was sly as she ushered me back out of the house. "You know how I do" was her cryptic answer, but after being around her for three years, I knew exactly how to decipher that. Poppa had been laying low for a minute while she worked her ass off—undoubtedly to produce the next Grammy Award–winning single—and hadn't been on her usual shenanigans with women. Pussy was definitely the goal for the night. I didn't judge her for that at all, even though I didn't move the same way.

Things were a little different for me though. After Samir and I split, I dated a few people who were nice but left me feeling unfulfilled. Either they were great in bed but boring to talk to, or cool to party with but looked down on sex workers. I'd been surprised and disappointed by how many people could meet an exotic dancer *while she worked*, yet judge her for the job she did. Not wanting to continue wasting time with temporary people who only brought me temporary pleasure, I stopped dating and focused on finding joy in being single. It was the best decision that I'd ever made, after moving to Houston.

I took myself on a date every week and made sure that I learned what made me happy. Rediscovering Juleesa was a journey that I thoroughly enjoyed. I hadn't had sex in almost a year, and most of the time I didn't even think about it. *Most of the time.*

The rest of the time…let's just say that the person I end up with might need to schedule a few sick days so that I can re-lease my pent-up…emotions without rushing.

They might also need to have a recovery massage lined up.

"Here," Poppa called, tossing me her keys and simultane-ously breaking me out of my thoughts.

I climbed in the passenger seat of her car and cranked up the engine while she pulled my car into her garage. From the out-side looking in, it might have seemed chivalrous, but the truth was that she regularly talked cash shit about my driving and once said that she'd rather move my car herself than have me scratch up something of hers. There was nothing wrong with the way I drove; Poppa was just particular. Some might—and have—call it controlling, but I didn't see it that way. I loved the way she took the reins of her life and steered it in the direction she wanted. As someone who had spent my formidable years living according to what my parents decided was right and wrong, I admired the hell out of Poppa for that.

Locking my door with the key fob, Poppa jumped behind the wheel and we headed south to Xeno and Trisha's house. They were already in the car and waited for us to circle the cul-de-sac before exiting the neighborhood. We made it to VR Club and Lounge and followed Xeno's bodyguard through the building and up to VIP. Once we were situated, the DJ shouted out Poppa and Xeno before playing Xeno's latest single. The volume in the building grew as folks cheered and began rapping along to the lyrics.

It was like a mini concert, with the energy getting even the most introverted person hype enough to start spitting lyrics at strangers. The VIP was just as lit as the dance floor. Status didn't matter when it came to appreciating good music, and what Xeno was doing for the rap game—let alone Houston—was too impressive to ignore.

Several rap songs cycled on before the R&B came out. That's when things became a little weird. We went from rapping to dancing, all of us up on our feet vibing out to the spectacular mix of tracks the DJ was spinning. It was nothing for me to bend at the waist and back it up on Poppa. I'd done it a million times before, and she usually just laughed and slapped my ass once or twice. Sometimes she caught it and danced with me for a few beats before waving me off with a laugh.

To my surprise, she didn't do either of those things that night. Gripping my hips, she ground against me, rolling her body sensually. And because I wasn't new to this, but tried and true to this, I rolled with her. We danced as if we'd had a brief interview on a black leather couch beforehand. My body was heated, primed, and ready to go. I forgot where I was until the side of her arm brushed my chest and the fear of Poppa feeling my erect nipples through my mesh dress and thin bodysuit snapped me out of my fog. Thankfully, the song came to an end, giving me an excuse to pull out of her grasp, and she didn't protest.

Why the hell was I so juiced up from a damn dance? I did this shit on a regular and by this point, a dance was nothing. Turning around, I pasted a grin on my face, prepared to laugh it off, but the expression on her face stopped me.

I had to be seeing things. That was the only explanation, because there was no way Poppa would be giving me the *Dirty Dancing* hungry eyes. Hell, there was no way Poppa—*my Poppa*—would've been giving me a proper daggering as if we were at a Caribbean fête either, and yet, here we were. My mind was racing, scrambling trying to come up with a logical reason for my body's reaction and now this look on Poppa's face. Her lips parted and my chest tightened, but Xeno clapped a hand down onto Poppa's shoulder, breaking the seconds-long stare-off we were locked into. Grateful for the distraction, I immediately excused myself to go to the bathroom, pulling Mercedes along with me. The dance floor wasn't too crowded, and there wasn't a line to nab one of the eight stalls. The bathrooms were single, unconnected rooms with frosted-glass doors along a dimly lit hallway. Mercedes primped in the mirror while I peed, and then we switched places.

"You gonna tell me when you and Cyn Tha Starr started fuckin' or are we still pretending y'all are just besties?"

Usually I was ready for Mercedes's random vulgarity, but I was caught off guard this time around and it was purely because I was distracted. My mind was back in VIP with Poppa's hands on my hips.

Frowning, I glared at Mercedes in the mirror.

"We *are* just besties!"

Smirking, Mercedes quirked an eyebrow. "The kind that bump coochies?"

Flipping her the bird, I didn't even bother answering her. After she washed her hands and refreshed her lipstick, we exited the bathroom.

"Girl, you are wearing the hell out of that dress!"

A gorgeous, caramel-skinned baddie stood in the middle of the hallway, a hand on her hip as she grinned at us. Instinctively, I knew the woman was talking about me. Hell, it was almost verbatim what I'd said to myself before I left the house for the night. That wasn't to say that Mercedes didn't look good, because my girl was bad, but it was an inexplicable feeling that came, along with the feeling that she wasn't being completely honest. I wasn't unused to random compliments from strangers, but something about this woman's declaration rang false.

Slim, with tig ole biddies, she wore a silver, sleeveless minidress with a heart-shaped keyhole at the base of her neck, which put said biddies on display. The dress stopped mere inches below her pussy and showcased the miles of oiled-up legs she possessed. Her rust-brown hair was styled in two massive afro puffs, and there were exaggerated swoops gelled at her temples. With glossy, two-toned lips and silver rectangular hoops in her ears, baby girl was capital-*F* fine. I might've been on a self-imposed sex sabbatical, but that didn't mean I couldn't look.

After giving her what was surely an obviously thorough once-over, I dipped my chin. "Thank you, gorgeous. I must say the same about you."

Her face brightened and smile widened. "Thank you!"

Sudden chattering sounded from her right and our left as a group of women came down the hallway in search of the bathrooms. Baby girl was all in everybody's way, but instead of continuing on into one of the stalls, she took a step closer to me and Mercedes. Confused why the moment wasn't over and the woman didn't just continue on into one of the stalls, I turned to meet Mercedes's eyes. She had an eyebrow quirked but otherwise didn't look nearly as lost as I felt.

"Oh, hey! You two were in VIP with Xeno, right?"

Mercedes instantly started cracking up and I rolled my eyes, giving her an exasperated look before swinging my gaze back to the woman.

Damn.

I'd thought we'd just experienced a beautiful moment of club bathroom appreciation, but it was all a ploy.

Baby girl was a groupie.

Don't get me wrong—I had nothing against groupies, I swear. Hell, I had a few myself despite only working during primetime one weekend a month. Sanity was one of the most popular strip clubs in Houston, which was saying a lot, so I was used to kicking it with celebrities from all mediums, and groupies were a part of the fame that couldn't be avoided. I wasn't judging baby girl for having stars in her eyes; it just stung a little to realize that my intuition had been right and her praise likely wasn't genuine, but instead only a means to an end.

Pasting a smile onto my face, I reached over and grabbed Mercedes's arm, nodding toward the end of the hallway as I took a step in that direction before I turned to face the woman. I didn't want to be rude, but the moment had dragged on long enough and now it was time to go.

"Yeah. We were."

Hiking the short strap of the silver bag she carried higher onto her shoulder, she nodded and took a couple of steps closer to us.

What the hell?

"Oh, okay. I thought so." Her eyes bounced from me to Mercedes and then back to me. "So, are y'all on a double date or something?"

My eyebrows shot up while Mercedes continued giggling

next to me. That was a really personal question for someone you'd just met in the bathroom. Groupies didn't care about shit like privacy, evident in her accosting us right outside the bathroom of all places and then attempting to follow us.

Tilting my head to the side, I eyed her. "Since it's clear you only complimented my dress to start a conversation, just tell me what you want to know so I can get out of this hallway."

The woman giggled but didn't even have the decency to look remorseful for her recon mission.

"Is the stud with the waves your girlfriend? Y'all were dancing kinda close and I don't want to step on any toes."

Mercedes shrieked, and this time I joined in, laughing heartily at the question. Whatever brand of audacity that men consumed on a regular, baby girl must've taken a shot of it before following us down the hallway. "Girl, if you truly thought she was my girlfriend, you wouldn't even be asking me this. But to answer your question, no. That's my bestie. And just in case you want to ask another question *that isn't really any of your business*, I don't fuck my friends." I might've had a bit of an attitude, but it was warranted. It wasn't like I'd planned to give her a chance anyway, but the way she went about trying to holla was all wrong and now I was just annoyed.

"She's telling the truth," Mercedes insisted. Clucking her tongue, she finally started moving, pulling me with her away from the stall since I still had my hand on her arm. "I tried to throw some pussy her way when we first met, but she said she don't fuck single moms." She tossed the last part over her shoulder, making the other women in the hallway who were waiting on a free stall break out into laughter.

I hollered, slapping her arm once we were clear of the entrance. "If you don't shut your lyin' ass up! Now you gon' have that girl telling lies about me on social media."

My friend rolled her eyes. "Trust me, talking about you on-line is probably the very last thing that's on that woman's mind."

I shot her a side–eye. "How you figure?"

Pursing her lips, Mercedes gave me a dumb look. "Girl, duh. She pressed you for information about Cyn 'cause that's who she's after. Lil mama is on the hunt and you were just the chum she used to reel in her catch."

Frowning, I released Mercedes's arm and grasped her hand, holding tight as we trudged through the now incredibly crowded dance floor to reach the stairs for VIP. Calling me chum was rude as hell but, more importantly, how had I read the situation so wrong? I'd instantly assumed baby girl was com-ing for me, but thinking the conversation over, she hadn't even flirted that hard. I shook my head in disappointment, hoping that my long–term singledom hadn't destroyed my ability to recognize real interest.

There was a twinge in my brain that whispered how I'd seen very real and clear interest in Poppa's eyes not even twenty minutes ago, but I blinked it away. That was…well, I couldn't blame it on the alcohol, since Poppa didn't drink. None of the Thomases drank, not since Carissa started on a path to sobri-ety ten years ago.

Thinking about the support of loved ones brought Poppa right back to the forefront of my mind. Lil Miss Afro Puffs was just her type, and I hoped I hadn't just set Poppa up for some bullshit by giving that girl more information than she deserved. Despite how attractive the unknown woman was, she could've been a crazed fan with ulterior motives. You could never tell these days. I felt another twinge as we trekked back across the dance floor, this time in my gut instead of my brain. The last thing I wanted to do was send yet another good-for-nothing woman in Poppa's direction.

When we arrived back up to Xeno's section, Poppa was missing and Trisha announced that we were going to do a round of shots. I talked her out of ordering tequila, which made Juleesa a Very Horny Girl, and convinced her that whiskey was the better option. The shots arrived quickly, but Poppa still hadn't returned. After tossing the shots back and placing the glasses on the tray, I went to Xeno, who was hugged up with Trisha, kissing on her neck. I hated to interrupt their super sweet moment, but I needed to know where Poppa was.

Just to be safe.

"Where'd Cyn go?" I asked, leaning toward them to help project my voice over the music.

Trisha met my eye and tapped Xeno's arm.

"Bae, she's looking for Cyn."

Blinking out of lovey-dovey bliss, Xeno looked over at me for a minute, as if she was processing the question.

"Oh," she said after a moment. "She went to speak to the DJ." With her finger, she pointed toward the dance floor.

Turning, I looked in the direction she indicated, squinting to see in the dim lights, sweeping my eyes over the crowd right in front of the DJ booth. I felt a thud in my gut when I spotted her. Trying to get a closer look, I walked over to the railing, both hands on top as I willed my sight to zoom in like those goggles in the spy movies. I didn't need to zoom in though, because the club wasn't so massive that I couldn't make out the image down on the dance floor.

Poppa was standing near the stairs to the DJ booth, a glass in one hand, while the other was on the back of a woman who stood in front of her, speaking into her ear. The woman in question?

Lil Miss Afro Puffs.

"Well, well, well," cooed Mercedes into my ear as she came to stand right next to me at the railing. "What do we have here?" Rolling my eyes, I shot her a quick glare before returning my gaze to the dance floor. That proved to be a mistake, and I watched as Poppa threw her head back and laughed at something that girl said to her. Jaw clenched, I spun around, putting the image to my back as I leaned against the rail. Mercedes smirked at me.

"What are you talking about?" I snapped, annoyance all up and down my tone.

"I'm talking about this—" she gestured at my face "—attitude you recently acquired." My frown deepened, and her grin immediately spread in response. "Could it have something to do with lil mama from the bathroom pushing up on your...*bestie?*"

"Ugh!" I hated the high-pitched tone she used when she said *bestie*. "Why do you have to say it like that?"

"How am I saying it, friend?"

"Like you don't even believe the words coming out of your mouth. Like calling us besties is bullshit. Like me and Poppa are cosplaying as friends but be scissoring in secret!"

Mercedes tilted her head to the side, the corners of her mouth drooping as her shoulders lifted slightly.

"I mean..."

I scoffed. "There's something about that girl that I don't like. I can't fully explain it, but it has *nothing* to do with her and Poppa being hugged up and *everything* to do with her lil recon mission earlier."

Lips curved in amusement, Mercedes dipped her chin. "Oh, okay. You not ready. It's cool."

My brows started straining and reaching for each other as Mercedes took a sip from the glass in her hand and cut her eyes to the left as she turned away from me. That's how hard I was frowning. 'Cause why would she try and play me like that? Why couldn't she just hear me and believe me? And more importantly, *why* didn't she believe me?

As that last question flitted across my mind, I turned back

to the dance floor and heaved a long breath as my eyes immediately found Poppa and Lil Miss Afro Puffs. Poppa had her phone out, likely typing in that girl's number. I felt my lip start to curl because I even realized that I was frowning.

"Oop! There it is."

Mercedes was right back at my ear, giggling like she'd figured it all out. And...I don't know, man, maybe there was *some* merit to what she'd been saying. Heavy on the *some*.

Because the way my stomach twisted when Poppa kissed that girl's cheek after she slid her phone into her front pocket felt a little like betrayal, and I wasn't quite sure if it was entirely friendly.

Chapter Seven

Cyn

Clubbin'

The moment Jucee and Mercedes disappeared down the stairs in search of the hallway where the bathrooms were located, a group of ball players arrived. The crowd on the dance floor seemed to double in size and the volume surged. I was out to chill with my people, but I couldn't turn my business brain off. With so many people in the building—including prominent celebrities—now was the perfect time for "The Rest of You" to drop publicly. It had done very well at Sanity, with Jucee tagging me in every comment on her social media that asked when the song was gonna be available. Since then, I'd put it up on all streaming apps and uploaded all of the details onto Shazam. It was go time and I felt confident that this song was going to catapult Ray right into the spotlight. Tapping Xeno on the arm, I leaned into her ear.

"I'mma go holla at High-Fee right quick." The DJ who'd been spinning when we arrived had wrapped up his set, and High-Fee was now in the booth.

Xeno nodded. "You finna slide her that track?"

I grinned. "You already know, my boy."

We both stood and slapped hands.

Xeno tapped my shoulder with the side of her fist.

"I can't wait to watch their faces from up here when the beat first drops."

"Already!"

I descended the short flight of steps from VIP and pushed through the crowd until I reached the elevated booth. There was a seven-foot swole dude guarding the entrance to the stairs, but he stepped to the side before I reached him. There wasn't even a need to flash my VIP wristband; he knew who I was already. I dapped him up and proceeded up the stairs. The DJ booth at VR was futuristic and functional as hell. LED lights ran underneath the rim of the countertop that ran the length of the eight-by-eight-foot space. There were multiple mounted, thirty-two-inch screens that could be connected to devices for larger viewing, which was an especially nice feature for dark clubs. The booth had a nearly 270-degree view of the dance floor and VIP sections, with a plexiglass shield across the front that rose five feet in the air. Fred Pierce had really put some thought into this design, and I applauded him for that.

"Aw, shit!"

The exaggerated exclamation pulled a wide grin out of me. She'd turned from her station to face me, bowing dramatically at the waist.

"I ain't know greatness was in the building! Let me show my respects!"

I couldn't help but laugh at her antics. DJ High-Fee, also known as Nacora, was about eight years younger than me, but instead of generation wars, we'd clicked from the moment we met and she'd been the homie ever since.

"Whatever, whatever," I laughed. "Please cut the bullshit."

Straightening, she cracked up and approached me with opened arms, her five-inch platform wedge-boots making her tall as hell with her titties hitting my forehead as we hugged. High-Fee looked like she was headed to a rave, and the neon-orange fishnets tucked into her mint green boots that matched her high-waisted miniskirt, the furry, cropped black coat over a white tank top, and the cat-ear head band were right in line with that.

"It's not every day that a Grammy Award–winning producer steps into my booth. I'm honored."

Groaning playfully, I waved her off.

"Chill out."

She took a step back before she'd made it over to where I stood and mimed taking pictures of me.

"Cyn Tha Starr! Cyn Tha Starr! Look this way!"

Cracking a smile, I hit a couple poses to the beat of the song playing as Nacora cheered and depressed the imaginary shutter. We both busted out laughing after the third pose. She stood from a crouch and beckoned for me to cross the small space and join her at her setup, where she immediately resumed mixing.

"So, what's up with you?" she asked, glancing my way. "How you been? How's that Grammy treating you?"

"What's up with me is that I have this new track I'm hoping you can slide in sometime during your set."

Her eyes widened and she rubbed her hands together, a sly grin coming onto her face. "Is this the track that the girls been asking for?! The one Jucee danced to?"

My nod was slow, my answering grin full of pride that the buzz the song had already gained was strong enough for Nacora to catch wind of it.

"One and the same."

Clapping, she bounced on her toes.

"Send it over! I been waiting to get my hands on this Cyn Tha Starr track."

Chuckling, I pulled out my phone and airdropped the file to her. I watched as a notification popped up on one of the screens in front of her. She accepted the file on the mounted MacBook directly in front of her, nodding in satisfaction. Selecting the song, she dragged it over to the software she was using for the night.

"What's the vibe?" she asked as I watched her scroll her queue.

"It's low and sensual. Think anything Victoria Monét or Bey's 'Speechless.'"

Lips pursed, Nacora gave a deeper nod and inserted the song where she wanted it. I didn't take it for granted that she was putting the song into her set without having heard it first. She trusted that I wouldn't give her some bullshit, and I honored that trust by making sure I never did. Grabbing a microphone, Nacora turned a dial to lower the music a notch.

"How y'all feeling?"

She paused and allowed the cheers from the crowd to float up to her. The building was packed and the people were feeling good. High-Fee was a damn good DJ and knew exactly how to move the crowd just how she wanted.

"I'm lovin' it, I'm lovin' it." Lowering her voice, she infused pure sex into her voice as she continued speaking. "I want to turn the heat up in here a little bit. Y'all cool with that?" There was whooping, some cries in the affirmative, and one person who screamed "Yes, lawd!" which had me cracking up. Nacora grinned and glanced back at me. "Aight, I'mma slow it down a little bit." Switching the mic off, she raised the music and faded one song out while the opening beats of 112's "Anywhere" faded in.

I shot off a text to Xeno, letting her know that "The Rest of

You" would be playing sometime soon, and then I watched Nacora spin through a couple of songs. A server in a black jumpsuit entered the booth and handed Nacora two drinks. I raised an eyebrow at her double-fisting as the server disappeared. Grinning, she handed me one of the glasses.

"What is it?" I asked while bringing the glass to my nose for a sniff before taking a tentative sip.

"Mocktail version of my huckleberry mule. It's good as shit, right?"

The tanginess of the odd fruit matched with the crisp bubbles and danced on my tongue. I nodded.

"Different, but not bad."

I started to ask her how she knew to order me a drink when it was just her up here, but she shot me a look and nodded at the crowd as she picked up the mic. Turning the music down, she lifted it to her mouth.

"Who's fucking somebody when they leave here?"

Straw in my mouth, I damn near choked when she asked that. There were a few whistles and several shouts that went up in answer of her question. The cheers from the crowd were almost deafening.

"Good," Nacora said, her hand moving across the trackpad. "Let me play some mood music." She cranked the volume up, and the opening beats to "The Rest of You" filled the air and the dance floor turned into the set of an early-2000s R&B music video. Bodies pressed together and writhing. The strobe lights went from flashing white and yellow to pulsing red and green to the beat of the song. Ray's voice had folks grinding and damn near fucking on the dance floor.

It was glorious.

Nacora turned to me, her face scrunched up like something stank to high heaven. All I could do was smirk and bob my head to the beat.

"This is a banger."

She was right, of course.

"Thanks, Nacora."

I'd made a radio edit that was only three minutes long, but the version I sent to Nacora was the full five-minute version, which included thirty-five seconds of Ray's vocal runs as the instruments played. It was actually me on piano for part of the song, because I'd wanted to channel the seventies habit of giving the musicians time to flex their skills.

Nacora allowed the entire song to play, transitioning into Victoria Monét's "F.U.C.K." so damn smoothly that you would've thought the two songs had the same melody. My phone buzzed in my pocket. I checked the screen to see it was a text from Xeno. Preferring to get her reaction in person, I got Nacora's attention and let her know I was leaving. She turned to give me a quick hug and then turned right back to her setup. I was down the stairs within seconds, feeling lifted from the crowd's reaction to "The Rest of You."

I'd taken two steps away from the booth before a woman stepped in front of me and blocked my momentum forward. Almost colliding with her, I held my hands up, half-finished drink sloshing around in the glass.

"My bad, sweetheart," I murmured, stepping to the side so she could get to wherever she was going in a hurry.

"It's all good," she remarked in a voice infused with sensuality. When she stepped with me like a mirror image, my eyebrows shot up and I leaned my head back to take her in. Face beat, titties sitting, dress serving sexy disco ball, and heels higher than my car note, she looked good. Real good.

How would that dress look on Jucee?

Instinctively, my eyes swept up toward the VIP section, where she was likely shaking her ass with Mercedes. The way the lights were situated, I couldn't even see up there, but I wondered what she thought of the club's reaction to "The Rest of You." I squinted, and the motion made me realize what I was doing. Blinking out of my thoughts—especially that initial random one that came out of nowhere—I acknowledged the woman in front of me. Her voice had what sounded like a natural rasp, the depth not matching her bubbly appearance. She sounded like she should be scatting at the Red Rooster, but she was dressed like a top-forty popstar.

As she stepped closer to me, I tried to place her face. It was possible that she was in the industry, but she didn't look familiar.

"You lookin' for me, or is this just a happy accident?"

Sauntering over to me, hips rocking from side to side, she licked her lips and shrugged. "Can't it be both?"

I cocked an eyebrow, lips curving into a smirk. "It's like that?"

"It *is*," she insisted, practically purring. "I've been looking for you all night, but running into you right now was a coincidence. Fate, maybe."

"Fate," I found myself repeating. "Oh, so you think this was meant to be." It wasn't a question. There was no need to ask, because clearly that was what she was telling herself. I recognized her point as one fans—groupies—believed in on a regular basis. It was a little unrealistic, but I rarely said no to a beautiful woman when she was so obviously interested in me.

She threw her head back and laughed uproariously as if I'd just done stand-up comedy, and my eyes widened as my head snapped back a bit. I was known to tell a lil jokey joke or two, but this wasn't one of those times. It was still wild to experience groupie shit, and this felt like that.

But there was something else wrong here though. Something was off. Like a Jacuzzi with no bubbles. The water is heated, so your mind registers that you aren't in a pool, but without the jets it's just a public bath.

Shorty was gorgeous, without a doubt. She was one of those aggressive femmes that I lowkey loved, pushing up on me and telling me how much she was feelin' me. The icing on the cake was that she was clearly down to fuck immediately.

It had been a few busy weeks since I'd been back, with me in the studio twelve to fourteen hours most days, and before that I'd been chillin' after me and a girl I met at H-E-B stopped kicking it. I wasn't exactly hard up for sex, but if she was down, then I was with it.

Except…

There was something in the rhythm of her laughter that made me cringe. It was in the wrong key or something. It was nails on a chalkboard, the way it grated at me. We were in a loud-ass club with hundreds of people around us and we'd just met, so I had no idea about her personality outside of her not being afraid to go for what she wanted, but her good looks could only take us so far. I took a step back, putting some space between us, preparing to make my way back up to VIP. She immediately clocked my movement and slid forward, getting right up on me, brushing her titties against mine as she fingered the crown medallion on my chain.

That was all it took for me to reconsider. I mean…if things were going right, there wouldn't be too much to laugh about, and hopefully her moan was more D-flat than E-sharp.

She put her lips directly at my ear. "So, whose place are we going back to? Yours or mine?"

Her breath tickled my neck, but instead of it being a sexy caress, it itched. It was perplexing. Tilting my head to the side, I placed my hands at her waist and leaned back.

"Tonight's a no go, but gimme your number and we can link another day." I'd never had such a negative response to some-one's laugh like this, so I needed to process this phenomenon.

I might not be interested in fucking her anymore, but I was definitely interested in testing this out.

Although I hadn't given her the answer she'd wanted, asking for her number brought a smile to her face.

"It's Jackie," she offered.

As she rattled off her digits, I typed them into my phone and jotted a quick note in the contact.

Wild ass laugh.

Satisfied that I wasn't planning to curve her, shorty dropped a sticky kiss on my cheek and strutted off. I stared after her, full of wonderment about our entire interaction, feeling like I'd just unlocked a new level in my brain. I couldn't wait to tell my daddy about this.

On my way back to VIP, I was stopped no less than four times by someone who either wanted to tell me how much they loved what I was doing for the city or wanted to get in the studio with me. As I told the latter to hit my DMs, I heard Xeno's voice in my ear call me extra friendly. I'd accept that. There was no way to predict which package talent was going to arrive in, and I'd dealt with being underestimated enough in the music world to know not to do the same.

Trisha met me at the top of the stairs, pushing a shot into my hand.

"Everyone already took one. You gotta catch up."

I eyed the brown liquid in the glass and raised an eyebrow at Xeno's girl.

She grinned. "It's just Coke."

Relieved, I brought the glass to my nose and sniffed out of habit. The tell-tale notes of the cola hit me, and I quickly tossed it back. My hesitance wasn't because I didn't trust Trisha, but I knew all too well how easy it was to accidentally drink in environments like this one. With the low lights, it was nothing for glasses to get mixed up, or vodka to be mistaken for water or bourbon for apple juice. I handed Trisha the empty glass, and she shot me a wink before tilting her chin over her shoulder.

"Jucee was looking for you."

Laughing at the smirk she wore during her announcement, I nodded. Jucee and I were never too far away from one another when we went out. Not even just on a buddy system type of thing, but we were always on the same vibe, so it happened that way. My mind flashed back to the dance we'd shared before she left to the bathroom. It was out of the ordinary like a muthafucka, but even then, when I rocked, she rolled. I couldn't even explain why I'd been on her like that because that definitely hadn't been my intention, but it felt right in the moment.

My eyes swept the section until I found her. She was off near the railing that looked over the dance floor, dancing with Mercedes and some women from a nearby section. Although each of them looked good, Jucee stood out. She was a sunflower in a field of daisies. I frowned, because why did it suddenly feel like I was seeing her for the first time? I'd had a good look at her outfit when she'd came to my house and I've objectively acknowledged that she looked good, but for some reason, staring at her now, watching her wind her hips under moving strobe lights, I was struck by how sexy she was.

The sheer tube dress did a masterful job of displaying all of the skin Jucee wanted to be visible, and I was entranced.

"Whatchu lookin' at, bro?"

Xeno's sly question was accompanied by an elbow poking me not once but twice in the ribs. Smirking, I rolled my eyes and shook my head.

"You know damn well I'm looking at the group of baddies over there."

Dipping her head, Xeno acknowledged my words.

"You're right, I should've asked who you lookin' at? 'Cause I know damn well you ain't staring that hard at the whole group."

My eyebrows met as I slid my gaze over to my friend. There was something in her voice that caught my attention. A hidden message, as if she were speaking in code.

"The hell you tryna say, bro?"

Xeno laughed. "Nah, don't play dumb. You know exactly what I'm asking you."

I looked at her, wondering what the hell she was going on about and why she thought I knew it.

"Aight, man, you'll tell me later, I guess."

Leaving Xeno's side, I approached the group of dancing women. Phones were out recording Jucee as she bent at the waist and twerked her ass a few times. She straightened and moved out of the center of the circle as another woman replaced her and started dancing. I rounded the group of women until I came to where she and Mercedes stood laughing and rocking side to side. Sliding up behind her, I dropped my chin onto her shoulder.

"You were looking for me?"

Her eyes slid over to me for a brief moment before sliding right back to Mercedes as she gave a half-shrug with one shoulder.

"I guess. That was before I saw you all booed up though. I'm good now."

Confused, I frowned, my brows furrowing. *What the hell was she talking about?* "Booed up?"

"Mmhm," she murmured. "With Lil Miss Afro Puffs."

It clicked then who she was referring to.

"You talking about Jackie?!"

I watched her roll her neck as she sucked her teeth.

"Oh, is that the raggedy heifer's name?"

I tossed my head back as I laughed. "You know damn well that girl wasn't raggedy."

I was cracking up. Not only because I'd been anything but booed up with Jackie and her discordant-ass laugh, but also because Jucee's lil attitude had me tickled. She was so damn jealous. If I spent too much time with any woman that wasn't her, she turned into a brat, and while that was a trait that would have me chunking up the deuce in a relationship, on her, I lowkey found it adorable. Because of her history, Jucee kept her friends close to the chest and was a bit overly protective of them. There were only like three people she even used the word *friend* with, and I counted myself lucky to be one of those people.

I might've been the love 'em and leave 'em type before I met Jucee, but now that a couple of the songs I'd produced had won awards, I was in the studio so much that I barely had the time for the love 'em part of that equation. Yet, if I gave the little time I did have to "some random," Jucee wouldn't be the only one to make her displeasure known. My family would have something to say as well. Hell, even Xeno would be giving me the side-eye.

Wrapping my arms around her from the back, I nuzzled Jucee's neck teasingly.

"Not you being jealous of a groupie."

She lifted her shoulder to squeeze me out of her space, but I didn't let her go. After a second she dropped her crossed arms and busted out laughing.

"Man, get off me!"

I froze for a second, not immediately releasing her as my mind raced with questions. I'd heard Jucee's laugh a million and eighteen times and never thought twice about it, but suddenly I was faced with the sharp realization that her laugh—while loud and goofy—was actually quite melodious, especially in comparison to Jackie's raucous laugh. It didn't just sound perfect; it *pleased* me. I dropped my hands from around Jucee as if she were fire and I was oil.

That was…new.

I'd never compared her to a love interest before—potential or otherwise. I'd never wanted to. Hell, I prided myself on having friendships that were truly *just* friendships and not loading docks for future romantic relationships.

Was I trippin'?

Yeah, I was definitely trippin'. I mean, things were weird because Jackie's laugh was jarring and had thrown me off of my natural rhythm, and Jucee was my safe space, so it made sense that my brain would use her to right my mental metronome.

That's all it was.

I was certain.

Jucee turned around, already saying something slick. I couldn't tell you what was coming out of her mouth. Couldn't recall a thing. There was a lot happening in my brain, but where I was usually more than capable of handling it all, now, I fell flat. I felt a little unsteady. Like I would stumble if I took a step. The legs that had supported me my entire life suddenly felt foreign.

When Jucee fully spun around, she stopped speaking mid-sentence. Didn't trail off, didn't choke. Just came to an abrupt halt. Her smile never faltered, but there was a subtle change in her expression. Eyebrows dipped just a fraction. Eyes narrowed a hair. She saw something on my face—in *my* expression—that gave her pause. This woman could read me like a book, and it was both a blessing at times and a curse right now. She didn't need to see this hiccup in real time. I needed to process and then tell her about it *after* I figured out what happened and fully bounced back.

Acrylics pressed into my skin, the familiar sensation comforting me, as Jucee wrapped a hand around my bicep, lean-ing into my ear.

"You good, Poppa?"

She pulled back as soon as the question left her lips, tilting her head to the side to watch my face as I answered.

Fuck.

It was a simple question asked in a low tone, but it felt like she'd sung the last lines of a love song to me. The adlibbed riff-ing at the end that wasn't planned, but I hadn't stopped record-ing and just let the artist do what she came to do.

I was so not okay.

Of course she wanted to see my face. One of her favorite phrases was "Lips can lie but eyes can't." This woman knew me so damn well that I couldn't even fake the funk with her. Shaking my head one time, and one time only, I gave her what I hoped was a reassuring smile.

"Nah, but I will be." Her already narrowed gaze shrank even further, and I hurried to calm her before she went into full mama bear mode. "It's all good, trust me."

I placed a hand on her hip and leaned forward to drop a kiss at the corner of her mouth. I called myself doing something normal to help cull her suspicion, but I'd fucked myself. The moment my lips touched her skin, a burning desire to shift my aim a little to the left shot through me.

It's not enough.

That prickling thought startled me more than Jackie's dis-cordant laugh. Where the fuck had *that* come from? And why did the thought bring an almost impossible-to-ignore urge to grab Jucee's chin and bring her lips to mine?

"Was it that groupie chick? Lil Miss Afro Puffs?"

Laughter bubbled out of my throat, and I mentally wiped my brow, grateful for the obvious annoyance in her tone, which was the perfect distraction from my wayward thoughts.

"So, it *is* jealousy?" I asked rhetorically.

Bringing a fist to my mouth as I continued laughing, I shook my head in mock disappointment. "Never thought I'd see the day."

She rolled her eyes and walked over to where Mercedes was twerking on Xeno's bodyguard, Lonnie, who stood laughing, his arms folded across his mile-wide chest. Neither of them was interested in each other, but Mercedes had been bothering that man from the day they met. The fact that Jucee didn't refute my words proved them to be true, and I know I'd just teased her less than ten minutes earlier, but dammit, why did the idea of her truly being jealous make me a little giddy?

Chapter Eight

Cyn

After the Party Is the After-Party

Even though Jucee was singing her heart out along to the mix I had playing, the ride back to my house was too quiet for my liking. I wasn't distracted enough to not be in my head wondering about Jackie's laugh and the suddenly inexplicable *feelings* I was feeling for my friend. Jucee was being extra playful, flailing her hands as she sang, leaning over the console to caress my face, and grinding in her seat. There was nothing over-the-top about it, but for some damn reason it was turning me on something serious.

We'd danced for nearly three hours straight, tearing it up on the dance floor and up in VIP, but somehow Jucee still smelled like she'd rolled around in flowers plucked from a pussy garden. The air was blowing in the truck and my lil air freshener was doing its thing, but tendrils of her scent still made their way to my nose. It fanned the flames of my arousal and brought illicit images of tasting fruit from that garden to my mind.

Had her perfume always been this heavy duty? This…sensual?

As close as we were, I couldn't exactly ask her that. Maybe she was tipsy enough to laugh it off, or, best case scenario, give me an actual answer. The more likely result was that question would make things awkward. I'd have to explain where the question came from, and that would take me down a rabbit hole of explaining the weird thing with her and Jackie's laugh. Yeah, I wasn't in the mood to deal with that, so I didn't say anything at all.

It was almost four in the morning when I pulled into my garage.

Climbing out of the car, I headed to the door and pushed it open before stepping back to let Jucee in first. When she didn't go in, I turned around to see that she hadn't even got out of the car. Laughing, I walked up to the passenger door and opened it. Her eyes were closed and her head was leaning back against the headboard.

"I'm not 'sleep," she murmured. "I'm just resting my eyes."

"Mmhmm," I hummed, reaching in and unbuckling her seatbelt. "Come rest your eyes in the house."

She stepped out of the truck but shook her head. "No, ma'am. I'm sure Lil Miss Afro Puffs is on her way over. I'd rather not hear y'all fuckin' all night, so I'mma just head home."

Rolling my eyes, I pushed her toward the door and into the house. For all the shit she was talking, she went without a fight.

"Man, be for real, ole jealous ass."

Jucee scoffed. "I'm into some kinky shit, but that's a bit more than I can handle right now. That don't make me jealous."

"Sure, Jan," I laughed, giving my best Marcia Brady impression.

In our three years of friendship, I'd never had a woman over while Jucee or Amani were over. Hell, I barely had women over, period. I was more lowkey than that, and on the rare occasion that I messed around with someone who didn't understand what casual and temporary meant, it was easier—and safer—for them not to know where I lived. The truth was, when women knew where you lived, they tended to pop up whenever they felt like it, and I wasn't one for unannounced visits from people I didn't like like that.

Inside the house, I dropped my keys and wallet onto the table by the door and trailed Jucee to my bedroom, where she headed straight for the bathroom while I went into my walk-in closet to remove my jewelry. I heard the toilet flush as I slid my shoes into their designated cubby in my built-ins, so I walked back into my bedroom to check on Jucee. I knew she was tired, but I wanted to confirm her level of inebriation so I could gather anything she might need in the morning. I'd only seen her fin-ish one drink and one shot, and that wasn't usually enough to get her tipsy, but there was always a possibility she had some-thing when I wasn't near her.

Eyes closed, Jucee sat on the edge of the bed with her hands clasped in her lap. The sight was hilarious.

"You know, you'd be more comfortable if you actually laid down."

Cracking open one eyelid, she peered over at me. "You laughing at me?"

I nodded and started to unbutton my shirt. "Absolutely." Jucee released a deep, exhausted sigh and moved to stand. I moved in front of her and grabbed her hands, pulling her onto her feet. She came faster than I was expecting, making me stumble backward a couple of steps so that we wouldn't col-lide. Instead of standing still, Jucee moved with me, dropping my hands and grabbing handfuls of my shirt.

"Damn, girl," I chuckled once we were steady on our feet. She didn't say anything, just stared at me, and that's when I realized just how close we were. Eye-to-eye. Chest-to-chest. We were so close I could feel how fast her heart was beating.

I watched her pupils dilate as she focused on my face.

I felt her nipples harden into pebbles.

My bra wasn't padded, so if I could feel hers, then she could definitely...

Shit.

Quickly, I stepped back, almost ripping out of her grasp in my haste to put some space between us. The last thing I needed was my reaction to her becoming public knowledge. I just needed to think, that's all. A couple of days of space between us so I could focus and figure out what this was and how I could make it go away.

I *had* to make it go away.

Whatever this was, I couldn't lose my friend because I was suddenly horny for her. So, yeah, I just needed to sleep on it.

Two sleeps, max, should do the trick. I was sure of it. This was just...my mind playing tricks on me because I hadn't seen Jucee in forever and it had been so long since I'd had a hook up. I'd been working hard for several months and had at least seven more weeks where my schedule was booked solid. I really did just need to rest.

As if she could hear my thoughts, Jucee blinked and her eyes focused. She shook her head like she was trying to shake the last few drops of water out of a bottle, turned away from me, and shimmied out of her dress.

Good Lord.

I was fucking losing it.

No. I'd already lost it! Whatever *it* was, it had fallen off, probably somewhere in the club.

I don't know what the fuck was wrong with me, but I couldn't take my eyes off of her ass. We'd been friends for years and I'd seen her in *various* stages of undress a million times. This was nothing new. Hell, the first time that we met, it was right after she'd been on stage at Sanity, so I knew that Jucee was draggin' a wagon, and yet it was like I was seeing her for the first time. Instead of her just being my hella thick friend, now she was this curvaceous, stacked, sexy as hell woman that was in my bedroom with me. And when those type of women were in my bedroom with me, it was because I was going to get to sample each and every one of those dips and curves that caught my attention.

But this *wasn't* that.

This was *my friend.*

I shook my head, tripping off the fact that I had to remind myself. I'd never had to do that before.

My friend who I was suddenly lusting over like a horny teenager. A teenager who had just discovered what attraction and arousal was. This was a little bit more than your standard, run-of-the-mill schoolgirl crush. It wasn't just hearts in my eyes when I looked at her; my pussy was beatboxing to the rhythm of how I'd sound saying her name while I was cumming. It was that intense.

And now that we were at my house, it was quiet enough for me to replay that laugh of hers, and all of our interactions at the club that led me to this moment. But I was doing the wrong thing—I wasn't supposed to be thinking of Jucee like this, because she was my bestie.

I would never—could never—think of Xeno this way.

But…Xeno was like one of my brothers.

And Jucee was…

Nope.

I couldn't finish that. Didn't really know how to—not if I wanted to retain any of my sanity that night. So, to distract myself, I started up my teasing again. Anything to get me from staring hungrily at the way those round globes of her ass ate up that black thong.

"Man," I drawled, slipping out of my button-down. "I still

can't believe you were actually jealous about that chick at the club."

I could tell from the way her shoulders stiffened that I had been successful in not only distracting myself, but also distracting her. Why I felt like I needed to distract her, I couldn't say, it was just a feeling that I had.

Jucee spun around, slapped her hands on her hips, and glared at me.

"You know what, Poppa? Maybe I *am* jealous."

"Wait, what?" I stared at her, my mouth ajar. I hadn't expected her to admit that in a million years, and even though I really did get a jealous vibe from her when we were at the club, it wasn't really a big deal. I was truly just teasing her, but now she actually seemed upset instead of just annoyed, and I was... intrigued. Because big emotions over something little like this were new. And if she was experiencing something new just like *I* was experiencing something new, then maybe we could figure this out and get past it together.

Jucee threw her hands up in the air and paced the length of my room and into the closet before turning around, coming back to me, and doing it all over again.

"I don't know—shit, it's just something about that girl that got to me. I didn't like she was hugged all up on you, and whispering in your ear and shit, and had her titties on your arm and pressed against your chest. I didn't like that at all." She spun around and stared at me, her face scrunched into a scowl. "It most definitely has something to do with the shady way that she tried to get information about you from me, but that's not all of it. I can't explain it."

I stared at her, my mouth gaped open, at a loss for words. She was serious, and suddenly, the need for distraction evaporated and something else crept up in its place. Something both unrecognizable and undeniable. As quickly as possible, I dropped

my eyes from my friend to the floor in an attempt to get myself under control. Because I did not understand what the fuck
was going on inside of my head, but I knew that if I didn't
stop staring at her, she would cease to be across the room from
me and would likely be in my arms. And we didn't do that—
I didn't do that.

Not with my friends, and *never* with Jucee. I couldn't lose
what we had. Refused to.

But also…

"I—" Before I could get out my words, Jucee blew out a
heavy breath and shook her head.

"Uh uhn. Don't even worry about it. Forget I said anything."
She waved a hand in the air and turned to walk back into my
closet, likely to find something to sleep in, but it didn't matter, because she didn't make it. I grabbed her hand to stop her.
Before I could even think about what I was doing. As I pulled
her back toward me, I moved closer to her, eating the space
between us in double the time.

"Jucee…"

"I said forget I said anything," she began, already shaking
her head when I opened my mouth to speak.

At that point, whatever she was talking about was no longer
a concern of mine. I shut off my thoughts and moved on im-
pulse, instinct. Honestly, I really had no idea what was going
on between us, and why I was pulling her to me, and why I
was staring down into her chocolate-brown eyes and giving her
an intense look like one I've never given her before. Looking
down at her plush-ass lips that were still painted with the gloss
and lipstick ombré. Why I was suddenly so turned on by seeing her in her bra and panties even though I'd seen her in this
and less over the years that we've known each other. But while
I had no idea why that was happening the way it was happening, I was very keenly aware of Jucee's response to what I was

doing. Her voice trailed off, words disappearing as she gave me a questioning look. But when I stood in front of her, peering directly into her eyes, I watched as her eyelids lowered and she went from being an annoyed friend to being a woman aroused.

The change was magnificent to witness. I could see it all over her and could damn near hear her heartbeat elevate. The stiffness in her shoulders relaxed, her nostrils flared, and her chin dipped. It was like she realized that she was prey and I the huntress, and she just…surrendered. Those pretty brown irises softened, flickered from mine down to my lips and back up before lingering on my mouth, and *my God* was that so fucking sexy.

I trailed the fingertips of one hand up her arm, gripping just above her elbow, while the other went right for her neck, resting at her nape, my thumb brushing the sensitive skin below her ear. I should've waited, should've asked if we were on the same page of the same book, but when she tilted her head back and licked her lips without me saying a word, the words in the rulebook blurred and my instincts took over.

Stretching my neck forward, I pressed my mouth to hers softly, intending to just…test it.

I just wanted to see.

I needed to know if the change in her sound meant something. If a different kind of kiss from this woman who meant so much to me would align with the shift in how I saw her tonight.

She pushed up on her toes just slightly, meeting me quicker than I anticipated, as if she wanted this just as much as I did and I was taking too damn long for her comfort.

I was unprepared for the jolt to my senses when our lips made contact. Why did it feel so familiar? Why did my body relax, unrealized tension draining out of me like water from a tub? Why did I breathe a sigh of relief, blowing the breath out through my nose to keep from breaking the kiss? Why was this kiss flipping switches and turning knobs in my brain?

I'd fucked up.

I realized it nearly immediately but was stubborn and kept going, relishing in her softness and the way her lips moved in against mine. It wasn't until the tip of her tongue slipped between my parted lips that I jerked back, dropping my hands from her body and putting some space in between us.

"Shit, Jucee. I'm sorry. That should've nev—"

Well, shit.

She shushed me and I snapped my lips closed with a quickness. Before I could reword my apology, Jucee had sunk her fingers into my tank top, pulled me back toward her, and kissed me again.

There went any argument I had. I kissed her back with a fervency that I hadn't experienced since the first time I'd eaten pussy. That's when time sped up and I got mental whiplash trying to keep up.

This was *Jucee*.

My bestie.

My ace.

And she was pulling my shirt out of my pants and tugging it over my head. She was kissing my neck, and licking my lips, and moaning when I grabbed her ass and massaged her cheeks.

And *fuck me*, I was grabbing her ass!

What the hell was I doing?

I had no answer, and after a minute, I stopped trying to figure it out and just...went with it. Yes, this was Jucee. No, this wasn't the type of relationship we had. But I loved her and I knew she wouldn't hurt me, at least not tonight. So I reached behind her and unsnapped her bra, palming her delicious-ass titties, kissing around her wide, dark brown areolas, and sucking her stiff nipples into my mouth.

Fingers gripped my biceps before sliding up my arms and over my shoulders. A hand cupped my chin and lifted my head up where Jucee took my mouth in another searing kiss. I replaced my lips with my hands, pinching and twisting her nipples as she sat on the bed and scooted backward. I moved with her, not wanting to break the connection of our lips—not wanting the moment to end. This felt like a fever dream, and I dreaded the moment the clock struck twelve.

In the middle of the bed, Jucee's hands fell from my face down to my body. I met her hands at my belt, and we worked together to get my bottoms off. Pushing up onto my knees, I broke our kiss to remove my remaining article of clothing. The moment my titties fell free from their binding, Jucee caught a nipple in her mouth like a baby bird who'd been waiting im-patiently for their turn to eat. A gasp caught in my throat, and my head fell back as pleasure shot through me. My back bowed, and I didn't even realize I was pulling back until Jucee's wide eyes were staring up at me.

"What you doin'?" she asked breathlessly.

"I—I'm just..." I snapped my lips shut as I realized I didn't have an answer—not one that wouldn't sound ridiculous. How did I explain that the way she was taking charge had my mind frazzled? I was a top. I ran the fucking show.

From the way Jucee licked her lips and twisted them into a sensual smirk, you'd have thought I'd spoken out loud. Had I spoken aloud? Had she read it in my eyes? Oh, duh.

She *definitely* read it in my eyes. Jucee knew me too damn well. Or maybe she knew me the perfect amount.

Because the way Jucee crawled toward me and placed her hands on my hips had me trembling. Yeah, I always topped, but maybe just this once I could try something different. She kissed me, and I was pretty sure my fucking knees almost gave out on me.

"Lay back."

Her command was punctuated with a nod of her head to-ward the pillows near the headboard, and I did what she said without hesitation. I settled in amongst the goose-downs, naked as the day I was born and filled with a sense of nervous anticipation. She trailed her hands from my ankles up to my knees before she pushed my thighs apart and straddled one. Leaning over me, she held my gaze in her own, and I was fucking stuck. My chest heaved under the intensity of her attention. We'd locked eyes a million and one times, but never had it felt like this before. Like she was peeling away the layers of my persona until there was nothing but my soul bared raw and vulnerable for her.

And when she found it—found me there—she leaned forward and captured my mouth in a searing kiss at the same time that she ground against my thigh and slid her fingers through the wetness between my thighs. I met her greedily, neck stretched as I stuck out my tongue to meet hers while I pushed up my hips, searching for more of her digits. Suddenly I wanted the friction, needed the pressure, wanted her to touch me more than anything in the world.

And because she knew me the way she did, she gave it to me. Her ring and index fingers breached me, and I gasped as her pointer finger brushed my asshole. It didn't go in, but the idea that it might sent me over the edge. It was so deliciously illicit and unexpected that her steady pumps coupled with her sucking on my tongue had me cumming within minutes, her name a curse and a cry on my lips. I didn't even have a chance to be embarrassed, because she immediately sat up and lifted her sticky fingers to her mouth to suck them clean before putting them right back while declaring that she needed another one from me.

My eyes fluttered closed and air whooshed out of my lungs. I pushed my head back into the pillow, moaning as she nipped at my collarbone before licking up my neck and taking my bottom lip into her mouth.

Who was this woman and what the hell was she doing to me?

Chapter Nine

Jucee

The Morning After

I couldn't remember the last time I woke up with a smile already planted on my face. Last night was everything, and the moment my eyes popped open I was ready to roll over and initiate round two.

Oh my God!

Covering my face with my hands, I squealed inside of my head.

I'd actually slept with my best friend! *Again.* Part of me couldn't believe that I had done this a second time, but another part of me knew this was different than it had been with Samir.

Shaking my head as if it were an Etch A Sketch I could wipe clean, I lowered my hands and turned to find an empty bed. Sliding my hands under the rumpled covers, I felt for warmth, my lips twisting when I found none. Staring at the closed bedroom door, I strained my ears and listened for any sound of life in Poppa's one-story house. The only thing I heard was the hum of the air conditioner. The realization that I was in that house alone sank onto me like the humidity in the summer after it rained during the day. It was heavy and oppressive and so damn disappointing.

It wasn't unusual for me to spend the night at Poppa's and wake up with her gone in the morning or the middle of the night. Sometimes she heard a melody or lyrics in her sleep and headed up to the studio to record them while they were fresh, no matter what time it was. I'd experienced this at least a dozen times over the course of our friendship, so I knew not to take it personally.

But that was before we'd slept together.

Before we'd shared something so intimate.

Before I'd had my fingers inside of her.

Before she sucked on my nipples.

Before we'd made each other cum.

Was this how she was with everyone?

This wasn't supposed to be like any other time that I'd spent the night because, for me, it was different. As I drifted off to sleep last night, I'd pictured this morning going quite differently, so her absence stung.

That last question pulled me up short. I had a lot of places to go today, and *there* was not one of them. I tossed the covers off of me and walked into the bathroom to start the shower and empty my bladder while the water came to temperature. When I stepped under the hot spray, I let the water wash over me while I took a minute to unscramble my thoughts. There were things I knew for a fact, and things I was assuming. I needed to make sure I didn't get them mixed up just because I was trying to figure it out alone.

Except, that was the fucking point.

It's all fine and well to try to keep an open mind, but the bottom line was that I shouldn't have been figuring that out on my own. Poppa should have been here when I woke up. Hell, she should have woke me up before she left, even if it was just to say goodbye and that she'd talk to me later.

But she didn't.

One thing I hated above all was confusion.

By the time I'd dried off, moisturized, and dressed in a jersey dress I'd left at Poppa's forever ago, an hour had passed and I still hadn't heard from Poppa. I gathered up my clothes from the night before, snagged the bottle of water from the nightstand, and left the room. I was met with empty silence as soon as I crossed the threshold of the bedroom, which killed any lingering hope that maybe Poppa was just out in the living room watching a movie, or in the kitchen cooking something that was magically devoid of scent. Still, I walked through the house, checking each room to be certain.

After confirming that I was alone, I opened the door to the garage and immediately huffed a humorless chuckle. My car wasn't inside of the small room. Closing the door, I sighed and left out through the front door. There was no need to worry about locking it, because Poppa could lock it remotely and would surely do so once the doorbell camera alerted her to my departure. My car sat in the driveway. I didn't know how to feel about that. Poppa only moved my car out of her garage when she knew she wouldn't be back before I was ready to leave. I usually found it thoughtful, since I had no way to close her garage after leaving her house, but today, it just confused me further.

Where was she?

Why wouldn't she tell me that she was leaving?

And *why* didn't she want to be here when I woke up?

The only person who could answer those questions was Poppa, which meant I needed to find her. For a brief moment, I was annoyed at myself for not being one of those clingy friends who continuously shared my location, because it would be so

You could just call her.

I blinked at that logic whispered from the back of my mind, and then immediately shook my head.

Nah. I needed to see her face when I talked to her. She could say anything to me over the phone, but she couldn't hide her expressions when she spoke. My stomach rumbled, reminding me how long it had been since I'd eaten. I downed the bottle of water and set my GPS for my favorite coffee shop. As soon as I backed out of the driveway, I instructed my Bluetooth to call Nana Cherry. It rang twice before she answered.

"Mommy!"

Hearing Amani's sweet voice instantly brought a smile to my face.

"Good morning, my baby. Did you enjoy the movie and ice cream last night?"

"I did, Mommy! It was so fun! And Nana Cherry let me get two ice creams!"

His exuberance made me laugh. My mood was lifted just by witnessing his innocent joy. I had a brief reprieve from being pissed that my *bestie* had dipped on me after a night of carnality. Instead, I was grinning from ear to ear while talking to my favorite boy in the world.

"Ooh! That sounds pretty awesome. Are you ready for me to pick you up?"

"Ummm..."

Amani dragged the word out so long that I wondered if he forgot what I'd asked him.

"Dang, 'Mani." I pouted. "You been gone for a week and you still not ready to come home?"

His giggle was so precious, I smiled through my pout.

"Hold on, Mommy," he instructed.

The sounds of shuffling hit my ears, and then Nana Cherry came on the line.

"Good morning, baby."

"Morning, Nana Cherry."

"You not on the way to take my baby, are you? We were just about to head out to service, and you know how much he enjoys children's church."

Laughing, I just shook my head. Nana Cherry would cart Amani all over the world with her if she could, and he would go without complaint.

"Well," I drawled. "I guess not."

She made a noise of approval. "Good. The Texans are playing today, so you know service will only be about an hour. I already cooked this morning, so just come round the house to eat. We'll be back no later than eleven."

Glancing at the clock on the dashboard, I shook my head. It wasn't even nine yet, and Nana Cherry had probably cooked six different things from scratch. I wouldn't be surprised if she'd risen before the roosters.

"I'll be there!"

"Good. Talk to you later, baby. 'Mani, tell ya mama 'bye and that you love her."

My baby's sweet voice filled the interior of my car again.

"Bye, Mommy!" he chirped. "I love, love, *love* you!"

"I love, love, *love* you too, my baby. I'll see you this afternoon."

The call disconnected, and I sighed. Amani was the sun in my solar system; no matter how dark things seemed to be, a moment in his presence—even distantly—brightened my entire mood. Feeling better, I sang along to my favorite playlist as I made the fifteen-minute drive to one of my favorite places in the city.

When I arrived to Black Coffee, the place was packed, with nearly all of the wrought-iron tables filled with people. In the back corner of the room, near the door that led to a patio area, was a group of older men playing board games across two tables that were pushed together. The volume inside was high, but not louder than the nineties R&B flowing through the speakers. Stepping into Black Coffee was always so comforting, like walking into my granny's house and seeing all my cousins chillin' on the couch. It made so much sense to me when I found out that it was a family-owned establishment ran by three sisters.

The aroma of freshly ground coffee beans called me toward the counter. There was a short line of only three people, but the five people behind the counter were moving at a constant pace, which let me know just how busy they were. I stepped up behind two teenagers who were discussing what they could order with their limited funds when the woman at the register waved at me as the person in front of her moved down to the end of the counter.

"Hey, Juleesa!"

Grinning, I waved back and took a step forward as the line moved.

"Hey, Tasha!"

Tasha Black, along with her older sisters, Tonya and Toy, ran the cafe that had been started by their parents. She was the sweetest person, with a kind smile, soft eyes, and a soothing voice. We'd met two years ago when her and her father, Mr. Cyrus, delivered coffee to Sanity during one of my day-shifts. After that, visiting Black Coffee became a part of my weekly routine.

The boys in front of me stepped up to the register, but before they could say anything, I leaned around them and caught Tasha's eye.

"I'm getting their order today."

They turned toward me, mouths falling open.

"Order whatever you want," I told them. "I'm paying."

"Oh, snap!"

"Thank you so much!"

Tasha grinned at the flabbergasted boys. "You heard her. Ball out."

I laughed as both of the boys started talking rapid fire. Somehow Tasha caught everything they said, keying in elaborate, secret menu–style recipes without stumbling or asking them to repeat anything. When they finished, they both turned to me with another round of thanks before heading off to sit at one of the few unoccupied tables.

"You in a good mood today, huh?"

At Tasha's question, I immediately shook my head. More like the complete opposite. I was here for sugar and caffeine in the hopes that they would help.

"Not at all," I answered honestly. Her eyebrows shot up.

"But that's why I need to do nice things, so I can feel better." Her lips turned down for a brief second as her chocolate-brown eyes roved my face. I don't know what she was looking for, but she must've found it, because she pursed her lips and nodded her head.

"Can I choose your drink today? I'd like to make you something special."

Surprised, my eyebrows shot up, but I quickly nodded. One thing I'd learned by frequenting Black Coffee was that the Black sisters knew their stuff. Each of them was the coffee equivalent of a sommelier, and having a custom drink prepared by them was a privilege. Tasha keyed a third drink into the computer and gave me my total. I tapped my card and then went to the end of the counter, leaning against the wall as I watched Tasha squirt different syrups into a large hot cup before steaming milk and pulling shots.

Tasha called out to me as her sister Toy placed the two large frozen concoctions and bag of pastries the boys ordered down and went back to the coffee bar. They grabbed their wares, thanked me, and practically skipped out of the cafe. Chuckling, Tasha handed me my drink, waggling her eyebrows as she waited for me to taste it.

Dutifully, I brought the cup to my lips and took a sip. My eyes widened when I realized what the flavor reminded me of.

"It tastes like a cherry cordial!"

Her red-brown face lit up as a pleased grin spread across her face.

"Good job!"

The warmth of the cup in my hands and the drink making its way through my body helped to brighten me up a bit more, and I felt a surge of gratitude for my favorite barista.

"Thank you for this, Tasha. You don't know how much I needed it."

Her grin didn't falter, but her eyes softened. "Anytime, friend, and I mean that."

Heart warmed and tastebuds dancing, I left the cafe and headed straight for Rhythm & Rainbows. I needed answers, and I needed them immediately. Poppa and I were supposed to be able to talk about any and everything, and to have her disappear on me like this—after what we shared—was something I couldn't let slide. We were friends above everything else, and right now, I didn't like how my friend was handling me.

Lonnie let me inside the building, and I followed him back to Missy, my shoulders tight in anticipation of seeing Poppa after last night. I knew a confrontation was unlikely to happen inside the studio, since Lonnie's presence meant that Xeno was there, but at least setting eyes on her would give me some semblance of an answer. I was disappointed to find Xeno sitting alone at the soundboard. She looked up when I entered the room and stood, spreading her arms for a hug when I moved further into the room.

"Aye, what's up, Jucee?" she asked as she returned to her chair.

For a split second, I debated on how to answer that. There was no way for me to know if Poppa had told Xeno about us sleeping together, and I didn't want to accidentally disclose that if she hadn't, but I also wanted it known that I was looking for her.

"I'm just making my rounds as I search for one Cyndi Thomas."

Xeno double blinked and then canted her head to the side. "Come again?"

Laughing at her antics, I shook my head.

"I stopped by in hopes of catching Poppa, but it looks like I missed her again. Has she been in today at all?"

Shaking her head, Xeno leaned back in her chair. "Nah. I actually thought she was with you today."

Sighing, I took another sip of my drink and shook my head. "Alright, let me go find this girl."

"Uh oh," Xeno drawled, leaning back against the counter and crossing her arms over her chest. "She in trouble?"

I swiped my tongue over my bottom lip. That was something I could answer honestly. "She will be if I don't see her today."

Xeno whistled. "Do I need to warn her?"

Brows furrowed, I headed for the door. "Warn her for what? I'm not about to do nothing to that girl!"

Chuckling, Xeno pursed her lips. "Sure, Jan."

That made me laugh. Waving goodbye, I left the studio. Once inside my car, I headed to the only other place I was likely to find Poppa. If she wasn't at her parents' house, then we would *really* have a problem.

There wasn't a soul to be found once I made the thirty-minute drive to Mission Bend. The driveway was empty when I pulled up along the curb, but I still gave it a shot and rang the doorbell anyway, just in case someone was inside. No luck.

Walking back to my car, I was hit with a wave of emotion that made me want to cry. Why the hell was I driving all over the southside trying to find this woman? Why was I fighting so hard to accept the obvious? The moment that I woke up in an empty house, things were clear, yet I was on a hunt, looking for an explanation for something that could be understood without confusion if I would just stop and think.

Poppa didn't want to talk to me.

She hadn't called me. She hadn't texted me. She hadn't even emailed me or sent me any memes on social media. All of the things that made up our daily interactions, and all of it outlined how different things were now. One night changed everything for us.

I went from being her *best friend* to being just another of the women that she fucked and then discarded. Back in my car, I bent over the steering wheel, my chest aching as if I'd been punched. Despite the years I'd known Poppa and the bond we had, she was treating me just like every other woman. Our history—the love we had, the care we showed—meant nothing.

I started to text her but stopped myself. I was teetering into dramatic, and this wasn't a conversation I wanted to have over the phone. My heart was already sinking at her avoidance, but before I came to a full conclusion, I needed to see her face. She was an expert at modulating her tone, but her eyes could never lie. Lifting my phone, I swiped through my contacts and placed a call. It rang twice before it was answered.

"Hey, sweetie. I was just talking about you."

Carissa's friendly rasp greeted me, instantly bringing me a measure of comfort, even as her words made me pause for a moment.

Why had she been talking about me?

Who was she talking about me with?

What was being said?

I forced a chuckle, switching the phone from one hand to the other. My nerves had me restless. A dozen scenarios entered my mind, each of them more depressing than the last.

"What you sayin' about me?" I asked teasingly, my playful tone belying the true state of my emotions.

Her deep laugh washed over me. "I was just asking Cyndi why you didn't join us for breakfast."

My steadily sinking heart picked up speed and plummeted directly into my shoes. Poppa was not only avoiding me but was keeping me away from her family. *Had being unreasonably horny ruined my friendship?* Before I could formulate a response that wouldn't sound as hurt as I felt, Carissa continued on.

"I know, I know. Y'all aren't attached at the hip—"

"Is that what she said?!" I interrupted, lips pursed, ready to cuss. It was one thing to cosplay a damn ghost—it was another to try and play me off entirely. The list of words I had for Poppa grew longer.

Somehow, Carissa was still laughing, completely unaware that I was in distress behind her only daughter.

"Oh, she didn't even get a chance to fuss like she usually does because you called. Your ears must've been ringing."

I relaxed—marginally—and offered a little laugh.

"No. I just pulled up to the house and saw that the driveway was empty. I know Nana Cherry is at church, so I was just calling to see where y'all were at before I drove off."

"Oh, you're at the house!" she exclaimed before the sound grew muffled, as if she'd pressed the phone to her chest or something. I could hear her speaking but couldn't really make out her words. Finally, she returned. "We're heading home now and should be there in about ten minutes."

I started to shake my head even though she couldn't see me.

"You don't have to rush home on my behalf—"

"Girl, hush! We were only heading to H Mart and Cyndi was already complaining, so you're really doing her a favor." I heard Poppa's voice in the background, and my chest squeezed a little.

"What are you mumbling about back there?" Carissa sassed.

"You're lucky I love Juleesa, because otherwise I'd drag you to nine different stores just for all this complaining you're doing."

"Babe," Marvin's deep voice soothed, likely from the driver's seat.

That single word was all he said, but Carissa immediately paused her fussing and took an audible deep breath before blowing it out slowly. I marveled at the way one calming word from him could reel her in when she was on the cusp of going full Killa Carissa.

"I'm cool," she murmured.

"We'll drop her off to Juleesa, then we'll head over to H Mart, and when we leave there I'll take you to Tout Suite for those macarons you like."

His tone was so sweet and loving that the tears I'd held at bay ten minutes earlier almost burst forth, only this time out of pure envy instead of sadness.

Marvin's Cadillac turned onto their street, but Carissa didn't hang up the phone. I listened as she thanked her husband and gave him loud kisses, a soft smile on my face at their unfettered display of love. Instead of pulling into the driveway, Marvin rode down to the cul-de-sac and made a u-turn before rolling to a stop beside my car. I stepped out and walked over to the passenger side. Opening the door, Carissa climbed out of the car and pulled me into a tight hug.

"Thank you, Daddy," Poppa chirped from the backseat.

Swiveling around, Marvin glared at her.

"Get yo tail outta this car."

Despite the pain in my chest, I laughed lightly, and Carissa hugged me tighter.

"Please take her away, 'cause I'm 'bout ready to clock her."

"Dang, Mommy," Poppa tsked from my left. "Two hours in your company and you ready to beat me already?"

My brain was torn between wanting to crack up at their antics and not finding much humor in anything at that moment, so all I managed to do was shake my head. "What am I supposed to do with her? She don't wanna come with me."

Leaning back, Carissa pursed her lips and rolled her eyes.

"Oh, please. You're all she talked about the whole time she was with us. She done got on my last nerve!" Carissa glared at her child before pulling me closer for another tight hug. Her declaration wouldn't have been out of the ordinary had it come anytime before today, but I found myself skeptical. When she released me, I leaned down to wave at Marvin through the opened door.

"Bring me back some shrimp crackers from H Mart!"

Chuckling, he nodded. "Will do!"

Carissa climbed back into the car, and I took a step back so they could drive off without rolling over my feet. Once they turned the corner, I took a deep breath to gather my thoughts before I slowly spun to face Poppa. To my surprise, her eyes were already on me. I mean, it shouldn't have been a surprise, because she looked at me all of the time, but after the last seven hours and all of the scenarios I'd cooked up in my head, I would've bet money that she'd avoid looking at me. My surprise was valid and…even more surprising was the hungry look in them. Surprising…and confusing. I had so many questions, so many thoughts whizzing through my brain that I didn't know where to start. Slapping my hands on my hips, I frowned and dropped my head to the side.

"What the fuck, Poppa?!"

Chapter Ten

Cyn

What Had Happened Was

"Jucee..." I interjected, hoping to get ahead of her rightful explosion.

She paused, and I know it was to give me the chance to speak, but the only words on my mind were different adjectives that described how fuckin' fine she was. It had never escaped me that Jucee was bad, but now that I'd experienced her as a lover, it was impossible to look at her in any other way. Shit, the sun even seemed to hit her different, glistening on the skin left exposed by that clingy dress that had been sitting in my closet for six months. She stood in front of me looking edible and so damn pissed with her hands on her hips and her face pinched in anger, but all I wanted to do was have her for breakfast. I couldn't say that shit to her right then though, not while she was mad, so I did the next best thing.

I closed the small space between us and wrapped my arms around her, resting them against her lower back as I pressed my face into her neck. Inhaling, I breathed her in, allowing her familiar scent to fill me up and settle me. And it did just that because, although she was pissed, the rhythm of her breathing was my internal metronome. She let me hug her, so it wasn't as bad as it could be. I wanted this hug to be our reset. I needed it to make things make sense again, because it was our thing.

We hugged. We held hands. We kissed. We cuddled.

I'd never had any relationship that was this...intimate, this affectionate, without being sexual. Had never known it was something that I would be even down with, let alone come to look forward to. Even just describing it aloud sounded wild if you didn't know the context. When Jucee and I first started kicking it, I thought she was tryna get at me because she was always touching me in some way. It was Trisha who told me that physical touch might be Jucee's love language and suggested that I ask her about it instead of making assumptions. She was right.

I went from looking forward to it to needing it.

Like right now.

With Jucee in my arms, I pressed a kiss to her cheek and then to her neck because I couldn't help myself. I had gone so long without being able to touch her that I had taken it overboard last night, and yet...I still couldn't fucking help myself.

She didn't make a sound, but I felt the way her breath stuttered in her chest, noticed the strain in her neck as she fought not to tilt her head to the side, the way she swallowed down whatever noise in her throat that my touch incited. The hug lasted all of ten seconds before she cleared her throat and stepped out of my embrace. Losing her warmth was like stepping out of the sun and into a walk-in freezer. It was a shock to my senses in a way that I couldn't verbalize, and I was torn between giving her space to think and pulling her right back into my arms. It was my comfort versus her comfort, and though I could be called selfish by many, putting Jucee first had never been an issue until now. My main source of restraint came from that thick vein of hurt that she was trying so hard to mask beneath her anger. I heard them both loud and clear. "I repeat," she gritted, her arms folded her across her chest to show me she meant business, "what, the, fuck?" We spend the whole night fucking and you just dip without so much as a text message? That's how we treat each other now? It's gotta be me, 'cause I know damn well that's not how you treat them women you run through—not the way they stay tryna spin the block. That's what sex with you gets me?"

Shit.

She wasn't pulling no punches with me this morning, and because I knew I'd fucked up, I had to eat every blow. I ran my hands down my face, pulling in a deep breath as I did so. As I released it, I stepped over to her car and leaned against the driver's side door.

Dropping my head back against the car, I stared up at the canopy of trees. She was in my peripheral, but I couldn't look her dead on while I said the shit on my mind. It was bad enough that I'd initiated last night. "I woke up this morning, looked over at you, and I panicked."

She gasped. Just a single, sharp inhalation that managed to convey quite a bit.

"You regret it."

The words were so soft they might've wanted to be a whisper when they grew up. Three little words that slid from her lips with unfettered conviction and quickly struck a chord inside of me. Pure, uncut bullshit that had me immediately twisting my head to face her. The only thing I regretted was the fact that I caused the hurt she was so poorly hiding.

"Hell no! Seeing you lay there, in my bed, where you'd been a million times, fucked with me. It was the same as always and also something I'd never experienced in my life. You were naked and sexy as fuck, looking and smelling delicious, and snoring like you always do and I'd wanted to spread you open and go again." Closing my eyes, I shook my head at my admission. "And that's when I realized how far gone I was. I'd forgotten who you were, and I had to reel that shit in."

"Uh…excuse me?"

Her mouth gaped open and her eyes were rounded to saucers. My words had her in complete shock, and guilt crowded in on me. "I know! I'm sorry! I feel like shit about this and that's why I've been MIA all morning. I've been trying to figure out a way to fix this. To fix us. I'm—"

She held up a hand to stop my rambling, and I reached for her. It was an instinct, but this time it backfired. Throwing her hands up in the air with a frustrated yell, she turned on her heel and stomped up the driveway and into the yard. Underneath the large oak tree in front of the house was a two-seat swing, and I watched her from the street, waiting until she sat down before following behind her. My parents had built that swing when me and my brothers were in elementary, back when the three of us could fit comfortably while they pushed us. Fifteen years later, it took a concentrated effort to fit all the hips me and Jucee possessed, but I was determined. Once seated, I scooted closer to her and dropped my forehead onto her shoulder, and it was cramped and maybe a little uncomfortable on my back, but I ate that shit because I was scared that I'd broken us irreparably and I needed to feel the rise and fall of her chest as she breathed. I needed my metronome. Needed to be settled. As our breaths synced, I pushed at the ground with my right foot, sending us gently rocking back and forth in the early-morning breeze on the quiet street of the neighborhood that would always be home to me.

I relished the couple of minutes of quiet, holding my breath when Jucee sighed and shook her head.

"Poppa, I need you to explain it for me like I'm five. Talk to me like I'm Amani."

Confusion knit my brows as I lifted my head and stared at her. I didn't know how else to apologize for going against the bounds of our friendship and promising never to do it again. As I racked my brain to think of something else to say, she blew out a frustrated breath and turned to me.

"What are you really worried about here? You said a lot of things, and I can't keep up to figure out what I need to correct."

Oh. That was easy enough to answer.

"I'm worried that I ruined our friendship." I was also concerned that I'd tasted something I'd never be able to forget, but the status of what was me and Jucee's bond was my greatest worry. The smile she gave me was small but earnest, and my eyes started to sting a little as hope and relief manifested as tears.

"Well, let me ease your mind," she said in a warm, sure voice. "You did nothing of the sort. We're still besties in my eyes. Nothing will change that."

She never broke eye contact with me. She didn't blink. She meant it. The relief was so overwhelming that my shoulders sank and I melted into the seat. Just a little bit, though. Nothing too dramatic. Jucee dropped her head back and laughed. It was wet and lightly stuttered, and it gave me immediate pause. There was something, I don't know what, but it sounded...off.

"Are you sure?" I asked, unable and unwilling to hide the skepticism in my voice. "Because I've been kicking myself over whether or not I took advantage of you."

I was trying to joke to lighten the moment, but the way her eyes ballooned made me think I'd maybe gone about it the wrong way.

Uh oh.

"You what?!" Two words full of pure disbelief.

"*Man...calm down.*" I placed my hand on her knee and squeezed, the urge to cup the back of the joint and pull her legs open startling me enough to pull my hand right back into my own lap. Clearing my throat, I shrugged as nonchalantly as I could feign and tried to clarify. "You just had a few drinks last night, and I should've taken that into consideration before letting things go as far as they did."

"Damn," she murmured. "So now I'm a drunk who'll sleep with anybody after two lemon drops and a shot of tequila?"

Aww hell.

Jucee clearly wasn't in a joking mood, so I stifled my laughter with a groan and tried to wrap my arms around her. She didn't exactly snatch out of my grasp, but she did lean her body toward the opposite end of the swing and shoot me a mean side-eye. That shit almost made me burst into laughter, but I tried to hold it in. It was wild and outrageous, but her angry faces were so damn cute that as much as I hated to make her angry, I also loved to see her in that state.

Biting my lip, I vehemently shook my head. "No, man! That's not what I'm saying."

Rolling her eyes toward the sky, she pursed her lips. "That's exactly what you just said, Poppa. Literally, verbatim."

I couldn't help it. I dropped my forehead to her shoulder as I laughed. She was acting like I really insinuated that she was a slutty drunk, when the reality was that the numbers barely would've moved if she'd had to take a breathalyzer.

"You're so damn dramatic," I mused, finally giving in to those thoughts and sliding my hand around the back of her knee and tugging her until she leaned back toward me. For all her bellyaching, she came easily, lips twisted into a pout, head still turned away from me as I looped an arm around her waist and pressed a kiss to her temple. I wasn't trippin'. She didn't have to be looking at me to hear what I had to say.

"Jucee, the relationship we have means so much more to me than a nut. And I'm not saying that's all last night was, but that was a one–off when we've been tight for three years. I think we can both agree that last night was..." I stared at her, observing the way the sun fell upon her dusky brown skin as she looked off to her right to avoid looking at me "...unexpected."

It took a second, but eventually she nodded, and that small move meant a lot to me. If we were on the same page, then we could work on the missteps we made in the last chapter. And by work on them, I meant strictly avoid putting ourselves in a similar situation.

"Right." I continued wanting desperately to grab her chin and make her face me, because I suddenly had a mighty need to feel her eyes study my face. I wanted her to look at me and know how sincere I was in this. "And, while I won't say it was a mistake, I think we should just—I think we should keep things in perspective."

That pulled her eyes to me. I looked at her, waiting, knowing that I was right but needing her to outwardly agree. Because when we laid all of the facts out, it became hard to ignore the obvious. Fact number one, Jucee had been single since her and Samir split three years ago. She'd dated since then, but none of those encounters ever got off the ground because—despite us never talking about it—I knew that Juleesa Marie Jones was a serious-relationship woman. She was a lovergirl who longed to be boo'd up, and she deserved to have exactly what she wanted.

Fact number two, I was married to my career, and I was as faithful as a music producer could be. Women came into my life for orgasms and the experience and left soon after. I had the best example of what a loving relationship looked like and knew down to my core that I could never give that to someone. And because of how much I loved Jucee and needed her in my life, I would never ruin what we had—what was essentially the longest friendship I'd ever maintained with a woman I actually found attractive—for a night of sex. I refused.

So I stared at her, eyes pleading, mentally begging her to get it so that I didn't have to say it out loud. My girl didn't make me wait long, finally offering me a soft smile and a nod.

"Yeah, you're right. Last night was…"

She trailed off, and my brain immediately filled in the space as if I were the one speaking. *Amazing. Fantastic. Perfection. Not enough.*

Blinking rapidly, I turned my head to the side and coughed over my shoulder to keep her from seeing any of that in my eyes, wishing that I could eliminate the words from my brain as easily as I could expel phlegm from my throat. Thankfully, Jucee continued as if uninterrupted.

"—something that happened that we won't let change us, and that's all that matters."

Her smile was still soft and tentative, but it grew marginally as if she was forcing it at gunpoint. I wanted to protest, but I also understood more than I wanted to, and because of that, I had no choice but to return her smile. She allowed me to pull her into another hug and she didn't even roll her eyes when I kissed her cheek. That had to count for something. And when I pulled back and our eyes met, I ignored the way my body seemed to heat with desire—with longing—and I dropped my eyes to the grass so that she wouldn't be able to read how dissatisfied I was with the conclusion we'd come to—no matter how necessary I knew it to be.

Chapter Eleven

Cyn

Faking the Funk

My world was spinning out of control, and my fingers were too greased up to grab ahold and set it to rights. I hadn't seen Jucee in a week, not since we'd had our talk in my parents' front yard. Maybe I was a coward, because when I realized she was putting space in between us, I just let it happen. As much as I wanted things to stay exactly as they'd been for years, the desire for more of what we'd shared—more of experiencing her in a new, exciting way—grew with every moment that passed. It was wild and uncontrollable and it just seemed easier to let Jucee keep her distance than to be forced to reckon with the realization that I wasn't as unaffected as I portrayed to be.

There was no way that I could make up for not being there when she woke up and keep my hands to myself. Or kiss her in apology. I just needed time for the memory of what we'd done to wear off, is all.

Just a little time. A couple weeks or a month or something like that.

That's it.

Nothing too outrageous.

It was possible that everything was fine and I was just anxious and reading too deeply into things. I mean, we'd talked, but she hadn't come by the house or the studio, and that was unusual for us. She'd even missed Sunday dinner, which was an ordeal. Had everybody asking about her until they got tired of my hemming and hawing and Nana finally sucked her teeth at me and went to call Jucee for answers herself. I had no idea what excuse she'd given, but no one asked me another question.

I knew that Nana had seen Jucee since then, because Amani had been at the house a couple of times when I stopped by, but that was all I knew. Well, I also knew that I hadn't done anything to change the radio silence between us either. I'd texted— to which she always answered—but hadn't popped up on her or stopped by the club to see her. My reasons felt honorable. If she needed time to help her reset our friendship in her mind, then I would give her that and then some. More than anything, I couldn't lose Juleesa Marie Jones or her friendship.

My phone rang, which was weird, because I could've sworn I'd put it on silent. I lifted it off of the table to see that it was Jackie calling me. I held it for a second, trying to decide if I wanted to answer it or not. I could feel my daddy's eyes on me, and I knew that it was my indecision that had drawn his attention. Usually, my phone never rang when I was in the studio, with only a small number of people able to get through my focus session. All it took was a quick glance at the screen for me to know if it was worth breaking my concentration to talk to whoever was on the other line or not.

I knew it was suspicious as hell, taking as long as I was to decide, and it was even worse when I swiped my thumb across the screen and lifted the device to my ear.

"Whassup, Jackie?"

"Hey, baby," she crooned into the phone, the saccharine tone pulling my lips into an instant frown. "What you up to?"

I stared down at the soundboard for a moment, wondering when we'd moved to terms of endearment. "Uh...I'm in the studio working on some tracks for Hitta."

She gasped. "Ooh! I love him! Is he there with you?"

The excitement in her voice was off-putting. It wasn't just awe, it was fandom, and I hated that shit.

"Naw. He was here a couple of weeks ago to lay some stuff down, and now I'm mixing and mastering what we came up with."

"That's so dope," she breathed. "You ate lunch yet?"

As annoyed as I was by her, the sound of food perked me up. I could deal with her shit for a little longer if she was gon' feed me.

"Not yet. I need to eat something soon though. I've been in here all morning."

"Okay. I'll see what I can do about that."

I might've grinned at that. Just a little bit though. Food got me excited. "That's a bet."

When she hung up, I replaced my phone on the table and turned back to the soundboard.

"Hmm," came a judgmental hum from my daddy, who had yet to say a word.

I slid my eyes over to him.

"What, Daddy? What you got to say?"

His lips were curved at the corners as he nodded at my face-down phone.

"Who was that?"

"Oh, that's just Jackie."

"Just Jackie, huh?"

His inquiry made me laugh.

"Yes, Daddy. *Just* Jackie. I met her a couple of weeks ago when a group of us went out to Fred Pierce's club downtown."

"Mmm."

That was all he said before he returned his attention to the knobs and dials in front of us. That was my cue to drop it if I didn't want to talk about it anymore. Except, this was the perfect opportunity to discuss the phenomena that had been plaguing me about Jackie.

"Daddy?"

He slid his gaze my way. "Hmm?"

"Tell me if you've ever heard of anything like this before." I proceeded to explain my auditory reaction whenever I heard Jackie's laugh, watching his face carefully as I did so. His eyebrows shot up when I said her full laugh was equivalent to hearing nails on a chalkboard.

When I finished, I waited for him to process everything and tell me what he thought. I hadn't told anyone about this, but I knew my daddy was the one person who could give me some insight on what the fuck was going on. Not only was he a musical genius, but he was the wisest person I knew. After a couple of minutes, he leaned back in his chair and shook his head.

"Star Shine, I know this might be disappointing, but I've never heard of that before. I'm curious about Just Jackie now."

I busted out laughing. "Her name isn't Just Jackie, Daddy. It's just Jackie."

"That's what I said." He lifted his eyebrows and shoulders simultaneously.

I shook my head. He was being silly. "No, Daddy. Her name is Jackie. That's it. That's all."

"Ahhh." He nodded his head sagely, which only served to make me laugh harder.

"Let's get back to the music, old man."

We finished up the track and moved on to another, but just when Hitta's voice filled the room, my phone rang again.

"Come on, man," I muttered, praying it wasn't Jackie calling me back.

Eventually I was going to have to let her know that I wasn't interested, and not just because I hated the sound of her voice. I just couldn't get jiggy with the whole fandom thing she had going on. I knew plenty of artists and producers who thrived on that shit—hell, I was one of them before the Grammys came calling—but now that it was legit, I couldn't vibe with it. To my surprise, it wasn't Jackie who was banging my line this time around. Relief flooded my veins and I could feel the smile take over my face as I quickly swiped my thumb across the screen and lifted the phone to my face.

"Juleesa Marie."

Her indignant squawk brought immediate laughter out of me. I was so fucking excited to hear from her that my chest was thumping.

"Why are you saying my government like that?!" she yelled. My hand found its way to that spot between my breasts where my sternum sat and rubbed. "That's your name, ain't it?"

Jucee kissed her teeth. "One I only hear when I'm in trouble." There was a moment of silence where I swear I could hear the wheels in her head spinning so damn clearly that I could've bet money on the next words that were going to come out of her mouth. "Am I in trouble, Poppa?"

I would've won the bet and still lost, because her tone had dipped a little past playful into the danger zone where I'd managed to avoid being for almost a full week and yet, just the lower timber had my mind thinking thoughts. Dark and nasty thoughts.

As if it had been beckoned, my tone dropped to join hers in the gutter. "Not unless you wanna be."

Fuck.

I was so ready to meet her where she was at that my response had slipped out too fast for me to rethink it. But shit. Even if I'd been able to do just that, I might've still said it exactly as I had, because there was no more perfect response for what she'd said in the tone she'd said it in. My daddy didn't turn to look at me, but I felt his awareness like a wool blanket draped on my shoulders during a nap.

Double fuck.

Dropping my head back, I closed my eyes and cleared my throat.

"I—um…" Clearly I had thrown Jucee off as well, yet I was sickeningly pleased by that. *What the fuck was wrong with me?*

Jucee salvaged the conversation by getting right to the point of her call.

"It's after one, and I know you haven't eaten lunch yet. Tell me I'm wrong."

All I could do was laugh, and that was enough for her, because she knew me.

"Mmhm" was all she added before she hung up.

Pulling the phone away from my face, I stared at the device for a minute before placing it back on the table and turning back to the dials.

"Mmm," came from my right.

Chuckling, I turned to him. "What now, Daddy?"

This time, instead of asking me a question, he shook his head.

"Nothing. I don't have to ask who that was, so I'll mind my business this time."

Eyes narrowed, I stared at him, trying to figure out if he was being funny or attempting to apply reverse psychology on me. The little smile he wore pointed toward the latter, but I couldn't be sure, so I followed his lead and went back to the music.

It was twenty minutes later before another notification came across my phone. It was the chime from the security app to let me know the code had been used at the studio door. I was fairly certain I knew who it was, so I didn't even blink an eye.

Imagine my surprise when the door opened and Jackie strolled in as if she'd been here a million times and had every right to arrive unannounced. Behind her was a visibly annoyed Jucee, holding a plastic bag of something that smelled delicious.

Triple fuck!

The music faded out, and I turned to see Daddy with his hands on the knob. He gave me an expectant look and I returned it with one of pure cluelessness. I was lost. This felt like one of those situations you watch happen to other people; I had no idea what I was supposed to do. A chick who was into me and my best friend, who I'd—

"Hey, baby!"

Jackie broke into my thoughts with her loud voice. In the blink of an eye, I had a flashback to the time when I used to welcome random groupies into the studio with open arms. That was just a couple of years ago, and so much had changed since then. Not only because Jackie's audacity annoyed me instead of amused me, but because this particular woman got under Jucee's skin and I'd spent a week praying that things would improve between us sooner than later. This random popup felt like being knocked back six steps after only taking two steps forward.

Blinking, I stood to my feet and was nearly tackled by Jackie charging me for a hug. I didn't know she even knew where the studio was, but I guess I shouldn't be surprised. The location was public information, so anyone who wanted to know could find it. The real shock was seeing her inside, since that was a privilege only afforded to a small number of people.

"Whassup, Jackie?" I carefully avoided the term of endearment she'd decided to start using out of nowhere. A couple kisses didn't make you baby, and it was weird that she was trying to create a false sense of intimacy in that way. "What are you doing here?"

She giggled. I hoped my cringe wasn't too visible.

"You said you hadn't eaten, so I figured I'd come by so you could take me to lunch."

My eyebrows shot up, my daddy hummed, and Jucee snorted. *Take her to lunch?* That was presumptuous as hell. I pulled back from the hug and cocked my head to the side.

"I told you I was working, though."

"Yeah, but you need to eat. I figured you could stop working for an hour or two to share a meal with me." She shrugged, a clueless smile plastered onto her face. She didn't get it, and that wasn't her fault. She didn't know me well enough, or maybe she just didn't have anything that she was that passionate about, so she couldn't relate.

In my peripheral, I saw Jucee place the bag of food on the table against the wall and go over to my daddy. He stood to his feet and they embraced. The desire to know what they were saying was burning at me, but Jackie was in my face and I had to handle her first. Grabbing her hands in mine, I squeezed them.

"Listen. I appreciate you thinking of me, but when I'm locked in for work, I'm locked in. I can't just up and leave while tracks are unfinished. I can't do that to these artists."

Jackie pouted but nodded. Behind her, I saw Jucee walk toward the door. She glanced my way before leaving and gave a weak wave as she disappeared out the studio.

"I understand," Jackie said. "I'll do better next time."

I nodded and tried to hurry her to the door so that I could maybe catch Jucee before she was all the way gone.

"You're not gon' introduce me to your friend?"

My daddy's words stopped me in my tracks. Frustration rose up in me. He had to know that I wanted to try and speak with Jucee. He *had* to.

"Oh, my bad." I pulled Jackie over to him. Still standing, he held out a hand to Jackie.

She giggled as she grabbed it and shook.

"This is Jackie, Jackie, this is Marvin Thomas. He was bass player and lead songwriter for The Still Waters."

Daddy waved a hand at me. "Oh, she's too young to know about that old group."

Jackie just giggled harder, making my eye twitch.

"I'm actually twenty-eight."

Daddy gave her an indulgent smile. "Just a baby. You're younger than my youngest child."

Rolling my eyes, I smirked. He was quiet, but one thing for sure was my daddy could charm anyone.

"You don't look old enough to have kids my age!"

At that I snorted. My daddy might've been bald, but he had more salt than pepper in his beard. While his skin was beautifully moisturized and cared for, his sienna skin was wrinkled with signs of aging. I know that it was normal to tell older people they didn't look old, but for some reason it annoyed me coming out of Jackie's mouth.

Or maybe I was just annoyed by her in general.

And...if I were being honest, it was probably because I didn't really like her, but she kept my mind off of Jucee.

That was a terrible thought, and acknowledging it only made me more annoyed, so I shoved that to the back of my mind and hustled Jackie out the door, glaring at my daddy over my shoulder as he called out goodbye. I'd be having words with his instigating ass when I returned. Jackie chatted to herself about how sweet he was and how cool it was that I worked with pioneers from a time before me, and I just stayed silent. It was preferable that she thought he was just an older musician that I was working with and not my actual father. For some reason, I got the feeling that she would read too much into meeting my daddy, and I didn't need that additional drama. It was bad enough that I was essentially using her.

I walked her to a red VW Beetle and pulled her into a brief hug that hopefully said "goodbye." When I tried to step back, she gripped the sides of my shirt and kept me close.

"When am I going to see you again?" Dropping her chin, she blinked at me from under long lashes. There was no denying how attractive Jackie was, and ordinarily, this little move would've had me biting my lip and giving her a concrete date and hour.

Unfortunately for her, this wasn't an ordinary time.

"Uh…"

"What about tomorrow?"

I was off my game. This was a level-one question in the game of finessing, and I should've had three different responses ready to hit her with, yet I couldn't think straight. My eyes searched the parking spaces up and down the strip, praying Jucee was still around. Jackie squeezed my sides, bringing my attention back to her.

"That's fine," I finally said, not even entirely sure what I'd agreed to but fully aware that the desperate way I was searching for my friend was out of line. I needed to focus on Jackie if I wanted things with Jucee to go back to normal.

Pleased with my answer, Jackie hugged me and climbed into her car. I waved her off and headed back into the studio. I found my daddy sitting at the table, an open container of loaded baked potato casserole in front of him. Ignoring him, I grabbed my phone off the counter and called Jucee. It rang six times before I hung up and called again. It went to voicemail.

Okay.

I took a breath and calmed myself before I started getting heated. It was possible that she was calling me back at the same time that I was calling and that was why it had gone straight to voicemail. That's all. She hadn't blocked me or anything.

After convincing myself that everything was cool, I turned to join my father at the table.

"What is this?" I asked, sliding into the seat across from him.

"The lunch Juleesa brought with intention to eat with you."

I twisted my lips to the side as he leveled me with a gaze. "Man," I drawled, pulling out the other chair and sitting down. "Why you say it like that?"

"How did I say it?" His eyes were on me as he scooped a forkful of potatoes, cheese, chicken, and barbecue sauce into his mouth.

"Like I fucked up or something. Like you're disappointed in me."

"The way you let Juleesa come in here, bring you something to eat, and leave without saying one word to her? I *am* disappointed in you."

His voice was in an even, practical tone, his words uttered matter-of-factly. And he might as well have punched me in the chest.

"Daddy..."

"I don't often see y'all with your women—and I'm sure that's by design—so I have no idea if this is how you act on a regular basis. What I will say is that I didn't raise y'all to ignore your friends and the people who mean the most to you just because you got some new pussy—"

"Daddy!" My mouth fell open and then I busted out laughing.

He shrugged, as nonchalant as ever. "All's I'm saying is that you don't ditch your homies for a new relationship."

Groaning, I sat back and dragged my hands down my face. While he was right, he had it all wrong.

"First of all, me and Jackie aren't together."

Huffing a laugh, he took another bite. "I hear you saying that, but does she know that?"

Brows furrowed, I stared at him. "Of course. We just met two weeks ago. If she thought we were together, I'd be seriously concerned."

He nodded, head toward his food. "And what about Juleesa? Does she know you aren't with Just Jackie?"

I gaped at him. "She knows better than anyone. She was there when I met the girl! Why would you even ask me that?"

Lifting his head, he turned his piercing gaze onto me.

"I ask because I saw the look on Juleesa's face when she walked into this room."

My nod was slow as I thought back. "Yeah…she was definitely annoyed."

He just looked at me, those eyes boring into me as if he was searching for something. After a moment, he chuckled and shook his head.

"It's funny because, to me, it looked like she felt betrayed. But I guess that's crazy, right?"

He quirked an eyebrow and went back to his food as if he hadn't just dropped a wildly inaccurate bomb on me.

"Daddy," I whined, feeling a little embarrassed and a lot exposed. "You know me and Jucee are friends. Just friends. She's one of my best friends." It didn't matter that those words suddenly felt foreign like cotton on my tongue. That had nothing to do with anything.

"Mm."

With his eyebrows up, he gave me a look that said he clearly didn't believe me, but thankfully, he didn't say anything else. I wasn't going to address his hum, because that would open the door for him to keep going, and that was the last thing I wanted.

Reaching across the table, I dragged the unopened container toward me and popped off the plastic lid. The aromas from inside smacked me in the face immediately. I groaned a lil bit. Just a little though.

Jumbo shrimp and strips of tender, medium steak sat atop a bed of fluffy potatoes that had been scraped out of their skin and stuffed into a rectangular container and drizzled with a garlic aioli. It was my favorite dish from the potato truck on the southeast side. Glancing at my daddy's container, I recognized the Cajun chicken potato that Jucee loved. She must've already been on the south side of town to have picked these up and gotten here as quickly as she did.

Damn.

Finally seeing my friend after a week of no face time, only to miss the opportunity to speak to each other, was a sick sort of irony. Jackie's presence only made it worse. And my daddy's commentary didn't help.

And maybe the worst of it all was the fact that none of this would be happening if I'd just kept my lips to myself.

Chapter Twelve

Jucee

Breaking the Seal

We're just friends.

We're just friends.

We're *just* friends.

I had to keep repeating it to myself in hopes that the chant would actually affect the pure, uncut rage I'd felt at seeing Lil Miss Afro Puffs at the door of Rhythm & Rainbows. That pure, uncut rage I'd felt when Poppa was compounded by the pure, uncut rage I'd felt when Poppa hugged her and barely spared me a glance. That wasn't how we treated each other.

Well, it wasn't before.

And, like it or not, things were different now. It likely didn't help that I'd been missing in action for the past week. I'd needed time to process, but time did not heal these wounds, because being away from Poppa felt more like a punishment than a necessary device for healing. It was because I missed her as much as I did that I called her back a couple of hours after ignoring her call immediately after leaving the studio.

"You mad at me?" was how Poppa started the conversation. Surprised, I burst into laughter and felt the tension in my shoulders lessen. I could handle humor.

"No, Poppa. I'm not mad at you."

"So then you're coming over later to watch the music awards, right?"

My lips parted as I tried to work that out in my head. I didn't actually have a reason to say no, other than my concern about being alone with her.

We are just friends.

We are just friends.

We are *just* friends.

With my mantra repeating in my mind like stock market ticker tape, I agreed to go back to the scene of the crime. It was dramatic, but it was exactly how I felt. However, if I wanted to maintain our friendship, I was going to have to get back to doing the normal things we did together. That meant saying yes when my mind was asking me if that was such a smart idea.

Saying yes is precisely how I ended up in this predicament. You know when you go out drinking and you're throwing 'em back all night without having to pee and shit is cool? You're having a great time, laughing, twerking on your friends, and singing every song the DJ plays at the top of your lungs. Your bladder is being the MVP of the night, holding you down, allowing you to stay on the floor having a good-ass time, but then you have that one drink that puts you over the top and suddenly you have to pee so bad you might not make it to the bathroom in time. And once you pee, it feels glorious, like you've poked a hole in a water balloon and the swollen bubble is deflating at a rapid pace.

The problem is, once you pee that first time, you're no longer able to hold it in for longer than fifteen minutes, and now you're running back and forth to the bathroom all night.

You broke the fucking seal.

That's how I felt about sleeping with Poppa.

Nearly a year without having sex had made me mellow. Even with grinding my covered pussy in folks' faces for a living, I didn't even desire to change that fact. One night with Cyndi Thomas changed that. I'd been activated, and now I was in go mode. We were just supposed to be watching an awards show, but I was unreasonably horny and unable to do anything but fantasize about the things I hadn't gotten the chance to do to Poppa.

Each scenario of how I wanted to twist her up like soft pretzel from a baseball concessions stand was playing on my mind the entire time that I sat next to her that night. I couldn't even pay attention and definitely couldn't have told you who won what, even if I needed that information to save my life. If Poppa noticed I was distracted, she didn't say anything, and I was too zoned out to catch any curious looks she may have aimed my way. I didn't even know the show was over until the lights came on and Poppa tapped my foot. Her touch got my attention, but it took me a second to come out of thoughts of her calves on my shoulders.

"You aight?" she asked, eyebrows raised, her expression a mix of concern and amusement.

Lifting my arms above my head, I stretched and nodded. "Yeah, I'm good." I stood up and grabbed my keys off of the coffee table. "I'm getting sleepy, so I'mma head out though." I was the furthest thing from sleepy but what I was wasn't something that could be addressed in her presence, so it was best if I bounced. Amani was with Samir because Pooh had a recital and it didn't make sense to bring him home late, and I was off on Wednesdays, so there was no other reason for me to leave but to keep from trying to jump her bones again. That was a good enough reason, to be honest.

Poppa stood up as well and frowned. "Since when do you need to leave just because you're sleepy?"

I refused to answer that. It had only been a few hours since I'd seen her all hugged up with another woman, and I clearly wasn't as strong as she was. There was no way I could have a fucking sleepover like we hadn't just been hunching less than two weeks ago. Grabbing my shoes from the side of the couch, I bent to step into them and tie my laces. Righting, I faked a yawn and headed toward the front door.

"I have a bed, I'm gonna go sleep in it. No biggie."

If she wanted to say more, she'd have to say it to my back, because after I quickly pecked her on the cheek, I damn near sprinted toward the front door. I could feel her presence at my heels as she followed behind me, and I for sure felt her eyes on my ass with each step I took. It had been in her eyes that she didn't want me to leave, but just like me, she was holding back in an effort to preserve something that I hadn't thought was in danger. That was okay. I didn't want her to feel backed into a corner, but I had my boundaries and if I did nothing else, I was gonna stick to them. Curled up under someone who was adamant about us keeping things in the box they'd always been in wasn't a brand of torture I wanted to subscribe to.

I was steps from the door, hand extended toward the knob to let myself out, when Cyn grabbed me and pulled me over to the side, out of the path to the door. Startled, I blinked at her.

"Wha—"

Shaking her head, she cut me off. "I know you said we're good, but this shit still don't feel right."

My brows shot up but I stayed silent, giving her time to work out what she wanted to say. To say I was surprised that she even brought it up would've been an understatement.

She pulled off her fitted and scratched her scalp before sliding the hat back on.

"Jucee," she began in a somber tone that made my heart pound a little faster with dread, "you mean so much to me, you can't even understand. I don't want to lose this shit we have. I don't want to lose you. Worrying about it has been hell, not seeing you for a week even though we're in the same city was hell, and I don't want to experience no shit like that ever again."

Her words wrapped round me like a warm blanket. Avoiding her hadn't been the easiest thing for me either, but it was comforting to know that I wasn't the only one who suffered from the distance.

Her fitted was kind of crooked and her eyebrows were furrowed a little, like she was thinking hard about what she wanted to say, and I'd be lying if I said I didn't get a little hopeful. Lawd, but I hated it. You know that feeling when you were a kid and you'd been begging ya mama for an Easy Bake Oven for Christmas and she repeatedly told you that it was too expensive, but then The Big Day arrives and there's a box under the tree that looks about the size of an Easy Bake Oven and feels about as heavy as you imagined an Easy Bake Oven felt and you look over at ya mama and she's sitting on the sofa giving you this look—you know the look—that makes this flower of hopefulness bloom inside of you, but you're afraid to let it grow because you heard her tell your granny that she worked two jobs just to make ends meet, and although you didn't know what that meant, you knew what "too expensive" meant and it was possible that it was just a big-ass box of socks and underwear and frilly dresses for church, but *that look*?! That's how I felt as I stared at Poppa's face. She was back to being Poppa—*my* Poppa—and the uncontrollable hope had me stressed.

Twisting my lips to the side, I slid my hands into the back pockets of my jean shorts. "What are you saying?" I wasn't in a position to guess. I needed her to lay it all out for me.

She licked her lips, the gesture making her nerves plain, but she never broke eye contact with me as she said, "I want us to try for something more. Something...beyond friendship."

I felt my cheeks bloom like that hope in my chest as a slow grin spread across my face. "You thought about it and decided you wanna let me eat that pussy, huh?"

Laughter burst from her mouth as she covered her face with a hand and dropped her head back. The move exposed the smooth skin of her neck, and my lips tingled with the desire to kiss her there. It was only the need for confirmation from her that held me back.

"I mean..." she drawled, her voice suddenly low as she returned her gaze to mine. "Yeah. Among other things."

The look in those dark brown irises coupled with the outright suggestiveness in her tone, plus her admission and the vision of me doing exactly that, had me throbbing with want. Sucking in a breath, I placed a palm on each of her shoulders and pushed her back against the wall.

If she wanted it like I wanted it, then she could get it right now.

Trailing my hands down over her breasts and her torso, I settled them at her waist. My grip was firm and I watched her face as I spoke. So far, nothing but anticipation looked back at me. I dipped my fingers into her waistband.

"You sure this is what you want?"

Her immediate nod was unsatisfactory. While I was glad she didn't hesitate, I wanted to hear that voice. Thankfully, she knew me as well as she did, because when I quirked an eyebrow at her, she grinned and shook her head.

"Yeah, man. I know exactly what I want, and it's this right here, with you."

I didn't even realize she'd raised her hand until her fingers found my chin and she used it to pull me toward her. My heart was beating so hard I was sure it would burst through my titties. Her lips found mine, and I sighed. It was perfect. Like that first breeze of air conditioning touching your skin after you've been outside playing all day in the summer. Or getting the first cup of ice-cold Kool-Aid that was made by your baby brother who's always heavy-handed with the sugar. The way our mouths seemed to fit like the most important pieces of a heart-shaped puzzle that only had the center missing just made sense. Like this was already written in the code of whatever simulation we were living in. It was a relatively chaste kiss, only ending when she licked the seam of my mouth before pulling back as soon as I opened for her. The teasing was right up my alley, and I wanted more of it.

I almost melted into a puddle of pure happiness and lust.

"I want you, Juleesa Marie Jones." The corner of her mouth tipped up. "And I *really* wanna see what that mouth do."

I was laughing before I realized it, and it wasn't until that moment that it hit me how important that was for us. Poppa and I stayed clowning so much that laughter was like another language for us. That wasn't something that I wanted to lose just because we decided to jump the platonic ship and land on deck of the romantic one.

Still chuckling, I pursed my lips and began to unbutton her jeans. Watching her face was like observing a world wonder. Her laughter petered out and she sucked that juicy-ass bottom lip into her mouth as her eyes became hooded with lust. Even if she hadn't told me, it was as clear as glass that she wanted me—at least in this moment. And with the way I wanted her, nothing could've prevented me from pushing her pants down her thick-ass thighs and squatting in front of her. I glanced up, waiting for some sort of protest, but when she remained silent, her eyes begging me to continue, I did as I'd intended.

First, I reached around and palmed her ass, something that had been on my mind for a while. I'd felt her ass before but it was different in this context. This wasn't an accidental grope in the middle of the night as we slept next to each other. This was intentional and purely for pleasure—mine and hers. I only spent a short time kneading her cheeks, but when Poppa huffed a soft breath through her nose and grunted, I knew it was something I'd be returning to as soon as I was able.

Sliding my hands around her hips, I reached the front of her boy shorts and ran two fingers along the slit between her fat lips through the material, moaning at what I found. She was already so damn wet, my mouth watered in anticipation. The brand of underwear she wore was from an inclusive designer and had a buttoned hole in the front. I quickly undid the two buttons and used my two index fingers to separate the fabric as I leaned forward and stuck my nose inside. The intoxicating scent of her arousal was expected—finding her completely bald was not. That's not what I remembered from a couple of weeks ago. Grinning, I shook my head. One thing about Poppa, she was going to defy stereotypes when you least expected it.

From the positioning of the hole and because Poppa's pussy was so fat, the only thing I could reach was the very top of her slit. With my fingers rubbing her through the shorts, I gave her one slow lick. You would've thought I'd bit her with the way she hissed and jerked against me. Pulling back, I met her gaze.

"You okay?"

Her chin dipped, but she stopped mid-nod and gave me a smile. "I'm better than okay. I'm just—I don't get a lot of action down there, so it's sensitive."

My eyes bugged, but I quickly lowered my head to hide my reaction. With all of the women who constantly hovered around her everywhere she went, I expected that Poppa got head as a part of her daily vitamins. Hearing that the truth was actually opposite shocked me.

And fueled me.

I was already going to put in work, but now I wanted to give Poppa brain so good she called my mama begging for my diplomas. I was about to spell my name on her pussy with my tongue, and no woman who came after me would be able to erase it. Poppa had no idea, but she'd just unlocked a side of me that I'd kept under wraps for good reason.

It was now demon time.

Yanking her shorts down to her knees, I pressed a kiss to her fupa before using one hand to spread her lips and expose her wet clit, while the other dived for her now-uncovered opening. I gave her open-mouth kisses while rubbing through her wetness. Her flavor was an intoxicating salty-sweet that had my eyes fluttering closed as I devoured her. Her hips bucked against me and her hands came to my head, but nothing stopped me from my mission of cleaning my plate. When Poppa's grunts turned into strained mewls, I sucked her clit into my mouth at the same time that I slid my middle and ring fingers inside of her.

"Oh, shit, Jucee! Fuck!"

Her words came at the same time as she thumped her head against the wall, but it was all drowned out by my contented humming. This was where I wanted her. Thrashing and undone and quivering. Knees shaking, chest heaving. She only had one hand in my hair and had used the other to lift her shirt and cup one of her heavy breasts, her fingers tugging at the bar through her nipple. It was such an erotic sight that I was liable to cum just as I was, squatting between her legs with a mouthful of her pussy and my fingers thrusting inside of her. I was so tempted to slide a hand into my own panties and bring my release to the surface, but my plate was almost clean, and I'd be damned if I left behind a single solitary crumb.

Curling my fingers inside of her, I released her clit and replaced my mouth with my fingers, rubbing at her swollen nub while I licked and sucked around it. It felt like only seconds of that passed before Poppa let out a cry that sounded almost painful. Eyes up, I watched her come apart in my hands, relishing each and every expression on her face, twist of her lips, and the couple of tears that spilled down her cheeks. I gave her a minute to catch her breath before I completely pulled off of her. After redressing her, I stood to my feet and stared at her. Her fitted was barely hanging on, one of her titties was hanging out of her bra, and her eyes were blown. She looked completely wrecked, and I loved it.

Without saying a word, I fixed her bra and straightened her shirt. Then I leaned forward and placed a soft kiss on her lips. "I'll see you tomorrow" was all I said before walking out the front door and using my key to lock it behind me.

Chapter Thirteen

Cyn

The Girls Are Fighting

Good head cured many a thing, but even getting ate out like a Jell-O pudding cup couldn't erase my daddy's words from my mind. Daddy seeing betrayal on her face was fucking with me. It wasn't like I'd invited Jackie to come over, but if her presence rubbed Jucee the wrong way, then it was still my fault. I wasn't even fucking with Jackie for real, but because I hadn't told her that, she felt comfortable enough to show up to the studio. That was on me. I needed to fix that with Jucee and simultaneously needed to get us back on track. So when I texted Jucee the next morning and asked her to meet me at the newest food hall downtown for lunch, I held my breath. Wednesdays were her off days and usually the day we'd grab lunch together; things hadn't been usual, but after our conversation last night, I had high hopes. After fifteen minutes, my phone vibrated as Jucee thumbs-upped my question and responded.

Jucee Baby: …

Jucee Baby: What time?

Me: One?

Jucee Baby: Okay.

Maybe I was a little anxious, but it seemed like the driest interaction we'd had in a long time. It was enough for me. For now. My plan had been to spend another full day in the studio working on Hitta's album, but my daddy was right about one thing. I needed to make sure my friendship was righted. No matter what had transpired between us, the bottom line was me and Jucee were locked in, and nothing was supposed to be able to shake that up.

I tried working up until it was time to leave, but I couldn't even concentrate, so I went ahead on to POST Houston early. It was an entertainment venue with a food hall and was located in the old Barbara Jordan Post Office on Bagby. It was an amazing space, with coworking offices, a massive skylawn, and of course a large food hall. I'd heard of them when Trisha, Xeno's girlfriend, brought in spicy chicken wings from a spot called Lea Jane's, which was located at POST.

I was knuckle-deep in hot sauce when Jucee slid into the metal chair across the table from me, holding a tray with a plate of beef panang curry and jasmine rice, blackberry lemonade, and a basket of hot wings. She placed the basket in front of me and settled into her seat, fork already in her freed hand. Casting a cursory glance at the wings, I frowned at her. Never mind how she knew I wanted more of those, I was more concerned with the state of her arrival.

"So you're just gonna sit your ass down and eat without even giving me a hug or a kiss? That's what we're doing? That's how we're treating each other today?" Eyes narrowed, I waited for her response on bated breath because I wanted—needed—something normal. I needed to know that she was still rocking with me. That sex didn't mean we completely ruined our shit. I waited to see what she would do, and my heart split in half when an undeniable grin came on to her face. She rolled her eyes, but there was amusement there as well.

Tossing her head back, she hooted with laughter before shaking her head and pushing to her feet. Coming to stand behind me, she bent at the waist, wrapping her arms around me in a tight hug as she pressed her lips to my jaw. I saw it coming and still couldn't prepare myself. Her movements were slow—almost deliberately so—giving me ample time to categorize each and every moment before, during, and after her body heat and scent engulfed me. That pillow-soft bottom lip lingered just a fraction of a second longer than the top, searing a brand onto my skin. The weight of her limbs enclosing mine, holding me in place while she did what she wanted to me without my interference. The moment lasted less than two seconds, but from the way my eyes fluttered closed and my brain shifted into slo-mo, it felt like ten minutes of pleasure.

If I was unsure about my feelings before today, this moment absolutely solidified them for me. I'd just lived out a scene from a nineties Black rom-com in my head off of an innocent touch; if love was a destination, I'd moved in with my luggage in tow.

Dammit to hell, I was so fucked.

"I'm sorry, Poppa," Jucee murmured into my ear, amusement woven into her naturally melodious voice. "I forgot for two minutes what a brat you are."

The contented cloud of pining that had fallen over me cleared with a quickness, and I was back to glaring at her as she chuckled and returned to her seat.

"Or," I emphasized, "I just want your love and affection at all times."

With her attention on her plate, she nodded. "You know you got that already."

I harrumphed, but didn't otherwise say a word. I heard the deeper meaning in that loud and clear and my heart was swelling too big for my chest, but I didn't know what to do with that reaction. It was a precarious situation I was in. On one hand, I was trying to hold on to one of the most fulfilling relationships I'd ever managed to maintain, and on the other, I wanted to explore something I'd never had before with the most important woman to me. It could very likely end in disaster. Twisting my lips, I watched Jucee take a bite of her dish, the way her eyes closed as she savored the amalgamation of flavors and spice causing me distress. Of course I knew that she loved me, and I loved her too, but this was different. *This* was something that made my heart feel too big for my chest and had me up writing love songs at three in the morning.

"Poppa, can I ask you a question?"

When she lifted her gaze from her plate, I realized that I'd been staring at her. Shifting in my seat, I returned my attention to my hot wings.

"What's up?"

"Are you a no-touch stud?"

My eyes widened, and I started choking on the chicken. Jucee grabbed the glass of water on the table and shoved it into my hand. Then she jumped to her feet and ran off, returning with a glass, artesian bottled water. My coughing had subsided, but I still took the bottle and drained it quickly.

"Seriously, Jucee?" I wheezed, tapping at my chest.

"What?" She looked genuinely confused.

"You can't say shit like that out the blue! That's the kind of question that needs a warm-up. Prep me first, dammit!"

Grinning, she shrugged and sipped from the blackberry lemonade. "Prep first. Got it. I'll file that away for future refer-ence."

Rolling my eyes toward the heavens, I groaned. *"Marie…"* This called for her middle name, because she was really out of pocket for that question.

Folding her arms on top of the table, she leaned forward, giggling at my exasperated expression.

"Yes, Poppa?"

Dropping my eyes from the ceiling, I swung them toward Jucee, pulling a smile outta her. Her attention was glued to my face. The expression on her face said that all she wanted to do was put her mouth on me, and my skin heated at the thought.

"Why would you even ask me some shit like that?"

I spoke the question in a low tone in an attempt to mask how turned on it had me. We didn't talk about this kind of stuff. On purpose. Somehow I'd always known that it would be awkward, and now I knew the real reason was that I'd want to do whatever it was we were talking about.

"I asked 'cause I wanna eat your pussy again, and from the way you acted last night, I figured it wasn't something you received often. I know you get pussy, so I could only assume why that was."

My lips parted and my mouth fell open. Sitting back heavily, I cast my head from side to side, flitting my eyes around the wide-open space, trying to see if someone might've heard her. How in the hell did we get here? And why was her declaration that she wanted to give me another round of head heating me from my toes to my fitted?

Actually, I knew the answer to that second question. I wanted it. I wanted her.

Finally, after a full minute of feeling unexpectedly shy at her bold question and avoiding her gaze, I faced her, licking my lips nervously as I did so.

"I..."

Raising her eyebrows, she waited for me to continue, but nothing followed. I didn't know what to say. Couldn't even form words beyond *yes* and *please*, neither of which I could say because they had nothing to do with what she'd actually asked me.

"You...?" she prompted.

"You're one of my best friends——"

"Your *best* friend."

I chuckled and shook my head, glad to have something else to focus on. "Don't let Xeno hear you say that shit."

Rolling her neck from side to side, Jucee squared her shoulders. "She know what's up. Besides, she don't want these problems. I'm short but I can fight and these hands are rated E for Everybody."

My chuckle grew into a boisterous laugh, and I cocked my head to the side and eyed her in amusement. She sounded serious too.

"So, you'd fight for the title of my best friend? Seriously?" She quirked an eyebrow and met my gaze.

"I'd fight for that, among other things of yours."

Like your heart went unsaid, but I felt that shit with my entire being like she'd shouted it up to the rafters. It was corny as hell but I got it because that's how these newish feelings for Jucee made me feel as of late. Hell, that's how I felt during my songwriting sessions these last couple of weeks. Goofy, and corny, and giddy, *and* horny as fuck. Which was why I wanted to eat her for breakfast, lunch, and dinner before taking her for a long ride that ended with soaked sheets and the both of us passed out from exhaustion.

I groaned, running a hand down my face as I tried to clean those thoughts from my brain. The mental images seemed seared into my mind's eye. The numbers six and nine floated past my eyes, and I thought that maybe I needed to schedule a visit to my optometrist.

"Jucee! C'mon, man!"

Maybe it wasn't that serious, but why did it feel like she wasn't interested in taking things slowly? I was tryna preserve what we had and slowly introduce something new, and she wanted to just throw all of that away on a whim! Frowning, I clutched my chicken wing in my hand and sighed loudly. Jucee sucked her teeth in response.

"Seriously, Cyndi? Kill all of the dramatics. If you're not interested, you can straight up say no. All the extra shit is so rude and unnecessary." Her over-the-top display of displeasure made me sit up straight and look at her. She was trying to mask it with annoyance, but there was slight hitch in her voice that tugged at my heart.

"Wait. Are you being serious right now?"

She narrowed her eyes into slits. "You know that I am or you wouldn't be acting an ass."

Dropping the chicken, I opened a moist towelette and wiped off my fingers. She had it all wrong.

"I'm sorry. For real. I just..." I shrugged. "I don't know, man. You caught me off guard and I..." A heavy sigh pushed from my lips. "It's obvious you're not just playing and that shit threw me because..."

"Because what, Cyndi?"

My bottom lip curled up. "Aye! First off, stop calling me fucking *Cyndi*. It's Poppa from you or nothing else."

"When you *act* like Poppa, I'll *call* you Poppa. Right now, you're giving me big Cyndi Thomas aka *Cyn Tha Starr* energy."

She'd leaned forward, her hand curled into a fist on the table top, genuine fire blazing in her eyes. I didn't want to be turned on by the way she was tryna charge me up, but I'd be lying if I said my pussy didn't throb a lil bit. My lips quirked up of their own accord.

"Don't do me like that." I could admit that it was silly, but when she called me anything other than Poppa, it pissed me off. Like full on grated on my nerves. I didn't even get that mad when my mama called me my full government. *You know what?* Fuck it. If she wanted to go there, we could go there. I sat forward, ready to throw caution into the wind, when I heard someone call my name. Confused, I looked around until my gaze landed on Jackie.

"Are you shitting me?" I heard Jucee mumble under her breath, letting me know that I wasn't imagining things. Jackie was actually here at POST and headed right for us.

When she reached our table, she launched herself at my side, wrapping her arms around me and aiming a kiss for my lips. It had caught me off guard and all I could do was let it happen, my stomach sinking with each second that it lasted. Pulling away, I patted her back and shot a glance over at Jucee to gauge her reaction.

Following the path of my attention, Jackie turned her head and finally acknowledged Jucee.

"Oh, Jucee!" she gasped. "I didn't know you would be here!" My eyebrows furrowed as Jucee's shot up.

"I could say the same about you," Jucee responded, folding her arms on top of the table and leaning forward as if she was preparing to watch a good show.

"Uh, what are *you* doing here, Jackie?"

Instead of immediately answering my question, she grabbed a chair from a nearby table and situated it right next to me first.

"I asked you yesterday if we could get together today and you said yes. You don't remember?"

Jucee's eyes flew to me and I slapped a hand against my forehead.

"Shit," I muttered when I realized what Jackie was talking about. I'd forgotten all about that. Likely because I hadn't meant it when I'd answered.

"Yeah, I did. But how did you know I'd be here?"

Jackie laughed and looped an arm through mine, hugging up on me.

"I didn't. I'm meeting a friend on the skylawn for yoga and I saw you on my way to the stairs."

Relief flooded me. I thought she'd been on some stalker shit, but luckily it was just a coincidence. Her being here wasn't ideal, but it was like a wake-up call. It was unexpected, but maybe this was a good thing. Jackie's presence kept me from saying and doing something that I didn't need to be doing.

Jackie leaned into me and nuzzled my neck. It tickled, so I jerked away and immediately looked up at Jucee. I don't know why I felt compelled to look her way. I'd been with women in front of her before; she was always chill about it. But this time just felt different. It felt wrong on several levels and my daddy's voice echoed in my brain when he described the look on Jucee's face from the day before. I could try and explain it away, but even if it didn't make sense, it still felt wrong. And that wasn't the only thing.

The blood wasn't exactly bad between her and Jackie, but the vibe was off in a way I couldn't describe. Little shit like having my neck kissed on felt performative. I had to wonder if Jackie's display was for my benefit or Jucee's. And if it was for Jucee, then I had to wonder why Jackie felt like she needed to put on a show for her. Those thoughts took me down a rabbit hole that I just didn't have the wherewithal to travel, so I reeled it in and focused on my friend.

I watched Jucee press her lips together before she turned away. She only did that when she had things to say but figured it was best if she kept those things to herself. Usually I was in on it, sharing a look with her as she failed to keep the judgment off of her face. This time, I was the subject—or I was entertaining the subject, as Jackie was practically in my lap. Either way, I didn't like it.

Pushing back from the table, Jucee hiked her purse up onto her shoulder.

"I'm going to go." Standing, she took her tray to the nearby trash can, emptied her refuse into the bin, and slid the tray onto the waiting rack.

Disentangling Jackie from my limbs, I stood to my feet, not liking the random panic that shot me in the gut at the abrupt way Jucee had gotten up from the table. If she tried to walk out of the building without giving me some affection and a proper goodbye, I was going to riot. I wasn't going for that shit two days in a row. I couldn't explain the feeling—wasn't at all sure why it even seemed like a possibility when we didn't move like that.

She turned from the bin and headed right back to our table—right back to me—and I blew out a relieved breath. When she saw me standing, the corner of her mouth quirked up. I spread my arms, not even giving her a chance to do anything other than hug me. Her arms encircled my neck as she stepped into my hug, laughing when I squeezed her to me tighter than was necessary.

That laugh was the right one. The force of the thought knocked the wind out of me.

Her head fell backward as her laugh tapered into a giggle as I dropped a loud kiss on her cheek.

"You really do the most sometimes," she scolded as I released her. "You know that?"

Though she glared, I could see the amusement on her face, and better than that, I could *hear* it in her voice. My panic had subsided, allowing me to mirror the grin on her face. We were good. That's all I needed.

"I'm well aware," I replied before tilting my head to the side, offering my cheek for the kiss she'd yet to give me.

Snorting, she grasped my face a little roughly, causing my brows to furrow as she pulled me closer. But when she leaned in quickly and then paused just before her lips made contact, I found myself holding my breath. A million and seventeen thoughts flitted through my brain in the millisecond that passed before she brushed her lips across my cheek, in what was *barely* a kiss but also felt like *so. Much. More.*

An abstract beat popped into my head, and I closed my eyes to focus in on it, not wanting to lose it just because I was out in public. Jucee released me, putting some space between us, making my eyes pop open at the loss of her energy in my bubble. She wore a knowing smile.

"Mmhm, I recognize that look."

I chuckled, because of course she did. She knew me too well.

Her smile stretched into a sticky sweet, false imitation of the one I was used to seeing as she turned to the table. To my surprise, Jackie's head was bent as she stared at her phone. It had only been a few seconds, twenty at most, but somehow Jackie had checked out. Jucee stared her way for a beat before shaking her head.

"Enjoy your yoga session, Jackie." When the woman neither peeled her eyes from the screen nor offered a nod of acknowledgement, Jucee slid her gaze right back to me.

She didn't have to say a word—everything she was thinking was written all over her face. And, to be honest, I'd get it even if I hadn't looked her way. Jackie was being incredibly rude. I shook my head, ready to apologize, but Jucee lifted a hand to stop me.

"Nah, it's good. I'll call you later, Poppa."

At that, Jackie lifted her face from her phone and finally looked at Jucee. In my peripheral, I could see her face scrunch, her nose wrinkling as if she'd heard something bad. She turned to me, her expression suddenly more confused than disgusted.

"Why does she call you *Poppa*?"

Jucee's eyebrows shot up, and she gave me an indecipherable look before huffing a laugh that was anything but amused. It wasn't her usual laugh, didn't have the same melody that had made my heart pound at VR that night. The notes of this laugh were short and sharp, coated in annoyance and riding a resigned rhythm.

"*She*," Jucee emphasized, her head cocked to the side as she stared at the side of Jackie's face, "is right here and fully capable of answering a question."

Eyes wide, Jackie turned to Jucee and lifted her hands, clearly not wanting the smoke she'd ordered.

"Oh em gee!" she squealed, straightening up. "I didn't mean any disrespect!"

Bullshit.

I didn't understand the animosity that Jackie apparently held for Jucee, but one thing I did know was she meant each and every shred of disrespect she'd launched at my friend over lunch.

"Mmhm," Jucee hummed, unconvinced. Without saying another word, she spun on her heel and walked off.

It took me a second to realize she was actually leaving, but I caught up to her before she passed the second set of columns in one of the halls that bracketed the main area of food market.

"I'm sorry," I was saying before she even had a chance to come to a full stop.

Turning to me, she quirked an eyebrow and patted my cheek. "I know. Handle your shit, Poppa. If that means that we can't do more of these forced, fake-ass happy-go-lucky-looking-ass lunches until then, so be it."

To say she was irritated would have been an understatement. And I got it. I swear I did. For the second day in a row, Jackie had not only shown up unannounced, but she was kind of stealing my attention that should've been reserved for Jucee. But that shit pissed me off so bad. There was nothing fake or forced about the time she and I spent together. Never. My jaw clenched, and I blew a heavy breath out through my nose before I spoke.

"Nah, man. Shorty is on her way out." I hope that Jucee knew that I meant out of my life and not just out of POST. "This won't happen again." When she didn't respond, I felt compelled to get her to understand. "I'm serious, Jucee. I'm not with her. You know that, right?"

"Mm," she hummed noncommittally, her disbelief woven into the short sound making me want to double down.

"Juc—"

She shook her head and pulled out of my grasp. "Get back to *Shorty* before she has a fit." Jerking her chin over my shoulder, she gestured for me to go back in the direction where I'd left Jackie.

I didn't want to do that shit. That wasn't what I'd had in mind when I'd planned this meet-up. It was supposed to happen differently, with us back hugging and kissing and comfortable enough to cuddle while she binged reality TV and I scrolled social media.

What the hell did I have to do to get us back there?

Chapter Fourteen

Jucee

Dance for You

I might've been dumb enough to sleep with Poppa, but I wasn't dumb enough to think it would be easy to fall back into the easy camaraderie of our friendship in the aftermath. In fact, I'd fully expected it to be pure torture. Even if we somehow managed to keep things from being physically awkward, I knew that mentally I'd be a wreck. I figured that my newfound knowledge of the way her pussy felt and tasted would be too distracting for me to just "get back to normal." I thought that would be the hardest part.

Fun fact: it was even worse than I could've imagined.

It never really occurred to me how much time me and Poppa spent together on a daily basis. Not until I was wishing for some space between us. I needed reprieve from the constant bombarding of emotions I suffered every single time she dropped a kiss onto my temple or slung an arm around my shoulder. All I was asking for was twenty-four hours without taking into consideration that we spent an average of nine hours a day in each other's presence. Maybe not every single day, but at least four days out of the week. And since I'd assured her that our friendship was still intact after our little…incidents, it seemed like she wanted to spend even *more* time together being friendly as fuck.

I hated to say it, but it was driving me crazy.

I needed to breathe and she was suffocating me. The thing is, I couldn't even be angry with her because she just wanted to make sure we hadn't ruined our friendship while wanting something beyond it, but dammit, I felt so cloistered! I needed space to get my mind right, but if I asked for some breathing room, Poppa would think the worst and try to double down on "quality time." On top of that was the underlying threat of the investors trying to buy Sanity from under Mal. The threat of losing my safe space and the stress from my Poppa overdoing it was too much for me.

She'd left me no choice but to lie. Which was how I ended up at work on a Thursday. Poppa had wanted me to come over and watch some show with her, but I begged off, telling her that I had to help Mercedes with something. In reality, I was calling Mal and asking if I could come in to work. I needed the distraction, and the night crowd at Sanity would give me exactly that. I loved my day-timers, but it was a completely different vibe after nine. The place wasn't packed to the rafters, so it wasn't quite like a Friday night, but it definitely could hold its own. The crowd near the stage grew when my name was announced, and the love I received once my dance was over was more than sufficient.

Emerging from the back, I worked the room, the high from my dance relaxing me better than any drug could have. As I was heading to the back of the main floor where the paid sections were at, a woman stepped into my path with an earnest expression on her face. Caramel-skinned with a halo of kinky coils, she barely reached my chin.

"Omigosh, Jucee," she breathed. "I love you!"

Grinning, I dipped my head. "Thank you, gorgeous."

Turning, she pointed toward the elevated section. "Today is my baby sister's twenty-first birthday, and I want to buy her a lap dance to celebrate."

"Aww," I cooed. My heartstrings were sufficiently tugged. What better way to help someone bring in a new year of life than with ass shaking in their face? "That's so sweet. Let's go see baby sis."

I followed the woman up the steps to a cluster of about ten women who had pushed two tables together that were topped with two platters of wings, sides, and assorted drinks. Most of the women were in good spirits, immediately telling me how much they had enjoyed my set, but the one who I'd come to see was noticeably silent. There was no need for the eager woman to point her sister out, because it was quite clear which one she was. Sitting at one end of the joined tables with birthday balloons tied to her chair and wearing a sash that announced it was her birthday, a baby butch with a matching head of coils slicked up into an afro puff and her hairline tapered at her temples, wearing a bowtie, looked visibly uncomfortable the closer I came toward her. The other women began cheering as I approached her, but the way her fingers tightened on the table edge brought the mama out of me.

"Hey, birthday boo," I said, bending at the waist to speak directly into her ear.

Her eyes flicked from my face, down to my titties that were strategically busting out of my rhinestone triangle bikini top, and then over to her sister before landing back on my titties.

"Uh...hey."

"Happy birthday."

Prying her eyes from my chest, she quickly glanced at my face as she said, "Thank you."

"You okay?"

"Yea—" She cleared her throat and tried again. "Yeah, I'm cool."

Tilting my head to the side, I caught her eyes. "Your sister wants me to give you a lap dance, but something tells me you don't want that."

She didn't say anything for a moment, just shot a quick glance over at her sister as she sucked her teeth.

"I told her not to."

Just as I'd suspected. "Okay. It's your birthday, what do you want?" When her eyes dropped down to my glittering titties again, I laughed. "You want a hug?"

Her grin was slow to spread from the corners of her lips, but once she decided to let it fly, it lit up her entire face. When a sure nod followed, I spread my arms open and leaned forward. As I wrapped my arms around her neck, she pressed her face right into the valley of my chest. I squeezed my upper arms together and shimmied my shoulders. Her laugh was so sweet that it warmed my heart. It was amazing how a little motor-boating could lift your spirits. After she took a deep breath, we separated.

"When you're feeling up to it," I spoke into her ear, "come back and see me and I'll give you that birthday lap dance."

Ducking her head, she nodded, and I straightened and left the section without even looking at her sister. Any words that left my mouth might be a lecture, and I wasn't on that type of time. Stepping down from the elevated section, I locked eyes with Cody in an armchair less than ten feet from the steps. His face immediately lit up, but panic seized me when I saw who sat next to him. Poppa's eyes were zeroed in on my face, but I couldn't read her expression from so far away. Or maybe it was because I was actively avoiding meeting her eyes.

Fuck on a stick, why did I feel guilty? I hadn't really done anything wrong.

Except for bailing on hanging out with her tonight.

And lying about the reason.

And not telling her that I was coming to work.

But other than that…

"Hey, y'all!" I chirped, hugging them both. Cody returned my embrace with the same eagerness as he always did, but Poppa's hug was a little dry. Preferring not to make a big deal and call attention to it, I held my tongue and just moved to stand between their chairs, not missing the way Cody's left eyebrow quirked as he eyed us.

"What are you doing here? I've never seen you on a Thursday before."

Poppa snorted at Cody's question, but Cody just laughed her off.

"Yeah, yeah. You already knew. Whatever, man. I wasn't expecting to see her."

Offering a shrug that was anything but nonchalant, Poppa relaxed further into her seat. "Shiiid, me either."

Oh. She was giving mad attitude and practically ignoring me. Yeah, it was time for me to move around, because one thing I didn't do was drama at work. Shifting my weight from one foot to the other, I took a step back.

"Aight, I'll holla at y'all later."

I was a half-step away when Cody sat forward and wrapped his hand around my wrist. Looking over my shoulder, I glanced back at him.

"What's up?"

He gave me a curious look, like he was trying to figure something out, before sliding his gaze over to his sister, whose attention was now on the screen of her cellphone. When he looked back at me, there was a sly look in his eyes that let me know he was up to no good. And because of that look, I knew what he was going to say before he even parted his brown lips and said it.

"Can I get a lap dance?"

That calculating, observant bastard. I would've laughed if I wasn't so pissed. He released my wrist, and I twisted around so that I was fully facing them again. I looked from his expectant face over to Poppa, who *still* hadn't looked up from her phone, despite the fact that she'd undoubtedly heard her baby brother's request. While I was inclined to give her that same energy back, Cody had other plans. With one hand still on my wrist and a shit-eating grin all over his face, he dug into his pocket and pulled out a roll of money. He released me briefly and peeled off a hand-ful of bills before sliding the $500 into the garter on my thigh, then he grabbed me again and leaned toward his sister. It was as if she'd suddenly lost her peripheral vision, because she didn't even move until he slapped the side of her knee.

"Say, Cyn."

With no way to continue pretending she didn't hear him, Cyn lifted her eyes as slowly as possible from her phone to her brother, telling us that she didn't appreciate the annoyance of his touch without saying one word. Though she worked hard to appear bored and unaffected, I saw the moment that she noticed Cody's hand on me and the way her eyes narrowed in response. Then she blinked slowly and was back to a bored expression.

"Sup?"

Grinning, Cody seemed completely unfazed by her behavior. "I asked Jucee for a lap dance and slid her $500 for it. I'm just making sure you're cool with that." Then he lifted both of his eyebrows as he waited for her response.

The fact that she didn't immediately say no was the first indi-cator that she, too, was on some bullshit. Shrugging, she didn't even look at me before returning her gaze back to her phone.

"That's up to Jucee."

Oh.

Bet.

Cody turned toward me, a little uncertainty on his face. Clearly, he hadn't been expecting that from Poppa, and to be honest, neither had I. But it was all good. I was at work and lap dances were a part of my job. I only ever skipped out on dancing for Cody because Poppa clearly felt a way about it and always gave me more than whatever he offered so that I didn't lose out. If she wanted to be an asshole because I chose work over a movie night, then she made the decision easy for me. I wasn't turning down money to kiss her ass.

Instead of saying anything, I climbed into his lap, straddling his thighs. His eyes widened in surprise, and he immediately shot a glance over my shoulder.

"Don't look at her," I commanded directly into his ear. Tightening my thighs, I leaned forward and pressed my breasts into his face. "I want your eyes on me while I ride you."

"*Oh fuck,*" he whispered, making me giggle.

Good. I needed him to know that he'd fucked up. A dance from me wasn't just a game he was playing with his sister; it was an experience that he'd never forget.

I rolled against him, moving with the down beat of the song, which was slower than the faster pace of the lyrics. Planting my knees in the oversized armchair on either side of his hips, I bounced in his lap as if I was actually riding his dick, making sure I held his eye contact the entire time. I was no longer thinking of anything beyond the man beneath me and giving him something he'd never forget for the rest of his life.

Biting his lower lip, Cody lifted his hands, reaching for my waist, but I grabbed them and pressed them against the arms of the chair.

"No touching," I reminded in a firm but easy tone.

Standing, I turned around and bent at the waist, putting my ass right at his eye level. His answering groan was exactly what I needed to hear. I shook my cheeks from side to side a couple of times before bending my knees and slapping my ass onto his lap. The heavy thud that sounded with each connection was like music to me. Each slap the distinct *ka-ching* of an old-school cash register. Five hundred dollars for three to four minutes of work was already mind-blowing, but the potential for more wasn't anything to sneeze at. The way I could feel him harden beneath me felt like a bank deposit. In three years of dancing at Sanity, I learned that if you could turn a man on, you could empty his pockets.

I finished my dance by settling into an elevated split, balancing each of my legs on either arm of the chair while I held his knees and made my ass clap in his face. Then I swung my legs over to one side and stood up. When I looked down at him, I almost busted out laughing. He sat there dazed with his eyes glossed over, staring at the space over his lap that I'd just vacated.

Bending, I spoke directly into his ear. "You okay?" I didn't usually ask, but this was Cody. I knew him beyond the club and actually cared about him. I might've also went a little harder than I usually did because his sister had pissed me off. Just a little bit though. Nothing too crazy.

Except, with Cody staring up at me with stars in his eyes, it was possible that I'd overdid it. He'd gotten dances from other women, but I'd never seen him look like this before. I prayed he didn't start acting weird after this.

He nodded and I chose to take him at his word, but when I tried to walk away, he grabbed my wrist again. Eyebrows lifted in question, I turned back to him just in time to see him fish that roll of money out of his pocket and slide the entire thing into my garter. Grinning, I gave him a quick kiss on the cheek, which I *never* did, but again, this was Cody.

"Thank you, Cody."

Clearing his throat, he waved me off. "Yeah, yeah. You earned that and more. Get away from me, though, 'cause I'm two seconds away from sliding my Amex in there too."

I busted out laughing and did as he said. Only pausing for a brief second when I glanced over at Poppa for the first time since before I started the dance, only to see that she wasn't where I'd last saw her. Her chair was empty. That took a little of the wind out of my sails. Her disappearing like that felt like a slap in the face. She knew this was just work for me, and she really couldn't get mad after pushing the decision off on me when she never hesitated to make it herself every other time.

Feeling justified in my actions didn't make that little ache at the implications of what her absence meant go away though. I needed to take another turn about the room, but instead, I headed to the back to clear my head. After drinking some water, emptying my garter into a sack in my locker, and using the bathroom, I was ready to hit the floor again. When I stepped into the hallway, Milly was coming in my direction from the main floor.

"Oh, hey," she said, lifting the tablet in her hand into the air. "I was just looking for you. You have a private dance waiting for you in Tranquility."

Nodding, I shook out my arms and rolled my shoulders back as if I were shedding the distraction of the crap with Poppa like an unwanted blanket. It didn't take me long to make my way to the private rooms. There were three, each in graduated sizes with names that made you think you were in a spa instead of an adult club. Serenity, Tranquility, and Relaxation were all decorated in soothing earth tones with plants and lighting that invoked a different type of vibe from the one present on the main floor.

Pulling open the door to Tranquility, the midsize room, I froze in the doorway and seriously contemplated spinning on my heels and heading back out front.

Poppa stood in the center of the room with her eyes trained on me. I couldn't read her expression, but seeing her was a punch to the gut that was a mix of confusion, apprehension, and desire. Oh, and annoyance. Because why the hell did she look so damn good in a sleeveless basketball jersey and sweat shorts when she was being an asshole? She was supposed to be less attractive to me right now, but that was anything but the case, and that annoyed me.

"What are you doing here?" was the first thing out of my mouth when I finally stepped into the room and closed the door behind me.

Sucking her teeth, she folded her arms across her chest.

"Shit, I could ask you the same thing."

Pursing my lips, I counted to ten. Clearly, she was spoiling for a fight but I'd have to disappoint her, because I wasn't here for this shit.

"I'm here because you paid eight hundred and fifty dollars for me to dance for you in this room."

"And I'd pay ten times that to keep you from grinding on Cody like you wanted to fuck him right there in front of everybody again."

I threw my hands in the air. *Now* we were getting somewhere. "It was a dance, Poppa! It's my job to be grinding on folks. You knew that when you met me and it's never been a problem before, so what's the problem now?"

"Not on my damn brother, Jucee! You know how I feel about that!"

It was my turn to shrug. "Nah, I know how you *felt*. Today

it seemed like you didn't care, and if you don't care then again I ask, what's the problem?"

"You already know what the problem is. I shouldn't have to say it every time."

Oh, she really had me fucked up today. "Wait, so you want me to consider your feelings when you can't even respect me enough to look me in my face and speak? Girl, be for real."

Canting her head to the side, she nodded. "Let's talk about speaking for a minute. Did you really have to help Mercedes with something tonight? Or was that just an excuse?"

Rolling my eyes, I walked over to the digital display on the wall and scrolled through the playlists for the right one. I had a couple of favorites when it came to giving private dances, but I wasn't in the right mindset for either of those. Annoyance ran through my veins and I needed something that was going to calm me down so that I could make it through this hour with Poppa and the next two hours of work. I chose Mercedes's mix and turned back to Poppa. After what happened on the floor, I barely wanted to look at her. My feelings were still smarting from the sting of her dismissal, and now my hackles were up thanks to this surprise attack. Tryna keep a cool head while dealing with the myriad of emotions she'd invoked in me over the past few days was giving me whiplash and a hell of a headache.

Hands on my hips, try as I might, I couldn't help the heavy dose of attitude in my voice when I asked, "Does it really matter?"

Her brows furrowed. "If you felt like you had to lie to me about something so basic, then hell yeah, it matters!"

Blowing a breath out through my nose, I counted to ten.

"Listen, I get that, but things have been weird between us lately and I didn't know how else to get out of going to your house to watch a movie tonight."

If I hadn't been staring right at her, I would've missed the way her eyes widened with surprise before she shuttered her expression from me. *Fuck.* This is exactly what I had been trying to avoid, which was why I'd lied in the first place. She wasn't open to hearing anything that pointed out the flawed way we'd handled this. I got that she wanted things back to the way they were, but trying to do that was exhausting the hell out of me.

"Poppa, now isn't the time for this. I'm at work and I'm supposed to be dancing."

"Well, shit," she drawled, a hard edge to her voice. "If this is the only place I can get the truth out of you, then maybe this *is* the right time."

I reeled back as if she'd slapped me. All of the sacrifices I'd been making to make sure she was good and *that's* how she wanted to play it? I was in hell, grappling between wanting so much more from her and accepting that she wouldn't ever be able to give me that, and she couldn't even give me the space to process this change in our relationship!? I was working on her terms, tiptoeing on eggshells to keep from spooking her, living a half-life with the "something more" that she'd asked for, and she couldn't even understand that I needed a breather. Absolutely not.

Shaking my head, I crossed my arms over my chest.

"Nah, not while I'm on the clock. You know I leave the personal shit at the door when I'm at Sanity."

Her answering shrug was nonchalant as fuck. "You're still getting paid—what difference does it make?"

"It's not about the money," I shouted, fully incensed by her callous words. Did she think she owned my time because she'd paid for a dance? Had she forgotten that I could walk out of this room whenever I felt like it and there wasn't shit she could do to stop me? How could she ever fix her mouth to say some shit like that to me? "It's about the principle!"

"Oh, you wanna talk about principle now? How about we start when you lied to me today? Huh? How about that?"

I gritted my teeth to keep from screaming. We didn't do this. We didn't fight—never had a reason to. This wasn't us. But...we also didn't lie to each other, and kiss in the mouth, and we definitely didn't fuck. So maybe this was us when we stepped outside of the bounds of our friendship. And maybe Poppa was right, and we did ruin our friendship to an extent.

That thought hurt me more than fighting with Poppa did, and it effectively took all of the wind out of my sails. Shoulders sinking, I licked my lips and offered an olive branch.

"Do you want the dance?"

She stared at me, not saying anything for a minute. What killed me was that I couldn't decipher what she was thinking. It was such a foreign concept for her to actively hide herself from me, and it was an even further point of proof at how far removed we'd gone from our norm in such a short amount of time. Was she coming to the same conclusion as me? Did she realize that maybe we'd crossed a line that we couldn't uncross, no matter how much we—she—tried to pretend we didn't? I had no idea. And that fucked with me.

So, when she nodded and sat in the center of the wall of couches, I was genuinely relieved. I hadn't been sure what path she would choose, but I was going to make the best of it. I could salvage this moment and hopefully we could have an honest conversation with all of our cards laid out on the table in a day or so.

Ciara's "Body Party" shuffled on, and I rolled my shoulders back in an attempt to regain my focus. I was at work and I was here to dance. So that's what I would do.

Swaying from side to side, I let the music wash over me, getting me in the zone. Private dances were about selling a fantasy. The point was to transport the other person into another reality—one where they could actually have everything that was on display in front of them. To make them feel deserving.

In that moment, in the Tranquility room with Poppa, the fantasy I was selling was one where everything was exactly as it had been for the three years that we'd known each other. One where we'd never slept together and there was no sexual tension keeping things from being normal. Where we were friends and friends only. It was a fantasy because we'd never be friends again. No matter the outcome of that future conversation that we needed to have, Poppa & Jucee of old was no more.

So right now, I was going to pretend.

And it was fine. I danced around the room, first with my back to Poppa, trying to lose myself in the music and forget the bullshit plaguing me, and then facing her, appreciating that the shadows in the room fell perfectly across her face when she was seated so that I couldn't see her eyes and read them on purpose. I danced toward her as the music transitioned into "Tell Me" by Usher, climbing over her similar to how I'd done to Cody just half an hour earlier, but having more room to move as I wanted. With my hands on the back of the couch behind her using it as an anchor, I rolled against her, throwing my head back and running a hand along my skin from my neck to my navel. Sliding down her body, I pushed her knees apart and massaged her thighs as I danced in front of her.

Quickly, I had a mental flash of me doing the same thing to her just days prior before I touched her and kissed her in her foyer. My breath hitched in my throat at the memory and I snatched away from her, turning around to clean the image from my brain and get myself together. Every bit of eight minutes, the song was still going, and I still had a job to do, so I bent at the waist and sat in her lap. Grinding on her while I faced the opposite wall was safe. I could do that.

Everything was fine.

But then she brought her hands to my ass, kneading each cheek, spreading them, exposing me to her, even with my thong on, and suddenly, everything was *not* fine.

And because the unexpected feel of fingers on the softest part of my body felt so fucking amazing after a week of us keeping our hands to ourselves, I moaned.

I couldn't help it; it just slipped out. I tried to keep it low, but Poppa had ears like a fucking hound because as soon as it happened, I knew she'd heard it. It was like something switched for her. She went from hesitantly touching me as if she couldn't help herself, to being very intentional with each brush of her fingers.

The same fingers that then followed the trail of my thong from the top of my ass down between my cheeks, where she hooked the fabric with one knuckle and used the pad of a second finger to rub at my already damp lips.

Gasping, I looked back at her over my shoulder.

"No touching," I moaned, knowing that the pure lust in my voice was likely in direct contrast to the words I'd spoken, but also knowing they needed to be said. Poppa knew the rules. Sanity was a hands-off facility; patrons were encouraged to look as much as they wanted but refrain from putting their hands on any member of the staff, be they dancer, server, bartender, etc.

She knew just like I knew, and yet...when she bit her lip and lifted those big, beautiful, sleepy brown eyes up to me, I realized in that moment that I was going to let her do whatever she wanted to do to me, consequences be damned.

"I just wanna touch you, Jucee. Please. Just the tip of my finger, I promise. That's it."

I'd fucked enough men in my life to know good and well that it was *never* just the tip, but still, I nodded, giving Poppa the permission to slide a single digit inside of me. Gripping one cheek, she used her knees to spread my legs further apart and rubbed her middle finger through my wetness before pushing it inside of me. Another moan fell from my lips and I turned my head forward.

"Uh uhn," she grumbled. "Face me."

And of course I did, my heart stuttering and pussy fluttering as I did so. How could I say no when she'd commanded me in that lust-addled voice? I was incapable.

We met eyes and she raised an eyebrow. "Sit down."

Immediately, I lowered my ass, sitting on her lap, swallowing her finger, eyes glued to hers the entire time.

"You want another finger?"

I did. Of course I did.

"Up," she commanded once I gave her a nod. She added her index finger and instructed me to sit back down. But I couldn't just sit, I needed to ride, so I did.

There were so many rules being broken, but I'd deal with that another day. Biting my lip so hard I was surprised I didn't taste blood, I rode Poppa's hand painstakingly slowly while maintaining eye contact with her. I don't know how we'd ended up back in this place we'd been trying to pretend we'd never been, but now that we were here, I was going to milk it for all it was worth. I wanted more, but I didn't know how that was possible in this room with an unlocked door and hundreds of people on the other side.

"Jucee."

"Hmm?"

I didn't stop moving, but the sound of my name on her voice when I was heating up quick, fast, and in a hurry had me elevated.

"I have something else you can ride, if you want it."

And then my breath hitched again and my movements stuttered for a moment because I knew exactly what she was talking about, and sweet baby Jesus in a manger did I want it. I wanted it so badly I was already whimpering from the idea of being filled when I nodded.

"I want it," I whispered. The music was loud and I wasn't even sure that words had actually left my mouth, but her eyes were on me, and the way she dipped her chin in response let me know she'd received the message loud and clear.

Pushing me up just a little, she pulled her fingers free from me and unbuttoned her jeans, shimmying them down her hips until her boxer briefs were completely exposed. Twisting, I watched in fascinated anticipation as she reached into the material against her thigh and pulled a six-inch strap-on from a hidden pocket sewn into the leg of her briefs. Within moments, she had clicked the device into the mechanism that sat low on her underwear harness and was spitting into her hand and rubbing the saliva over the tip and down the shaft of the strap.

She reached for me with her free hand, palming my ass before tugging me backward by the strap of my thong. I bit my lip the moment I felt its tip breach me.

"Sit on it," Poppa commanded once again, releasing my thong and settling her palm on the small of my back. There was no pressure from her hand as I slowly lowered myself into her lap, moaning as I stretched to accommodate the silicone. Once I was fully seated, I blew out a breath and dropped my head forward.

"Julesa, gahdamn. You look so fuckin' sexy."

My name was a harsh groan from behind me as Poppa's hands found their way back to my ass, once again kneading my cheeks for a brief moment before she reached around me to peel the cups of my bikini to the side and bare my breasts. My already hardened nipples tightened even further at the rush of cool air, but Poppa immediately covered them when she scooped them into her hands and played with the turgid points.

There was an unexpected vibration at the base of the strap

that seemed less for me and more for Poppa's pleasure, and the knowledge that we were both being stimulated was heady. It fueled me as I began to bounce in her lap, slapping down hard, trying to put as much pressure on that little buzzer against her clit as possible. I wanted her to cum just as much as I wanted to cum.

I felt reckless and wanton, dangerous and so deliciously sexy. This moment with Poppa was the only thing I could process. Her hands on me, playing with my ultra-sensitive nipples, her strap filling me up, her hips snapping up to meet me with each descent, her titties pressed into my back, her goddamned lips on my neck. I was floating.

And when she grunted as if she'd just taken a blow to the gut, legs straightening in front of her, toes pointed out like she didn't know which way to go, I knew she was cumming. She bit down on my neck and pinched my nipples so hard you would've thought she was trying to snap them off and put them in her pocket for a midnight snack later, and the sting— the sheer-fucking-pain was exactly what I needed to send me flying right behind her. I might've cried her name as I crested. Not too loudly though, just a little bit.

As I came down, I slumped backward, head on her shoulder, chest heaving as if I'd just ran a four-by-four. She released my nipples and began to massage them, instantly soothing the harsh treatment she'd just inflicted upon them. Her lips were back on my neck, licking and kissing the likely bruised areas, and I sat there in silence, welcoming her touch, basking in her aftercare.

This was what I'd missed the first time around, when we'd been exhausted after a long night of partying and subsequent fucking, and the eventual orgasm was equivalent to a healthy dose of NyQuil. *This* was what I'd been looking for the morning after.

And just like that, my bubble burst. The reminder of how things ended just a few days ago pulled me up short.

What the actual fuck was I doing?

Finally thinking clearly, I started to pull out of her grasp. I needed off her lap and out of that room. My head was clouded and in need of fresh air and space. Planting my feet, I braced to stand, only to be stopped by her arm snaking around my waist and pulling me back into place. Back against her.

"Where you going?" Her voice was heavy with lust and I felt my pussy contract around the strap.

"Poppa," I groaned. Or maybe I moaned. I don't really know.

"Mmhm," she murmured. Wrapping a hand around my neck, she turned my head to the side and captured my lips in a nasty kiss. She licked into my mouth like she was trying to get to the center of a Tootsie Roll Pop, and I definitely, without a doubt moaned that time. "I want you to say my name just like that."

Before I had a chance to ask her what she meant, she'd dropped her arm from my waist and slipped her hand into the waistband of my thong. My lips parted, because I *really* needed to know what she was doing, but then she sucked my tongue into her mouth and slowly pumped her hips as she did very indecent things to my clit. Instinctively, my thighs tried to close, but then she stopped everything. Stopped kissing me, stopping playing in my panties, stopped fucking into me. Even my breaths stopped, halting right where they were in my lungs.

"Keep these fucking legs open for me, Jucee. I want you cumming for me one more time. Do you understand?"

You'd have thought a draft blew into the room the way I shuddered from head to toe. What was happening? What—how—who—*why* was she doing this to me? I had no answers, but what I did know was that I nodded and opened my legs like she told me to. And she immediately resumed her ministrations. The combination of sensations was pure torture. Years of piano and guitar playing gave Poppa a particular skillset that I hadn't really appreciated until she was playing out a rhythm between my thighs that had my breath coming in stuttered pants and gasps. Her shallow thrusts were seemingly harmless, but every movement against my already sensitive walls was so overwhelming that I could have cried. I might have, actually. Just a couple of tears though. Nothing too dramatic.

The worst—or best, depending on how you looked at it—of it was the way she kissed me. She was worshipping my mouth as if it was the only way that she could ingest oxygen and kissing me was literally integral to her next breath. It made me dizzy and weak and *floatfloatfloat* away from my body with pure, unfettered love.

It made me delusional.

Cumming made it worse.

I jerked and seized and trembled in her arms, and she held me the entire time. As I caught my bearings, she kissed my cheek, the side of my nose, my jaw, my neck, my shoulder, and only then did she release my neck. Switching arms, she continued holding me against her while she pulled her hand out of my thong and brought her fingers to her mouth, sucking each digit clean.

When I tried to stand at that time, she helped me, supporting me from below as well as holding onto one of my hands to offer leverage. My legs were a little unsteady on my heels, but with her help, I eased up gingerly, groaning when the strap slipped free of me. Walking toward the door, I put a little distance between me and the couch and began to right myself.

I straightened my thong, rolling my eyes at how wet and ruined it now was, and then tucked my titties back into my bikini. "Dance for You" shuffled on, filling the room with sensual lyrics that felt a little too on the nose for my liking. Deep in my thoughts, I damn near jumped outta my skin when

Poppa wrapped her arms around my waist and pressed a kiss to my shoulder. It felt so familiar—so normal—that it made my stomach ache.

But also...was she hugging me as a friend or a lover?

I couldn't tell the difference and that was the problem. My head was a jumble of questions, and her confusing back-and-forth behavior didn't help. While I was in my head, Poppa circled me, settling her hands at the small of my back as she leaned in and captured my lips in a sweet kiss full of promise.

The desire to trust that promise was so strong that I found myself swaying on my feet and leaning into her. We both laughed as she helped to steady me, an undeniable smugness written all over her face.

"You know," I began, after eagerly kissing her back despite the whisper of caution flitting around at the back of my mind, "I really am supposed to be working."

Poppa smacked her lips. "Man, you worked! And we didn't even use the whole time that I paid for, so you don't have to rush."

She kind of had a point, but there was no way I could spend the whole time in that room with her, cuddling and kissing. I was already going to be in so much fucking trouble when Mal found out, and she absolutely would. Nothing happened in Sanity that she didn't know about. Nothing.

"You're right," I conceded. "I don't *have* to rush. But I do have to go get cleaned up before heading back out onto the floor." I gave her a knowing look.

Grinning, she dipped her chin twice and dropped another kiss on my lips before stepping back. "Okay, okay. You have a point." She eyed me for a second. "So...can we still do movie night?"

Tossing my head back, I cracked up. "The only thing I'm gonna want to do when I leave here is stop by Waffle House and then go get in the bed."

Joining me in my laughter, Poppa shook her head. "I didn't mean tonight—I meant in general. Is that still something we can do?"

Twisting my lips to the side, I thought on it. She seemed more open—more receptive—which was a good sign. I wanted to believe that we could get over this hump and have something defined and stable. So I nodded.

"Yeah. I think we can do that."

Chapter Fifteen

Cyn

Oops! Oh My

I wish I could say that having sex with Jucee in the Tranquility room eased my fears, but I couldn't. The thing at the front of my mind every time I closed my eyes for a brief second was how she looked dancing for Cody. And that shit was fucking with me. It was exactly why I didn't do relationships, because when you opened yourself up to someone, you gave them the opportunity to hurt you. I had no one to blame for this and I was pissed about it.

And that is what was in the forefront of my mind when Mal rolled up on me and Cody as we were heading toward the door. It was just after midnight and the club was still in the swing of things, and since we hadn't yet passed the bar, there were plenty of people around us.

"I should've known you'd be here tonight once your girl said she was coming in" was the first thing Mal said as we slapped hands and she clapped me on the back.

Your girl.

Mal had been calling Jucee my girl since we'd started kicking it way back when. It had never been a problem before, but that was then. Now, it felt different because things were different. *Now*, hearing it made me panic. Did she already know what happened in the Tranquility room? Was that even possible so soon?

"What you mean?"

With an eyebrow lifted, Mal smirked. "Where can I provide clarity?"

Cody snickered at my right but I ignored him, scratching under my right eye as I huffed a little laugh. "Nah, you good. I was just saying——"

"You were just tryna play like she ain't your girl now?"

At Cody's outburst, I glared his way. He was taking it too far per usual.

"Chill. That's the homie."

He shrugged like he didn't care, but the calculating look in his eyes was anything but nonchalant. "I don't know, man. The way you were mugging during my lap dance…" Twisting his lips to the side, he shot Mal a meaningful look that she chuckled at.

"Bruh, what are you even talking about? Jucee ain't even into women like that."

My brother's face twisted into pure disbelief as he stared at me, but I couldn't focus on him because just over his shoulder was Jucee herself, dressed in another outfit, covered in glitter, and staring at me as if I'd just slapped her. I knew without a doubt that she'd heard what I'd said, and it felt as if all of the blood drained out of my face.

Fuck!

I'd fucked up. Paranoia had me trying to throw Mal off the scent of us fraternizing and I'd fucked up big. Jucee shook her head and spun on her heel, walking back in the direction she had come. I closed my eyes for a moment, trying to calm my panic, telling myself it was just an accident and would be fine. Mal's expression was unreadable; she flicked her eyes over my shoulder and toward the hallway that led to the entrance of the club before returning to me.

"That's the reason, huh?"

Something in her question made me pause. It was... There was a note of disappointment woven into those four words. It seeped into my bones and settled heavy in my gut. It brought another level of instant regret in a way I hadn't seen coming.

Double fuck.

Could this night get any worse?

"I mean..." I stopped again, unable to add anything else. What *did* I mean? What was I even *saying*? I wanted to backtrack, to take back the flippant remark that had Mal looking at me as if she was seeing me anew. Had I fucked up a professional relationship in an attempt to shake off suspicion about the changes between me and Jucee? Dammit.

"I'll leave you to think that over. Drive safe." Mal clapped Cody on the shoulder and walked away, and I stood there looking stupid with my lips flapping like a fish.

"What the fuck was that?" Cody asked.

Heading toward the exit, I shook my head. "I don't know, man."

Cody was right behind me as we exited the club and headed toward our cars. "Nah, I don't buy that bullshit. What even was that shit you said about Jucee not being into women?"

Frustrated, I spun on him. "Damn, bruh! It was just some shit I said. It's not that serious."

He cocked his head to the side as he stared at me, his lip curled like something stunk.

"It is that serious though. Daddy told me what happened at the studio the other day, and now this. Not to mention the damn death lasers you were shooting my way earlier. What's up with you?"

I gave him an exasperated look. "You already know how I feel about you asking Jucee for a lap dance! You thought I would just sit there and clap and cheer? Hell no!"

His face scrunched up. "Oh. So you were pissed because you hadn't been expecting to see her, so you handled that by ignoring her and then getting mad when she gave me a lap dance. That sounds real smart."

"Man, fuck you," I sneered. I didn't like what he was trying to say.

"Yeah, okay, Cyn. You keep treating Jucee like shit and she's gon' dump your ass."

"We're not together!" I yelled, throwing my hands in the air.

He pursed his lips. "I meant as a friend, but you've made it quite clear that y'all aren't together. You're making it a little *too* clear, to be quite honest. Makes me wonder why you're protesting it so much." Quirking an eyebrow, he gave me a knowing look.

Yeah, I'd had enough.

"That's my cue."

Turning, I walked away from him and crossed the parking lot until I reached my car. I needed damage control and I needed it quickly.

Chapter Sixteen

Jucee

What's Tea?

One thing I didn't have time for was dealing with Poppa's bullshit when I had bigger problems on my plate. My job was on the line. Sort of. Mal had called for a club-wide meeting at seven in the morning that Saturday, and I was on pins and needles just wondering if Sanity as we knew it would still be in operation.

Sanity was open seven days a week, three hundred and sixty-five days a year. She opened at 11:00 a.m. Monday through Friday, and 10:30 a.m. on Saturday and Sunday, and she stayed open until four in the morning. Every major, minor, and made-up holiday, she was open. Food was served every day, and on Thanksgiving and Christmas, the meals were reminiscent of the familiar dishes found in homes across the nation.

When I first moved to Houston and learned about the strip club scene, I thought those hours were wild and unsustainable. I couldn't fathom that people would wake up ready to see titties and ass at lunchtime.

I was so naive back then.

It didn't take me long to get with the program, and now, three years later, I knew that folks not only woke up ready, but went to sleep with it in their plans for the following day. There were people who came to Sanity every day for lunch, and those that strolled in for Sunday brunch religiously.

"What do you think this is about?"

Sucking her teeth, Mercedes slapped the steering wheel. "Shiiid! It had better be about the dressing room thief we have yet to catch."

Over the last couple of weeks, several items had been coming up missing from the dressing room. They were all small things that weren't missed until they needed to be used, but once we realized what was going on, we started taking inventory. Most of the girls who danced on the weekend had been hit. Shoes, weave brushes, panties. The most random shit, but it was consistent. We'd mentioned it to Josey—short for Josephine—and she'd taken it to Mal.

The next thing we knew, Josey had sent out a text blast on Friday night, informing us that Mal had called an impromptu meeting. The message required everyone to confirm they'd received the information because it was mandatory that everyone be present. While it wasn't unusual for us to have meetings, impromptu ones were rare, and to top it off, the tone of Josey's text was urgent, which made me nervous. What was going on?

Since it was my off day, Mercedes picked me up on her way to the club. We stopped at Black Coffee and then made it to Sanity with ten minutes to spare. Inside, the scent of grits and butter hit my nose, making me stop in my tracks for a moment. There was something familiar about it that I needed to figure out where I knew it from. When it hit me, I squealed and rushed further into the building, catching up to Mercedes, who had already grabbed a plate. The breakfast spread covering the bar featured several of my favorites from the menu at Chicken Or The Egg.

"Good morning, ladies," Josey chirped from behind the bar. She was pouring orange juice into champagne flutes. "Help yourselves to the food and then have a seat over at the tables. Mal will be out shortly to start the meeting."

She didn't have to tell me twice. I fixed my plate of grits, fried catfish, scrambled eggs, and buttered toast and then took it over to a table. A few women were already in the section and waved good morning. Mercedes was already eating, so I sat my plate next to her and went back to the bar to grab two mimosas from Josey. By the time I returned to the table, Mercedes was done and the rest of the dancers and all of the staff and crew had arrived. Some were seated while others were in line to fix their food. It was seven o'clock on the dot, and every single employee of Sanity had arrived.

One thing about Mal was that she demanded punctuality. She was fair and accommodating, but when it came to playing with her time, she had no tolerance.

Mal came from out the back and walked around, greeting everyone. She spoke to each and every person, making eye contact and saying their name. The way she knew and acknowledged everyone reinforced the differences between Mal and the owners of other clubs. She wasn't putting on to give us a false sense of family; this was who she was. It was one of the things I loved about her that also made me not even consider wanting to work at another club. We weren't just dollar signs here. Mal didn't prioritize the highest earners and ignore everyone else. It was equal love on all fronts, and that's what made Mal, and subsequently, Sanity, one of a kind.

After speaking to everyone, Mal went to the bar and poured herself a cup of coffee from the travelers on the other side of the plates. She added a criminally small splash of cream and at least a half a cup of sugar before walking back to the section.

Standing at the handrail, she slid one hand into the pocket of her wrinkle-free lime-green slacks and addressed us.

"Okay, y'all. I'm sure everyone is wondering why I called this team meeting. I always want to be transparent with y'all. I never want anyone who works for me to say they don't have any idea of what's going on." She looked at each of us. "With that being said—"

"You sellin' the club?" yelled someone from the far right of the section. I didn't see who said it, but it sounded like one of the servers.

"What?!"

"I know you fuckin' lyin'!"

"Oh Lord, I don't want to find a new club. I'm too old to start over!"

"Girl, what are you talking about?! You're only twenty-seven."

"I said what I said!"

Mal removed her hand from her pocket and held it up.

"Hold on now," she urged, raising her a voice to get above the panicked shouts. "Let me finish. Sanity has been doing better than a lot of people expected. This is good news, but unfortunately it means that the people who invested in the club from the start are paying more attention now."

"What does that mean?" one of the bartenders asked.

Mal sighed. "It means they want to buy me out. They want to take over ownership of the club so they can have maximum profits."

It was quiet for a second while everyone processed, and then the noise level skyrocketed.

"Oh hell no!"

"Ain't that 'bout a bitch!"

"I hope you told them no!"

She let everyone yell their opinions out, waiting patiently as she sipped her coffee. Once the noise died down, she continued.

"Let me assure you all. They'll have to pry Sanity from my cold, dead fingers. This is my baby and I'm not letting it go for any amount of money."

We all cheered and I felt a bone-deep relief wash over me. Sanity housed and nurtured my chosen family. To lose it would be a devastating blow.

"I'm telling y'all this for transparency, and also so that you won't be alarmed when some changes start being made. There was a recent theft issue in the dressing room. I learned that it was connected to our former security system, which was a referral by one of the investors."

"Oh, hell naw!" yelled Mercedes. "That's a setup!"

Mal nodded. "I thought so too. Which is why that security company is no longer contracted with us and we are now on the hunt for a replacement. No need to worry—I expect to receive a few bids for service in the next twenty-four hours."

After answering any additional questions about the thefts, the meeting dispersed and we were free to go about the rest of our day.

Instead of immediately leaving, a few of us hung around the club, chatting about what had been discussed. The club didn't open for more than an hour, so a couple of the dancers decided to get some practice in on the pole. I refilled my coffee and my plate before Mercedes and I found ourselves sitting at a table near the stage talking as they danced.

"So how did last night go?" Mercedes asked me. She knew that I'd come in to work, but I hadn't told her about what happened with Poppa. I took that moment to catch her up. Her eyes popped wide open when I told her what I'd overheard Poppa say about me.

It was bullshit in the highest order, because I'd dated at least three women since I'd met Poppa, and it all counted, even if she pretended like she didn't see it. Everyone else of importance in my life knew that. She was the only one with blinders on.

And I got that, kinda. We didn't talk about this kind of stuff. I'd actually assumed that it made her uncomfortable to discuss sex with me for whatever reason. In the beginning, I thought she just came from a conservative family that wasn't open with those type of things, but after meeting her brothers and then her parents, I realized that it was just something about me that brought out the prude in her. However, after being her friend for the past three years, and having to hear about her conquests from the girls at work, I learned that not talking about sex didn't equal not having it. Cyn wasn't running through Sanity like a tomb raider, but she wasn't a monk either.

It didn't bother me then, and it didn't bother me now, because the way I saw it, whatever she did with the women before me could only benefit me if we ever took it there.

And Lord knows I was tryna take it there with her.

And that was my dilemma, because clearly she didn't see it for me. Not only that, she didn't see me either, and I couldn't get down with that.

From my peripheral, I noticed Mal enter the floor, her strides sure and determined. Her appearance didn't strike me as odd, so I returned my attention back to the pole, only to be startled when she appeared at my side, standing over me.

"Let me talk to you real quick."

Eyebrows raised, I exchanged looks with Mercedes before nodding and quickly standing to my feet. I followed Mal all the way to her office in the back of the building, where she motioned for me to close the door behind me. Suddenly, I was a little nervous.

Was I about to be fired?

Mal perched on the edge of her desk, folded her arms across her chest, and squinted at me.

"Why are you fidgeting like that?"

Dropping my hands to my sides, I shook them out and shifted from one foot to the other.

"My bad."

She shook her head. "There's nothing to be nervous about. I only called you in here because I didn't want the others to think I'm giving you some sort of preferential treatment."

That was the thing that made me stop fidgeting. Brows furrowed, I held my tongue and waited for her to elaborate.

"Listen, you've been here long enough that you could probably recite the rules in your sleep. There's only ten of them, but each one is equally important." Dropping her hands to the desk on either side of her, Mal pinned me with a knowing stare. "'Don't Fuck The Customers' is number one for a reason."

She knew.

A heavy weight dropped into my gut with a force so strong it nearly brought me to my knees.

"I—"

She lifted a hand, effectively silencing me.

"I didn't say anything for the past year because the two of you have done a great job of keeping it under wraps, and I'm pretty sure I was the only one who peeped it. But now there's obviously a rift between you and so I have to step in. From the comment Cyn Tha Starr made last night to the not-so-quiet conversation you just had out there on the floor, it's clear that I need to remind you of how things go here in Sanity." Lifting a hand, she pointed toward the door. "This building is sacred and that floor is a place of worship. We don't desecrate it by bringing the filth from our mishandled relationships in the door."

I was seconds away from boohoo crying. Shame consumed me and brought with it a sob that was slick trying to church-finger its way out of my throat. Mal was right. I knew the rules, and even though I couldn't help that I'd crashed headfirst into love with Poppa, I'd made the decision to bring my frustrations into Sanity when I was supposed to be working.

From the first moment I walked through those heavy double doors, the club had been my sanctuary, my saving grace. Beyond that, the club was a place where fantasy and dreams were sold. Just like fans didn't want to know that their favorite heart throb movie star was in a relationship, the "patients" that frequented Sanity didn't want the illusion ruined for them either. It was toxic and annoying, but it was the business, and I'd known that from day one.

"I tell all you girls that if you ever need help, I got your back, but you have to remember what's most important. We don't compromise the club for pussy. Understand?"

Feeling good and properly chastened, I nodded.

"Yes, I understand. You're right. I'm sorry."

Straightening, Mal shook her head and pushed off her desk. "Don't be sorry, be mindful. The rules exist for a reason. Remember that."

"Right." Still nodding, I backed out of her office and headed back to the floor, where Mercedes sat in a chair near the stage, giving tips to Kreme, who was upside down on the pole with her arms stretched out on either side of her.

"So," Mercedes asked as soon as I was reseated, "what was that about?"

"Mal was getting me together about this thing with Poppa."

My friend's mouth dropped into an O, and I didn't blame her. I shook my head.

"First of all, she thinks me and Poppa have been together for over a year, which is wild. We aren't even together now!" I shrugged. "After last night, it's not even a concern anymore. I'm through with her. Through with the whole back and forth, and I'm through with her family. I'mma tell each of them soon. Not Poppa though—she already knows what's up."

Mercedes blinked at me before shaking her head as if she was trying to clear out smoke and giving me a disbelieving look.

"Wait a minute, bitch! You're gonna do *what*?!"

Rolling my eyes, I gave Mercedes a blank stare.

"You heard me."

She shook her head and sat back in her chair. "Explain it to me one mo' 'gin, because I know damn well you didn't just say you're about to go to that girl's family and break up with them one-by-one. I just know that's not what I heard!"

Sucking my teeth, I tossed a balled-up napkin at her. "I ain't say that shit, and you know it."

Mercedes tossed her hand into the air, her shoulders inches away from her ears. "That's basically what came out of your mouth."

"Not even close."

"Eh." She made a so-so motion with her hand and then cleared her throat before pressing a hand to the base of her throat. "*I respect them too much to ghost them, so I'll just let them know in person that I won't be in their lives anymore.*"

A shriek burst from my lips before I busted out laughing.

"Mercedes! Why the hell did you use that sex line, phone operator voice to imitate me?!"

"Uh, duh. You have that nineties Toni Braxton, Grace Jones thing going on. Don't play dumb." Her eyes rolled to the ceiling as if she was annoyed with me, her clear exasperation cracking me up.

Bringing her warm brown eyes back to me, she pursed her lips. "I know what you're doing and it won't work. I'm not so easily distracted."

My laughter petering off, I sighed and reached for my drink. I took a long sip of the hot coffee, taking the time to get my thoughts together because I knew that Mercedes wasn't going to let this go without breaking down each and every word I'd said. When I'd stalled for as long as I could, I placed the glass back beside my half-consumed plate of fish and grits and shook my head.

"I just don't want to offend anyone."

I could feel my friend's gaze on me but I refused to look at her. Mercedes had a way of looking into my soul when she wanted to find answers, and I wasn't in the mood to be dissected.

"You're doing a lot of emotional labor for a bigot."

Shocked, my eyes flew up to meet hers. She was waiting for me, her arms folded on the table, her face the picture of concern. Groaning, I leaned forward, propping my elbows on the table as I buried my face in my palms.

"In their defense, they probably don't even know that she's like that."

Somehow, she heard my mumbled words perfectly fine because she responded. "Well, are you going to tell them?"

Immediately I shook my head. "Absolutely not. That's not my place."

"And why not?!"

Her shout startled me, and I sat up to face her. The concern had been replaced with anger.

"Why isn't it your place? You were just moaning about how you have to let them down easily because they love you and you don't want to hurt their feelings. Saying that you love them so much and hate to lose them, but you won't even tell them the real reason you're dipping out on them." Pinning me with a confused look, she continued. "You love them but you're gonna lie to them with a straight face? That's love?"

Sensing that she was only getting warmed up, I held up a hand, trying to stop her while she was ahead. "That's not——"

She powered on as if I hadn't said a word. "If you don't say something, who will? And, furthermore—",

"*Furthermore?*" I sat back, impressed. She was pulling out the dissertation-level jargon on me.

"*Furthermore,*" she emphasized, rolling her eyes—likely at the teasing lilt in my voice—before continuing, "your decision to keep silent is a direct contradiction to the characteristics you constantly claim them to have—"

"How is—"

"You can't say the Thomases are good people, inclusive, and accepting, but be afraid to continue engaging with them simply because you want to avoid Cyn."

"That's not it at all. That's a very base-level understanding of what I'm telling you. They can be good people and I not deal with them anymore. Besides, how good can they be if biphobia came out of their ranks?"

The look on Mercedes's face was skeptical but I waved her off.

"Don't worry about it. It'll be fine. And honestly, there's only one person I expect to get any real pushback, but it won't be too bad. Just you watch." Mercedes had met the Thomas clan a couple of times at barbecues, but she didn't know them a fraction as well as I did. It was best to let them each know individually that I was leaving out. If I tried to tell them all at once, they were liable to team up and overwhelm me with their protests. One thing I didn't want to deal with was too many people trying to convince me why I was making a terrible decision according to them.

I had a soft spot for the Thomases because of what they represented to me. They were the family unit that I hadn't had in so long, and losing them was going to be hard—I couldn't afford to be influenced.

Chapter Seventeen

Jucee

Family Feud

If it was in my DNA to be a heartless bitch, I would've cut every single Thomas off with no explanation like my name was MCI. Unfortunately, I was Juleesa Marie Jones, and I was raised better than that. I had to end things amicably because these were good people, and despite how shitty things were with me and Poppa, I loved them. Not only that, but they loved me back, and that counted for something. It wasn't enough to make me stick around, but it was worth at least letting them know face-to-face.

Well, I didn't have it in me to speak to all of them. Just thinking about talking to Carissa about this made my knees shake a lil bit—but the one person I absolutely *had* to talk to was Nana Cherry.

I hated it and I knew Amani would hate it, but I felt like I didn't have a choice. Nana Cherry narrowed her shrewd gaze on me.

"What did I tell you when you first started coming around

here and you mentioned that you were having a hard time finding affordable care for that boy?"

Her gaze was hard but kind, yet it didn't make me feel any better. One thing I didn't do was hang out with the family of my exes. Even with Samir. We ended things and stayed friends, and yet I never went to the birthday parties or barbecues that they still invited me to. It didn't feel right. So, why would I start doing that now? If me and Poppa—Cyndi—were done, then I had to be done with her family too. One band, one sound.

Did you forget that Poppa isn't your ex or . . . ?

A smug voice whispered those words from the back of my mind, and I could've slapped myself. That was the problem right there. I'm sitting here thinking of Pop—Cyndi—in terms and conditions that don't apply. Sighing, I rubbed at my forehead, fairly certain that FOOLISH was printed there in Times New Roman.

"I don't remember, Nana. That was a long time ago."

Nana Cherry sucked her teeth and poked me dead center of where the second O probably was. She could likely see it plain and in living color.

"Young as you is and I have a better memory than you? How'd that happen, Juleesa?"

Her teasing was so familiar and warm that I wanted to cry. Even as she ribbed me, there was love there. My bottom lip trembled and I looked away. Instantly, she gripped my chin and turned me back to face her. That sharp gaze that missed nothing, brown irises surrounded by a halo of blue, bored into me.

"Two and a half years ago, you sat in the backyard with my only granddaughter and told us that you loved your job but wished you could afford reliable childcare so that you could dance more. You had your chin lifted up when you said that, do you remember? You weren't the least bit shamed to admit that you dance with no clothes on. You remember that?"

Dipping my chin, I nodded as a couple of tears fell from my eyes, not because I was embarrassed, but because I suddenly remembered exactly what she was talking about. I sure did sit my ass on that wicker couch and hold my head up with pride as I answered Carissa's question about my line of work.

"Yes, ma'am," I finally answered, my voice a little shaky, forcing me to swallow back the flood of tears in my throat. "I remember that."

"You remember what I told you?"

I nodded again.

"Good," she said firmly. "I told you not to worry about that baby. I told you to go to work and do what you had to do and that I would keep him as long as you needed me to." Releasing my chin, she leveled me with a fierce look. "And isn't that what I've done?"

"Yes, ma'am," I repeated.

Canting her head, she took a step back. "Alright now." Propped her fists on her hips, she frowned. "I did what I said I was gon' do and you wanna take my baby away from me? That's how you thank me?"

Quickly, I shook my head and approached her, reaching to pull her hands into my mine.

"No, Nana, that's not it."

"Then what is it, 'cause I know it can't be something my knucklehead granddaughter done did."

Despite myself, I giggled. She cracked a smile and I felt a wave of relief that at least she didn't hate me.

"I just figured that if me and *Cyndi* weren't talking, you wouldn't want us still around the family. I just didn't want to make things awkward."

"Awkward?!" The way Nana Cherry's eyes widened, you would've thought I'd called her a harlot. "Let my hands go so I can smack you upside the head and hopefully knock some sense into you!" She wrenched her hands from mine and I jumped back to avoid her swing.

"Nana! Don't be so violent!"

Obviously annoyed, she huffed and repositioned her hands on her hips.

"Last I checked, wasn't no mathematics degree needed to dance on stage with your jugs hanging out, so I don't know why you thought you needed to do all that figuring!"

The way my jaw unhinged and my mandible hung loose had to have looked as ridiculous as I felt. Nana stared at me, waiting. My mouth was drying up, so I gasped and then immediately yelped.

She burst into giggles, her thin shoulders shaking.

"That was funny." I stated the obvious.

"Mmhm. Not as funny as you thinking you were going to take my baby from me without a fight." Her hands were hanging by her side after she finished laughing, and I watched as one of them curled into a fist.

Holding my hands up, I took a step backward. "Hey there, slugger. I wasn't trying to take your baby from you."

Eyes once again narrowed, she glared at me. "Whatchu call it?"

"I—" My eyes bounced around the kitchen in search of something to help me give her an answer that didn't sound ridiculous. There was none, and after a moment I gave her a pathetic look. "Self-preservation," I offered pathetically.

The expectant look she wore morphed into one of recognition and her lips formed an O. On instinct, I started to shake my head, but then stopped when I realized I had no idea what she was about to say. The recognition turned into sympathy; I became fairly certain that I didn't want to hear what was about to come out of her mouth. I didn't want sympathy; I wanted to get my baby and skedaddle. But I should've known that was easier said than done with this family.

The Thomases were good people. They were close-knit and deeply enmeshed in each other's lives but had a lot of love to give to outsiders. When they brought someone into the fold, they treated them like one of their own. They'd taken in me and my baby, and even Samir to an extent. In them I had something that I'd been missing since before I made it to double digits, and as I tried to avoid Nana Cherry's knowing gaze, I at least had the wherewithal to admit the truth to myself.

My sudden need to dig myself out of their family plot was because I wanted to cut them off before they did it to me. It would hurt less if I lost them because I chose to, instead of the other way around.

At least that's what I told myself.

"It is because of my knucklehead granddaughter, ain't it?"

Choking out a dry laugh, I shook my head.

"Why she gotta be a knucklehead, Nana?"

Pursing her lips, Cyn's grandmother quirked an eyebrow at me.

"Well, is she the reason that you're trying to take my baby from me?"

I didn't want to heap all of the blame onto Cyn's shoulders, nor did I want to throw her under the bus, so I rolled my lips into my mouth and shook my head.

It kind of wasn't a lie.

Not really.

"Did she make a pass at you?"

Nana's question roughly jerked me out of my thoughts.

"What?! No! Not at all!"

Jerking back, Nana frowned. Finger pointed at me, she leaned forward, her small frame intimidating the hell out of me despite her being half my size.

"Now, wait just a doggone minute! Don't sound so offended. My granddaughter is a wonderful woman. She's loving, and makes her own money, and she has a good head on her shoulders. Any woman would be lucky to call her their girlfriend."

"Except Poppa doesn't do girlfriends," I chuckled morosely. Or maybe she did, but she just didn't do *me* as a girlfriend.

Unaware that I was having a complete meltdown in my head, Nana grabbed my hand and led me to the dining room, pulling out a chair and motioning for me to have a seat. She returned to the kitchen and was back in a few moments handing me a glass of what looked like red juice. I waited for her to sit before sipping from the glass, only for my eyes to pop wide open as I gave her an appreciative look.

"Ooh, this is good!"

Her smile was proud as she dipped her head. "Ain't it?"

"Mmhm!"

I held the glass up to the light and peered at the pink liquid. "What is it?"

"It's a little something I've been working on. I call it strawberry wine."

"You made this?" I asked after swallowing another mouthful. At this rate, my glass would be empty within minutes. It was delicious and tasted like the strawberry candy with the chewy centers that my own grandmother used to keep in her purse and dole out to me when I would get restless during long church services. I had to be around Amani's age at the time. Mommie passed just before I went off to college, and yet the memory of her hit me in the chest with the impact of a baby kangaroo who hadn't yet figured out their strength. My soft inhale was choppy with unchecked sorrow. I lifted the glass to my lips to find that it was empty.

"That was so good, Nana," I mused, offering her the glass. My eyebrows rose in surprise when she took the empty glass and replaced it with a full one. She then slid a tub of chocolate chip cookies toward me. I had no idea where she'd pulled all of that from, but I couldn't deny that it was making me feel better. Maybe Nana knew that I'd been having a meltdown after all.

Old Habits

"Jucee, baby, wake up."

Pressure on my shoulder was followed by gentle shaking that managed to pull me out of the deepest slumber I'd had in a good minute. Rolling over from my side onto my back, I lifted my arms above my head and stretched like a cat, releasing a little moan when I felt the bones in my back crack. I'd been curled into a ball and my joints were a little stiff. Sighing, I opened my eyes and looked to my left, my breath catching as my vision focused in the low light coming from the lamp as I recognized Poppa kneeling beside me.

She looked so damn good. A red and yellow Clutch fitted was perched halfway on her head, the bill sticking up at a forty-five-degree angle, showing off her perfect waves. The matching jersey hugged her chest, involuntarily drawing my attention to her titties, where a gold chain hung, the golden crooked crown pendant that I'd had custom made as a gift for her thirty-first birthday nestled against them. Swallowing hard against the dry lump in my throat, I quickly averted my eyes, looking up at the ceiling before lowering my lids to get myself together.

"What time is it?"

In my peripheral, I saw her lift her smart watch to her face.

"After six."

"Damn," I muttered. "What the hell was in that wine?"

Poppa chuckled. "Wine? You talking about the strawberry drink?"

"Mmhm."

This time she laughed out loud, the sound sending a shiver down my spine.

"Man, that ain't no damn wine! That's hooch!"

Slapping a hand to my face, I groaned. I should've known that Nana Cherry was making her own liquor since store-bought bottles weren't even allowed over the threshold. "She set me up."

Nana Cherry wasn't slick. There was no doubt in my mind that this scenario was exactly what she'd been planning when she handed me the second glass of that delicious-ass concoction that she'd made.

"You okay?" Poppa asked, her voice laced with concern.

I nodded. Although I didn't have to be to work until ten the next morning, and didn't have any plans that night, I needed to get out of there. Taking a couple of deep breaths, I sat up and swung my feet onto the floor.

Aww, hell.

Because of the way Poppa was positioned, when I sat up, it put her right in front of the space between my knees. If she moved a couple of inches closer, she'd be bracketed by my thighs. We met eyes and the way her left eyebrow rose just a hair of millimeter told me that the realization hit us both at the same time. I blinked in what felt like slow motion and a thousand images of what could happen if the impossible happened and we managed to be on the same page flashed before my eyes. I sucked in a breath, inhaling the cologne I'd bought her for Valentine's Day, the one that I'd teasingly insisted would make girls wet at first scent, and I almost whimpered.

She looked good and she smelled *edible.*

Humpable.

Grindable.

Face rideable.

Lord, have all of the mercy and all of the grace.

I needed to clear my thoughts immediately, and not a second later, because it was entirely possible that every thought in my mind was playing out on my face, and that was...bad. So, so bad.

Closing my eyes, I blew out a breath through my nose. When I cracked open my lids, I watched as she raised a hand and brushed some of my braids off of my shoulder, her fingers lightly grazing my cheek just before she tugged on my earlobe with the tip of her thumb and the side of her index finger. The always innocent move that she'd made probably thousands of times at this point left the entire right side of my face—and the juncture of my thighs—blazing hot.

How the fuck had I never noticed how damn erotic it was for her to touch me there?

Jerking my head to the left, I lifted my shoulder to block her access to the space. Hurt flashed across her face as she snatched her hand back, and I steeled myself against the urge to wrap my arms around her neck and offer her comfort. These were the consequences of her actions. She did this to us.

"Sorry, baby girl," she said, her voice low. "It's a habit."

My lips twisted to the side. "Habits are meant to be broken."

An annoyingly sexy smirk played at the corner of her lips.

"I thought that was rules."

Quirking an eyebrow at her, I pushed off of the sofa and stood to my feet.

"I need to go."

She sucked in a breath, and I understood because I was never short with her. But I was *not* sorry.

"Juc—"

Shaking my head, I started toward the door. "Never mind. Forget I said anything."

"C'mon, man. You know that's not possible."

My back still to her, I shrugged. "I don't really know much

of anything anymore. Not when it comes to you." I was pissed at myself for sounding so damn dramatic, but it's exactly how I felt. What felt like forever ago, I was confident that I knew Cyndi Thomas like the back of my hand, and now, I was wracking my brain, trying to figure out how I'd missed something so crucial.

I'd made it to the door, but Poppa grabbed my hand and tugged me around to face her before I could let myself out of Nana Cherry's suite.

"Juleesa, wait!"

My eyes were closed again. I couldn't look at her. I was only here because I'd been trying to eliminate her presence from my life, but drinking that hooch Nana Cherry pulled from her secret stash while I cursed Poppa out in my head only led to her being in my dreams. Now, with her standing in front of me, I was so turned on that it would probably only take a couple circles rubbed on my clit for me to cum. But that was bad because I was still so mad at her.

Not to mention disappointed.

And feeling all of those things for this one woman at the same time had my mind in a tailspin.

"What?" I croaked, hoping that she thought it was because of the drinking and not because I was warring with myself over her.

"You . . ." The sound of her clearing her throat made my eyes pop open.

There was this look on her face. Something like wonder mixed with hope. I didn't know what to make of it. Didn't know what it meant.

I was so damn confused.

"What?" I repeated, my tone less harsh.

"The way you're looking at me . . ."

Dammit.

Air whooshed through my lungs, up my esophagus, and out of my mouth. She'd seen it. Seen me imagining my thighs locked on either side of her head while she sucked on my clit like it was a straw.

Double dammit.

Shaking my head, I dropped my gaze to the carpet and mentally scolded myself. Then, I looked up and offered her an apologetic smile. Hopefully, it didn't look as fake as it felt.

"'My bad. I didn't mean to make you uncomfortable."

And then, before I could think it through, I leaned forward with the intention of placing a kiss at the corner of her mouth. To my surprise, my intentions were clocked and then immediately foiled, as Poppa swiveled her head a few millimeters to the left just before I made contact.

You know that feeling when you've been traveling for days, or even weeks, and you've been sleeping in hotel beds and eating restaurant food for breakfast, lunch, and dinner, and you've been wearing your shoes more than ever because you aren't at home so you don't feel comfortable walking around barefoot in a strange place, but then. Then you get home, and you kick off your shoes, and you eat food you cooked, and you shower in your own tub, and you jump naked under your own sheets, and everything smells like home and warmth and *yours*?

That was the feeling that consumed me when my lips accidentally on purpose landed on Poppa's. It had only been weeks since we'd kissed in any capacity, but, no matter how hard I willed it to not be true, Poppa was my home and kissing her felt like getting my footing after stumbling over and over.

And when her arms encircled my waist and her hands splayed against the small of my back, I felt that very same rush of rightness I'd felt the first time our kisses took on a new meaning. Everything about me being in Poppa's arms, her lips urgently coaxing mine to open for her impending exploration felt *right-*

*right*right in the best of ways. And as instinctively as I bent to tie my shoe after stepping into it, I opened for her. The moment her tongue touched mine, the jolt of arousal shocked me into awareness and I realized that I was doing the very thing I'd been avoiding for weeks. How quickly I became weak in the knees when it came to this woman.

I froze, ceasing all movement, and to Poppa's credit, she echoed my movement, or lack thereof. Pulling away from her, I broke our connection and stepped out of her arms, averting my eyes, not wanting to see whatever expression she wore.

"Sorry," I whispered, sucking in a fortifying deep breath before I reached up and swiped at the lip gloss that had transferred onto her mouth. It had become tacky after the hours-long nap I'd taken and took a little pressure to get it all off, but I ignored how she stood there and allowed me to do it. "It's a habit."

Backing away from her, I pulled open the door and left the room, forcing myself not to turn around as I entered the kitchen and headed for the front door.

Chapter Eighteen

Cyn

Daddy's Girl

I was once again in that space where shit just felt...off.

There was an explanation this time, but no solution in sight, which was as helpful as a bag of nails when trying to change a tire.

I went the one place where I didn't have to think. Of course, that meant that I ended up in my parents' front room, an acoustic guitar propped in my lap as I absentmindedly plucked at the strings. My mama took one look at my face, stared me down for a long minute, and then pulled me in for a tight hug before setting me loose. She left me to my own devices and my daddy replaced her presence less than five minutes later.

"What's going on with you and Juleesa?"

Sighing, I closed my eyes and hung my head as I continued playing the random tune. I sought out this music room in hopes of escaping the signs of Jucee in my own home, but I should've known that I wouldn't be able to go too long without hearing her name. Not with how entangled our lives had become. And especially not with the way my mama had mugged me when she opened the door fifteen minutes earlier. I honestly expected my daddy to appear in the doorway sooner.

Unsure of how I wanted to answer his question, I boomeranged another back at him.

"What made you ask that, Daddy?"

My eyes were still closed, but I heard the soft slap of his house shoes against the wood as he moved farther into the room. The rush of air leaving the cushions of the chair on my right let me know he sat beside me. Once he settled, the slow, deliberate inhalation of breath through his nose alerted me that he was about to speak.

"Well," he began in that easygoing tone that always brought me comfort like a warm blanket on a cold day, "your mama said Juleesa has declined her invitation for lunch three times in two weeks. I thought she was being a little dramatic—that Juleesa is probably just busy—but hearing that solemn melody you're playing told me everything I need to know."

Immediately, my fingers stilled on the strings and my eyes popped open. That dull ache in my chest throbbed and I lifted a hand to rub at the spot. Twisting my neck, I turned to face my daddy. There was no judgment on his face. His brows were raised; the look he wore was expectant. He was waiting for me to tell him what was going on.

My face crumpled and eyes stung as I tried unsuccessfully not to cry.

"*I fucked up,*" I whined, setting the acoustic on the floor by my feet, feeling like I was eleven years old again and had to admit to my parents that I'd accidentally dropped a plate while washing dishes.

And just like he did back then, my daddy pulled me against his chest and let me cry it out while he rubbed my back and assured me that worse things had happened. Logically, I knew that he was right, but in that moment my world felt wonky. Everything was knocked off of its axis and nothing was running the way it was supposed to. It was weird because the only thing that changed was Jucee's presence, but somehow that affected every aspect of my life excluding the music.

Except…according to my daddy, that was affected as well. I sobbed harder. *What the hell had I done?* Every time I feel like things with Jucee are close to being perfect, they get fucked up. I fuck them up. Why couldn't I just let things play out? Why did I have to ruin everything?

When I finished, my daddy leaned back and looked at me. I watched his eyes rove my face, taking in my damp cheeks and red eyes.

"You feel better?"

It was what he'd always asked us after giving us time to cry, and the familiar question made me smile. I nodded and moved back to my abandoned chair.

"Good." He pinned me with a look. "Now, what are you going to do to fix things with Juleesa?"

"I don't know if I can."

"Did you try?"

Scoffing, I gave him a crazy look. "Of course I did! Nothing has worked!" Frustrated, I threw my hands up in the air.

His brows rose again, this time in response to my elevated tone.

"How about you start from the beginning for me, Star Shine? Help me understand what happened, because I'm in the dark here."

"Juc—," I paused and shook my head. There was no way I could start from the true beginning. I'd always been able to tell my daddy everything, but I wasn't so sure I was ready to admit out loud that this all happened because Jucee overheard me say something hurtful about her. I didn't want to color my family's impression of her, and I was certain that's exactly what would happen if they knew the whole story.

"I said something ignorant and offensive. My words hurt Jucee and she stopped talking to me."

"Ah." Daddy nodded as if everything made sense. "Did you apologize?"

"I did! It was really heartfelt and everything but she didn't respond."

A slight frown came across his face. "She didn't respond?"

I shook my head. "Nope."

"What did she do? Just...walk away after you finished speaking?"

My lips parted but I froze in place.

Oh.

Shit.

I suddenly felt as if I was watching myself walk headfirst into a wall with no way to stop myself. It was like an out-of-body experience. I knew what was coming and yet I couldn't prevent the crash from happening.

Groaning, I ran a hand down my face. "We weren't face-to-face, Daddy. I sent her a text message."

My daddy straightened, sitting up in his seat and facing me with his undivided attention.

"Did you offend her through text message, as well?"

The head-on collision was happening and all I could do was scream at myself to go the other direction. Closing my eyes, I dropped my head back against my chair.

"No. It was in person."

"Let me make sure I understand you correctly. You insulted Juleesa in person—"

"I didn't insult her—"

"—but instead of apologizing in person, you did it through

the phone. And not even on a call, but via text message, the most impersonal form of communication known to man."

"I think 'most impersonal' is stretching things a bit."

"What else have you done to fix this?"

Scratching below my ear, I lifted my gaze to the ceiling. There was a paper-thin line of incredulity that hovered just beneath his neutral tone. It was slight, and if I didn't know his voice as well as I did, I might've missed it. "I texted her twice."

I waited for a response from him, but none came. Peeling my eyes open, I glanced his way, startled to find his piercing brown gaze.

"Hmm."

I squinted at him. "What was that about?"

"What?"

"You made a sound. You *harrumphed*. What was that sound for? What are you trying to say, Daddy?"

He shrugged and leaned back in his chair, hands folded over his belly.

"You said something curious so I made a curious sound. Nothing more, nothing less."

Rolling my eyes, I picked up the acoustic and placed it on its stand.

"Stop beating around the bush and speak your piece, old man."

A slow grin eased onto his face, cheeks lifting high and making his eyes seem as if they were the sun disappearing behind a mountain. He was enjoying teasing me.

"Well, you said that nothing you'd tried had been working, but you only tried one thing." He chuckled, clearly amused at my expense.

"Well, I—"

I cut off my excuse the moment he lifted a finger into the air.

"If the one thing you tried didn't work, try something else.

Maybe go to her in person and apologize. Bring her flowers, take her to dinner, and stop pretending to be too cool for love so you can have a chance to salvage things with her."

I choked on the air. "Daddy—"

He pinned me with a look. "Yes, Star Shine?"

I couldn't speak. Talking to my daddy about Jucee in this context had me frozen solid. I was but a mere statue perched at a piano.

"Hmm," Daddy hummed. "I thought you were about to tell me that you weren't in love with Juleesa. I'm glad you decided against lying."

A strangled noise might've escaped my throat, but that was debatable.

He gave me an amused look. "When you're finished, let's go over your plan to get Jucee back. The sooner she starts accepting Carissa's lunch invitations, the sooner I can get some peace at night."

Chapter Nineteen

Cyn

Duke It Out

I didn't hear my phone when it rang, but its buzzing caught my attention, the vibrations making it bounce around on the table in my peripheral. It was two in the morning and I was alone in the studio. Ray and her dude had ducked out about an hour or so ago and, while I should've been right behind them, I had some music on my heart that I needed to record. Without pausing the music, I picked it up and turned it over to see my baby brother's face grinning up at me from the screen.

The sound of me sucking my teeth reached my ears before I even realized I'd performed the action. I was not in the mood to talk to Cody's ass, so I rejected the call and placed it back face-down. I hadn't even pulled my hand back when it started vibrating again. Still, I swiped my thumb across the screen. Yeah, a conversation between us was well overdue, but it could wait until after I fixed things with Jucee.

The phone buzzed a third time but I concentrated on the

music, not even bothering to ignore the call this time. He'd get the message eventually.

Or so I thought.

The screen of my business phone lit up with a notification. That was worthy of my pausing the music to check it out. It was a notification from the security app. Someone had just entered the front door of the studio. Pulling up the live footage, I groaned aloud at the image of my big-ass, hard-headed-ass, can't-take-a-hint-ass baby brother grinning up at the camera as he entered a code into the panel on the wall and walked his happy ass through the front door. Rolling my eyes, I swiveled around in my chair just as Cody opened the door.

His eyes swept the room quickly before narrowing in on me. "Oh, so your ass *ain't* in here half-dead, you're just being an asshole."

My top lip curled and I shot him the finger.

"How am *I* the asshole when you're the one who snuck your snake ass up in here in the middle of the night?!"

Cocking his head to the side, he lifted his left eyebrow. His expression immediately morphed from joking to serious. I blew out a breath, dropping my head back against the chair and running a hand down my face. I'd gone too far. I knew it the moment the words came out of my mouth.

"My bad. I—"

"Nah, you clearly have some shit to get off your chest." Nodding his head, he crossed the room and dropped down onto the couch. Spreading his hands, he gestured for me to continue. "You been too pussy to speak your mind, but apparently that's dead, so let's go. I'm a snake now?"

I damn near bit a hole in my lip to keep from taking the bait on that pussy comment. I wanted to light into his ass, but I couldn't because he was right.

Eyes on the ceiling, I sighed.

"I deserved that."

Air whooshed out of the cushions as he shifted in his seat. He sucked his teeth and I glanced over to see him stretched out, his arms spread across the back of the couch.

"Hell yeah. You been ignoring me but now you talking real spicy. That shit ain't cool. I ain't deserve none of that." He chuckled afterward, but he couldn't mask the slight grumble that belied his hurt. My heart clenched.

I *was* an asshole.

Cody was the biggest of us all, but he was also the most sensitive. I knew that and still lashed out at him instead of dealing with my insecurities. I knew better than anyone that age didn't equal maturity, but I was also too damn old to be acting the way that I had. I blew out a breath.

"You're not a snake."

"No shit, Sherlock." He pursed his lips. "What I want to know is why that even came out your mouth. Or better yet, why you been acting like you actually believe that for the past few weeks?"

I don't know why I thought that I had control over when this conversation took place. The last few months should've been clue enough that things rarely went the way I wanted them, the exception being music. Which, of course, is why I'd been trying to bury my head in the sand by hyperfocusing on the music.

That was clearly an epic fail.

"I was wrong——,"

"Say that shit again. I don't think I heard you right."

Glaring, I threw my hands up in the air.

"Say, fool, you gon' let me get a full sentence out or nah?! I'm tryna apologize to your waterhead ass and you won't even shut up long enough for my lips to form an *s*!"

He laughed and waved me on. "You been treating me like

the red-headed stepchild for a minute. You can deal with a little ribbing. Hell, you earned it."

"I'm sorry, Cody. I've been fucking up in more ways than one with too many people that I love."

To my surprise, he remained silent, his eyes on me expectantly. Letting out a breath, I ripped off the Band-Aid. "I was jealous and I was scared."

He sat forward, his elbows landing on his knees, his eyes piercing into me.

"Of what?"

"Of...what looked like you getting with Jucee."

"Explain."

I frowned. "Don't be bossing me, fool! You know what I'm talking about!"

"Hell nah! I have no idea what you saw and perceived as me 'getting with her' when every-damn-body know that girl only got eyes for your watermelon-head ass. I don't know why, since I'm the better-looking Thomas offspring, but I'm pretty sure she needs glasses." He shrugged like it was no big deal.

I gaped at him.

"Say what?"

Resuming his reclined position, he shrugged again.

"Where's the confusion? I swear your comprehension skills are lacking. If it's not music, you stay lost." He tilted his head to the side and eyed me. "Do I need to grab a guitar and sing it to you?"

In spite of myself, I cracked up. "Man, fuck you!"

"Aye, I'm just tryna meet you where you at."

"I can't stand your ass," I muttered darkly.

He smirked. "But you jealous of me though."

"*Was*," I emphasized, wishing I could take that confession back. "Not anymore."

His cheeks lifted, making his dark brown eyes disappear behind his lids, and his grin spread. "You say that like it matters."

"Man..."

He sat forward quickly, cutting me off. "Nah, Cyn. Be for real. Whatever reason you been beefing with Jucee don't have shit to do with me. You can try and pull that jealousy shit with someone else, but I know better."

I stared at him.

"Mmhm," he continued, nodding as he scooted to the edge of the couch. "Jucee is fine as hell. You know that, I know that, everyone who lays eyes on her knows that. And yeah, she's bi, but shit," he chuckled, "that don't mean a damn thing to me if the only person she's interested in is my disgustingly talented, but sometimes blind to the obvious, older sister. I mean—" he shrugged "—I worry about her taste since she chose the least attractive Thomas, but I'm not one to judge other folks' preferences."

The amusement dropped from his face as he pointed a finger at me. "You, on the other hand—"

At this point, I felt confident enough to try and derail the train before it made contact. Holding up a hand, I shook my head. "You don't even have to say it. I already know and I'm working on it."

Both of Cody's eyebrows surged up his forehead as if they'd heard that Beyoncé was performing a concert on the edge of his hairline and wanted to be first in line to buy their tickets.

He waved me on. "I gotta hear this shit. G'on then, tell me what it is you already know."

Amusement appeared in the wrinkles at the corner of his mouth. I wanted to be pissed—I was pissed—but my daddy's voice was in my head telling me the perils of leading with anger. So, I took a calming breath, blew that shit out, and spoke.

"My...preferences..." I trailed off as several paths appeared in the forefront of my mind.

My instinct was to defend myself, to explain away the explanation before I even got the words out of my mouth, but I knew better. It was too late at night—or too early—to be wasting time with bullshit. I'd fucked up. I could admit that. Had admitted it days earlier while crying on my daddy's shoulder.

This was different though.

Cody was my baby brother. He had the unique advantage of knowing me all of his life, and because of that, didn't see me the way others did. While he had a measure of respect for me, it didn't keep him from calling me out when he deemed it necessary. Where my daddy was invested in protecting me as much as helping me learn the lesson, Cody was much more interested in pointing out my fuck-ups.

I was pissed that I'd given him so much material.

Clearing my throat, I began again.

"I allowed my fear to cloud my judgment. I used that to unintentionally push away the woman I loved."

There it was. I'd laid it out there and admitted my fault to him. It was much easier to deal with when I told on myself. I felt like B-Rabbit at that final cypher when he took the ammo from Papa Doc. Smirking, I waited for Cody to respond.

Yeah, fool! Tell these people something they don't know about me!

The scoff that burst from Cody's throat was so disgusted that I reared back.

"You really think that's what I was about to say, Cyndi?" Frowning, I blinked. The inflection on my name was real aggressive, each syllable clipped like jagged fingernails that kept snagging threads from a beloved garment. "That's what happened, so what else could you have to say?"

His chuckle was less amusement and more frustration. The underlying resignation was a flashing marquee that he was fed up.

"If you think all you did was 'push her away,' you're more dense than I thought."

"You calling me dumb?"

"I'm saying, if somebody was out here playing with my *best friend* the way you been playing with Jucee, I'd be pulling up ready to plex."

Cocking my neck back, I narrowed my eyes. "Playing?"

He curled his lip. "Everybody *and Nana* been watching you toy with this girl like a kitten with a feather. Jucee wears her emotions on her sleeve, big and bold for everyone to see, but instead of you reciprocating her feelings, you've been punishing her for them. You wanna play house, fuck her, play step-studdy to Amani, and make everyone believe y'all are finally getting together, only to back out and pop up with another woman whenever you feel like it. And you think that shit is cool?" Shaking his head, he glared at me. "Be for real. If it was another woman doing this to Jucee, what would you tell her to do?"

I stared at him, his words settling in my gut like a fifty-pound weight. There was nothing for me to say; he hadn't uttered a single lie. Even if I'd never intended to play Jucee like that, that's exactly what had happened. Daddy had always talked to us about our intentions not superseding their impact whenever we made missteps that hurt someone, but here I was, a grown-ass woman, doing something I'd been getting warned about since I was in elementary.

"You're right."

I waited for the inevitable ribbing, but, to my surprise, he didn't gloat. Instead, he stared at me expectantly. Somehow, he knew that I wasn't finished.

"I fucked up." Grabbing my head, I groaned. "I feel like a broken record saying that shit again, but I don't know how else to describe it. I wasn't trying to hurt her, I was…shit, I was just scared."

"You tell her that?"

"You know I haven't."

"So, why are you here?"

I sucked my teeth as I gestured to the board on my left.

"*Man, I'm working.*"

He quirked one of his eyebrows. "What that mean?"

"It's the middle of the night."

Unperturbed, he blinked. "Again, what that mean?" When I didn't respond, he snorted. "You know what that sounds like? Excuses. And not even good ones." He shook his head. "*Pathetic.*"

All I could do was laugh, because he had a point. My excuses were pathetic as hell. That didn't stop me from lifting both middle fingers into the air and aiming them in his direction, but I did so knowing that he was right and I was wrong. It didn't happen often, but this was a special moment that I didn't take for granted.

"Why don't you tell me what I'm supposed to do then, since you know everything." If he wanted to act like he had all of the answers, then he could start spilling them.

Cody's eyes bugged.

"Bro, I had no idea you were this incompetent. How the fuck do you manage to bag bad bitches when you don't even know how to grovel?! You ain't never begged a woman to take you back?!"

Now I was the one scoffing. "Boy, please! I don't beg women to do anything but open their legs wider and stop running from what I'm making them feel."

"Yeah, yeah." Lifting a hand in the air, he waved me off. "That sounds good coming out of your mouth, but if you've never gotten further than a few orgasms and sleepovers with a woman, then I have to question what you plan to do with Jucee. Because that woman is a lot of things but one thing she isn't is the friends with benefits type. She's the type you marry and start a family with. You can't string her along. She deserves better than that."

The passion in his voice took me aback. We sat there, staring each other down as I tried to figure out how I felt about how he'd said what he said. Because if I didn't know better...

"You sure you don't want Jucee?" I asked bluntly. There was no need to dance around it.

I watched my baby brother purse his lips and suck in a slow breath, the inhalation almost noiseless in the quiet room. When he released the air through his nose, he leveled me with a point-blank look and leaned forward, resting his elbows on his knees.

"Are you saying I have to want a woman to see her worth? You think that's the kinda man my daddy raised?"

Shit.

Even if his words hadn't chastened me, the thread of hurt woven into the anger of his words shot a pang of regret through my chest. It hadn't been my intention to question his integrity, but, once again, intention didn't equal impact.

I licked my lips. "Not at all, I was just—"

"If I wanted her, I wouldn't be here."

That effectively shut me up. I nodded and sat back in my seat. A few beats passed before he echoed my nod.

"Aight then. What are you gon' do?"

Chapter Twenty

Jucee

Yes, No, or Maybe?

I hated pull-ups with every fiber of my being, but they were the one exercise that didn't allow me to think of anything else while doing it. There was no room to worry about the state of things with Poppa when I was mentally coaching myself through my least favorite body-weight cycle. Being a big bitch was all fun and games until you had to do a vertical on the pole, then you needed to be a big, *strong* bitch.

Hence, the pull-ups.

"Come on, Jucee!" my trainer called from behind me. "Give me two more. I know you have it in you! Let's finish strong!"

I definitely couldn't be in my head when I was getting yelled at—excuse me—*enthusiastically motivated* like this.

Concentrating all of my brainpower on my breathing, I sucked in a breath and released it as I slowly pulled myself upward until my chin was above the bar. As much effort as it took to go up, it was even more difficult to lower myself at the same pace as I gone up. The last thing I wanted was to tear a muscle or yank my arm out of its socket by dropping too fast. Once I was hanging back down, arms stretched above me, Jaz patted my hip.

"One more. Don't rest too long. Let's go!"

Nodding, I sucked in a breath and repeated the action one final time. This time, instead of hanging when I came down, I released the bar and dropped to my feet. As soon as I was standing, I allowed my knees to buckle and dropped down dramatically, falling first to my knees and then onto my side before laying spread eagle on my back.

Jaz stood over me, laughing at my antics.

"You made it. Good job."

Stepping over me, she disappeared out of my peripheral, likely to go check on one of the other girls, while I once again focused on my breathing. Today's workout had kicked my ass, but I'd loved it. Not only for the distraction, but for what I got out of it. The sound of weights clanking, feet pounding treadmills, and low music playing was all around me.

I gave myself thirty more seconds to cosplay a log before I rolled onto my side and pushed up on my knees. That's when I heard the commotion. It was the "oohs" that got me; they indicated something eye-catching was happening and my feeling of missing out kicked in. Twisting to look over my shoulder, I searched the room until I found the cause for commotion. And then I promptly gasped.

Mouth gaped open, I stared wordlessly as Poppa strolled her fine ass across the gym to stand in front of me. She held a bouquet of artfully arranged fruit in one hand and a paper shopping bag in the other, the unmistakable Crumbville logo stamped on the front.

My heart was beating fast as hell as someone stepped up to grab the bouquet so Poppa could grab my arm and help me to my feet. No wonder everyone was on their high school cafeteria steeze, coming from other rooms in the gym. This felt very much like receiving a promposal from your crush during the busiest lunch period.

Once I was upright, Poppa reached to hug me, but I immediately stepped back, putting my hands up.

"I'm sweaty!"

There'd been a quick flash of hurt in her deep brown eyes at my retreat, but then she blinked and it was gone, replaced with a narrowed glare.

"When have I *ever* been put off by your sweat, Jucee?"

The inflection in her words had my heartbeat drop below my waist as visions of her licking the sweat from my back as she—

"Ooh, she nasty," murmured Mercedes, pulling me out of my torrid thoughts. I turned to her, meeting her eyes as I twisted my lips to the side and gave her a knowing look.

Poppa was a lot of things and nasty was absolutely top of the list.

I laughed to myself before stepping into Poppa's outstretched arms. This was so far from lowkey that you would've had to zoom out on the map to see them both. And though this public display didn't fix anything at all, I loved a good spectacle. Get your grovel on, baby girl.

"Mmhm," Poppa whispered into my ear, her fingers digging into my waist, "she *real* nasty."

At that, I pushed back from her. Sex with Poppa was so easy. *Too* easy. Easier than it should've been, considering that I'd gone into it knowing how she felt about bisexual women. But that was why I knew I had to pull back, because if I let her, Poppa would fuck me into a raggedy amnesia-like, post-coital stupor that would have me giving her goofy grins and thinking we had it all.

Hell naw, I'd be damned!

"What are you doing here?" I asked the obvious, taking the

proffered bag of assorted, freshly baked cookies as she turned to retrieve the bouquet from Shay, the gym's owner.

Fruit in one hand, Poppa grabbed my bicep and led me over to an empty corner.

"I came to apologize."

I quirked an eyebrow, folding my arms across my chest as I jutted my hip to the side. "And you thought doing it in public was the best course of action?"

"*Man*," she drawled, sucking her teeth, "I ain't studdin' these folks and you ain't either. I know you like this type of shit, stop playin'."

She stared at me, waiting on me to deny it, but all I did was laugh. There was no need to lie when she knew me as well as she did.

"Yeah, well, you're lucky I was done with my workout."

She grinned and slid her hand from my arm, up my shoulder, and down my side, scorching a heated trail onto my skin with the soft caress.

"Except it wasn't luck. I had some help with that."

I followed the jut of her chin toward the front desk where Shay stood with her eyes on us. When she waved, I frowned, causing her to burst into laughter. Swinging my eyes back to Poppa, I shook my head.

"I can't do this with you here."

She took a step toward me. "I know—"

"No," I emphasized with a shake of my head. "You don't. This isn't a conversation I can have with you in public, even with all of this." I held up the paper bag and gestured at the vase in her hand.

"I know," she repeated, gripping my waist and stepping closer still. "I didn't come here to talk like that, I swear. I just came because I wanted to see you smile."

Ugh, those sweet words wrapped around my heart and squeezed.

"Poppa..." I trailed off, not even sure what I wanted to say, but feeling like I needed to say something.

"Shh," she murmured before leaning in and dropping a kiss onto my lips. I could be mad about her shushing me another time but at that moment all I wanted to do was siphon her unique flavor from those pillow-soft, plush-ass lips.

"_Awww!_" went up around us, making it clear that, while we'd moved out of the center of the gym and the women had started returning to their equipment, we still held everyone's attention.

Poppa broke the kiss before I did, her eyes open and on me as I swiped my tongue across my bottom lip like I was licking Cheetos dust from my fingers after emptying the bag into my mouth. She moved her hand up from my waist to cap the back of my neck.

"Go shower and get dressed. I'll follow you home and then take you to lunch so we can talk. Is that aight?"

Hell yeah.

The list of things that weren't aight concerning Poppa was very short—but those few items were pretty damn significant.

"Yeah," I said with a nod, "that's aight."

Rubbing the side of my neck with her thumb, and simultaneously increasing the pulsation between my thighs, Poppa smiled, dropped a swift peck at the corner of my mouth, and took the paper bag from me. She then nodded toward the hall where the showers and sauna were located.

"Take your fine ass on."

I rolled my eyes at the command, but you know what else I did? I took my fine ass on across the gym toward the hall, stopping first at the front desk where Shay sat on a stool, a smug grin on her face, looking pleased as punch. Propping my hands on my hips, I glared at her.

"You set me up!"

There wasn't an ounce of shame visible on her face. In fact, she preened a little, clasping her hands over her heart and lifting her shoulders.

"I did!" she practically mooned.

Her lovesick reaction was cartoonishly funny, so of course I busted out laughing.

"You're not even ashamed of yourself, are you?"

She tossed her head back as she joined in on my laughter.

"Girl, I've been watching you mope around here for weeks with a perpetually downturned smile, sad as a plant without the sun. Why in the world would I be ashamed of helping your girlfriend publicly grovel when it was clear that whatever was wrong with you was her fault?"

Shay stared at me, waiting for a response that I didn't have. There were several parts of her statement that I needed to address, most importantly, the assumption that Poppa was my girlfriend. But oddly, that was the one part that I *didn't* want to correct. I *liked* Shay assuming that me and Poppa were a couple. I *liked* hearing her refer to as my girlfriend even when I knew it was untrue. My foolish heart struck again.

Dropping my defensive stance, I nodded my head and blew out a breath.

"You have a point," I conceded. "I guess I should be thanking you."

Tilting her head to the side, Shay eyed me. Then she leaned forward, her palms flat on the desk as she held my gaze.

"Hey. If it's not what you want, know that it's okay to say no."

Eyes wide, I blinked at her. Unperturbed, she continued.

"Even if you wanted it before, but now you've changed your mind, you can say no. Nothing is set in stone."

My lip trembled as a wave of gratitude slammed into me out of nowhere.

"I appreciate you so much for this, Shay. Thank you so much for looking out for me." My voice was a little thick with unshed emotion, but I couldn't help it.

This went beyond standard client satisfaction. Shay wasn't giving me this talk simply because she wanted to retain my business at her gym; she was doing this because she genuinely cared about me. All of the worrying I'd done over the past few weeks, the hand-wringing as I thought that I would have no one left who loved me if I completely cut off the Thomases, was all for naught. Here was another example of the community I'd built in this city.

"Listen, if there are people in your ear, forget about them. Forget this whole display. None of that shit matters if you don't want her."

"But I *do* want her." Folding my arms atop the counter and dropping my head onto my folded arms, I sighed heavily. "That's actually the problem."

Standing to her full height, Shay peeked over my shoulder in the direction I'd come from. I twisted around to see what I could see and found myself ensnared in Poppa's intense gaze. That look—the undeniable love—beaming from those warm brown eyes struck me dead in the chest.

It was difficult to question things when she looked at me like that.

"*Gahdamn*," Shay muttered after letting off a low whistle. I snapped my head back to her, watching her eyebrows shoot toward the ceiling as she pinned me with a look.

"Baby, I'm not seeing the problem. She *clearly* wants you too." My chest inflated as I inhaled a deep breath. I pushed the air out through my nose.

"It does look like it, huh?" I chuckled softly.

At least this was further proof that I wasn't seeing things. I wasn't trying to make something out of nothing just so that my feelings didn't feel unrequited. It was one thing for her family to say they could see something between us, but it was a whole other thing for someone who didn't know us as *Cyn & Jucee* to say the same.

That should've made me feel better.

It didn't.

Tapping my nails on the counter, I smiled at Shay.

"I'm gonna go hop in the shower. Thanks for everything, Shay."

She gave me a soft smile, dipping her chin in acknowledgement. "Don't forget what I said."

She'd said many things, but I knew exactly which things in particular she meant.

"Yes, ma'am," I teased before finally making my way to the back of the gym and into the locker room.

I wish I could say that I took my time and made Poppa wait, but I did nothing of the sort. Pineappling my braids, I shoved the huge bun into a satin-lined shower cap and took my toiletries into a shower stall. Once I stepped into the spray of the shower head, it didn't take long for my brain to start racing. I was pretty positive that I knew why Poppa had shown up, but that didn't change me nor my anxiety about her being there. What was she going to say to me and what would happen afterward? I mean, I was pretty certain that I knew why she was there, right? We hadn't spoken, truly, in a couple of weeks, which was unheard of in the entirety of our friendship. It was obvious she wanted to change that, but a small part of me wondered if she was only here because not only had we not spoken, but we hadn't been having sex either.

Please stop acting like you're the only bitch Poppa can fuck.

That thought pulled me up short. Of course I wasn't the

only bitch that Poppa could fuck. I'd seen firsthand, at least hundreds of times, how pussy would literally fall into her lap, so why was I even worried about her being here simply so that we can have sex again?

That was ridiculous.

But that just went to show how all over the place my mind was. Then I had to ask myself, hypothetically speaking, if she was here specifically for the sex, what would I do?

Was I okay with a piece of a relationship with my best friend whom I was in love with? Was I okay with only having half of Poppa's heart? Would I be okay—would I be able to live with myself—if I took the offering of a piece of her relationship with someone who did not even see the entirety of my being?

That was the easiest thing for me to answer. And the answer was no, I wouldn't be okay. I wouldn't be able to live with myself and I wouldn't be able to live with Poppa. Every facet of our relationship would shrivel and die, and I didn't want that. So that meant I had to be prepared to walk away permanently.

Fifteen minutes later, after I'd scrubbed from head to toe, I sat on a teak bench and slathered on a shea body butter scented with jasmine and then quickly dressed in a pair of red bike shorts and a Houston Clutch oversized tank top in the team's red, white, and gold colors. White slides completed the outfit.

After placing my sweaty clothes into a mesh bag with my name on it, I dropped them into the designated hamper and exited the locker room. Thick n' Fit offered a laundry service for an extra fee and I regularly took advantage of it. I worked out four times a week and those clothes added up. I had no problem utilizing any convenience offered to me.

Back in the main gym, I swept my eyes over to the corner I'd left Poppa in, but she wasn't there. Instinctively, I looked over at the front desk. There she was, leaning against the counter, one hand in the pocket of her shorts, the other holding her phone,

head thrown back as she laughed at something Shay was saying. My gifts were on the counter by her elbow and she looked
relaxed and unbothered.

She looked so good.

And she was here.

That counted for something.

Right?

It did. It meant she was willing to make the first move, and
that? That was something Poppa didn't have to do. The fact
that she was doing it for me gave me hope that she maybe saw
something different for us. She wasn't handling this the same
way that she handled every other situation with every other
woman. Hell, most of her interactions with those other women
never made it out of the bed buddy stage, so her being here,
making a public display, said so much.

The only question was whether or not I was going to listen.

Chapter Twenty-One

Cyn

Big-Girl Panties

With my hands twisting the leather of my steering wheel, I followed Jucee home, trying and failing to tamp down the rambunctious gaggle of nerves taking up residence in my belly. She had been so quiet at the gym, and that was so unlike her, that I couldn't help but think the worst. Her eyes were as expressive as always, but I needed to hear her voice, and it felt calculated when she kept it from me.

Parking beside her in the lot, I trailed her up the stairs and inside her apartment. She didn't say a word as she toed out of her shoes and headed toward her bedroom, unaware that I watched her the whole time. When she disappeared down the hallway, I sighed and headed into the tiny kitchen, setting the bag of cookies onto the counter before crouching down and making some room on the lowest shelf in the refrigerator so I could place the bouquet of fruit on a stick inside to prevent spoilage.

Since I couldn't do what I *wanted* to do after I finished that task, I shuffled into the living area and plopped down onto the couch, my hand on my right knee in a failed attempt to cull the bouncing that had begun as soon as I tried not to think about the things we'd done the last time we were in a bedroom together. It didn't work, of course; I was failing at a lot of things these days.

I'd *wanted* to follow Jucee into her bedroom and push her onto the bed.

I wanted to climb over her, kiss her neck, and then her lips, and then her *other* lips until she forgave me and we were able to move forward and be together.

I wanted that so bad I could already taste her on my tongue.

But I couldn't do that; I *wouldn't*.

Because the sex with us was so perfect—so *easy*—and was often the palate cleanser at the end of whatever disagreement we had, I think Jucee thought that I used sex to manipulate her. I mean, she never told me no for anything after I gave her a screaming orgasm, but that was never my intention. I didn't want that to be the go-to whenever we had problems, but I couldn't deny that it worked in my favor more often than not. It wasn't on purpose and I didn't want to handle this with her the way I handled everything else with everyone else, because Jucee wasn't like anyone else.

She wasn't just my best friend, she was my heart. And because there was no way that I could lose a piece of my heart and continue to live as a whole person, I needed to make sure that everything was okay between us. Better than okay, actually. I needed to fix what I'd broken, and repair it in a way that made sure it never broke again.

The moment that she appeared, I jumped to my feet and started to head her way on instinct, but when she twisted her lips to the side and nervously rubbed her hands on her thighs, I stopped midstep. I'd been about to pull her into my arms and kiss on her, but I wasn't sure if I could—or even should—do that anymore, or at least right now. So, I stood there awkwardly for a moment, willing her to come over to me, to hug me and kiss me and give me some affection.

She didn't do any of that, of course, because we weren't in a good place. I'd fucked up and I had to fix it for any of that to become my reality again. When she dropped her eyes from mine, I swallowed down the hurt and moved over to the foyer with my keys in one hand and my other fist shoved deep into my pocket. I needed something to occupy me so that I didn't grab for her.

Jucee grabbed her purse off the couch and met me at the door.

"You ready?" I asked, even though she stood right in front of me looking more than ready, and maybe just as nervous as I was.

Instead of giving me the skeptical look my obvious question likely deserved, she nodded and opened the door. "Yeah. Let's go, I'm starving."

The walk to my truck was a quiet one and, for the first time in the three years that we'd known each other, the silence between us was awkward as fuck.

I hated that shit.

I fucking *hated* it and I had no one to blame but myself. I knew that, which is why I was here trying to fix things.

In the parking lot, we climbed into my truck and buckled in as I navigated out onto the street and headed toward the restaurant. It was quiet for a few minutes as we rolled along before Jucee spoke up.

"You're not playing music."

My eyebrows shot up and I stole a quick glance over at her. She was staring at the dashboard, her face pinched into a frown. Then she turned toward me.

"You never ride in silence," she uttered—no, accused. Her voice was a bundle of tightly woven cords. She sounded put off, as if I was doing something wrong by not having music on. Like I was committing a heinous crime. Brows lifted, I reached over and pressed the power button on the radio, instantly flooding the vehicle with the latest mix I'd made.

"My bad," I murmured, wondering why I felt so guilty. "I guess I just had a lot on my mind and I didn't even think to turn anything on."

Although my eyes were back on the road, I could feel the intensity of her gaze on the side of my face. It truly hadn't occurred to me that she would think anything of the fact that there was no music playing, and I wasn't lying when I said that I had a lot of my mind, but she was correct when she said I never rode in silence. There always needed to be some music in the background no matter where I was, always some new song that I needed to be listening to. There was always something.

But today, right now? That *something* was on pause until I mended this thing between me and Jucee. The regularly scheduled programming could resume when things felt regular again.

Besides, her breathing was a little heavy and slightly erratic. I might not have noticed it if the music had been blasting, but in the silent truck I could hear that very well. And maybe—this might make me sound like a psycho, but—hearing her breathe, knowing that those breaths were uneven and a little fast-paced, made me feel good. It warmed my chest a bit and took away some of the sting of her withheld affection, because it meant that she was nervous too. And if she was nervous then that meant she hadn't made her mind up about us, and if she hadn't made her mind up about us, then there was a pretty good chance that I *could* fix this. There was an in for me there, and that brought me some comfort.

Nothing else was said as I drove us into Third Ward and parked in a lot on Almeda. We got out of the truck and walked up a block until we reached Turkey Leg Hut. It was just after eleven on a Wednesday and there was no line at all. We walked right in and were seated immediately. We chose to sit on the right in and were seated immediately. We chose to sit on the patio, figuring it would give us more privacy to have our conversation. Under the white tents we were shielded from the sun and there were fans going, so it was bearable and not too bad at all. A few minutes after we were seated, a young guy with a thick afro puff gathered at the top of his head came over to us.

"How're y'all doing? My name is Denny and I'll be your server today. Can I get y'all started off with some drinks?"

"What's up, Denny? I'm gonna have this frozen strawberry lemonade that you guys have, 'cause this picture looks amazing." I nodded at Jucee. "And she'll have the sweet tea."

To his credit, Denny looked at Jucee with his eyebrows raised, waiting for confirmation from her. When she nodded, he returned the gesture and wrote the things on the notepad he carried.

"We'll also have two ice waters, please," Jucee added before he could turn and walk off.

Pulling out her phone, Jucee scanned the barcode sticker at the edge of the table and began to peruse the menu that popped up on her phone.

"I know you want to talk," she began, raising her eyes up to meet mine before dropping them right back to the screen, "but let me just figure out what I want to eat first."

I nodded. That was reasonable. I'd been to the Turkey Leg Hut before, but Jucee never had, even though she'd been in Houston for three years. It was a very popular restaurant that was infamous for its long lines and even longer wait for the food. Coming during the week was the perfect time to not only treat her to a meal she'd been waiting to have, but also to lay all my cards on the table. This was also a calculated move for me, because Jucee was always more malleable with a full stomach. Whether her stomach was full of laughter, my strap, good food, or drink.

"No problem at all," I said as I followed suit and scanned the QR code for the menu. "I was thinking we could share a turkey leg stuffed with crawfish mac and cheese, and you can get whatever else you want on the side. What you think?"

She moaned. "That sounds amazing! Yes, let's do that!"

Chuckling, I scrolled the page until I found the section of sides and decided what else I wanted to order. When I was finished, I darkened my screen and folded my arms on top of the table and stared at the woman across from me. Now that I'd accepted how I felt about her, and I allowed myself to feel those feelings, I was no longer scared by the depth of emotions I had just by seeing her. Watching her now, the way her eyes lit up as her thumb dragged up and down her screen, excited me. I loved it. I just loved looking at her.

Taking in the warm hue of her skin, the gloss on her lips, remembering the way they felt against mine when I kissed her at the gym, wanting to taste them again, the way her hair was styled. It had been in a bun at the gym, but she'd taken it down when she came out of her bedroom. The braided yellow tassel earrings that hung from her earlobes that matched her outfit. The way we sort of matched despite the fits not being exactly the same. She had on the city's basketball team colors and I had on the city's football team colors. It was as if we had planned it that way, but we were just on the same wavelength like that, and that said something to me. It meant something.

But just because we were on the same wavelength when it came to outfits, and because the sex was always amazing, and because she was my very best friend, it didn't mean that we had to be together. I wanted to be with her, more than I ever wanted anything in my life, which was saying a lot considering I always wanted to be in the music business. The way I felt about Juleesa Marie Jones was unlike anything I had ever experienced before, and that terrified me. But I loved her enough to fight past the fear.

I just needed her to love me enough to give me a second chance and an opportunity to undo the shitty things that I had done when I was trying to fight this thing between us.

"You two ready to order?" Denny placed our drinks on the table and then tucked the round server under his arm and pulled his notepad back out.

Pulling a pen from behind his ear, he looked at us and waited. I nodded at Jucee to go first. She rattled off her order as Denny scribbled everything onto his notepad and then turned to me. I gave him the order of the turkey leg and decided on sides of dirty rice and cowboy beans. Once he had everything, he started to back away when Jucee called out to him.

"Hold on now, Denny. Let me taste this tea before you go, because if it's not sweet enough I'm going to need something else."

Denny grinned. "Do you have diabetes?"

Eyes wide, Jucee shook her head. "No..."

"Well, let's just say you might after drinking that tea."

I cracked up. He was funny.

Jucee danced in her seat as she pulled the drink toward her and grabbed the straw Denny had placed on the table. She gave the drink a stir with the straw before taking a healthy sip. With her lips puckered, she sat back on the bench seat and bounced her shoulders.

"Oooh," she drawled. "Now that is how I like my tea! Thank you, Denny!"

"Yes, ma'am," he said with a slight bow before spinning on his heel and heading back to the restaurant.

Reaching for my own straw, I pulled it and the frosted glass that held my drink toward me. It was so hot outside that I could already see my drink melting back into pure liquid at the bottom of the glass. So, I used the straw to stir the drink back up and then tasted it. It was amazing. The perfect combination of tart and sweet, which was exactly how I liked my fruity lemonades. I drank it down a little bit more, loving the feel of the coolness traveling down my chest, fighting the heat. Pushing it to the side, I once again folded my arms across the table as I looked up at Jucee. It was now or never.

"So . . ."

Jucee sighed and linked her fingers on top of the table. The sound was a mixture of resignation and dread. There was a slight warble that indicated her nerves as well. Was she as nervous as I was? Was she anxious in the same way that I was? Did she have the same fear that this might be the end of us like I did?

So many questions. There were so, so many that I had, and the only way I would get an answer was if I started to speak. So I did.

"I love you so much, Jucee."

Her eyebrows rose and she sat forward as if she was preparing to speak, but I held my hand up to stop her. "Just . . . just let me get everything out first before you say anything. Even if it sounds like something that you're supposed to respond to immediately like a question or whatever, just let me finish, please. Please?"

She nodded but otherwise didn't say a word. Nodding my thank-you, I took a deep breath before continuing on.

"I love you so much, Jucee." She sucked in a breath, but to her credit she didn't say a word. She rolled her lips inward as she sat forward, propping her elbows on the table and bouncing her chin on her closed fist.

"I know it's been a bumpy road while we find our footing in this romance thing, and—" I grinned sheepishly "—I can admit that most of the speed bumps were caused by me." Lifting an arm onto the table, I opened my hand palm-up. To my relief, Jucee instantly placed her hand over mine, wrapping her fingers around my wrist. "But I want you, I want *us*, and I want to do all of the necessary shit to smooth the road and keep moving forward."

I waited for her to speak or give me some sort of a reaction that said she heard me and agreed, or *something*, but the only thing I got was her biting her bottom lip and looking out over the street. Trying not to immediately take it negatively, I blew a breath out through my nose and squeezed her hand.

"You don't have to say anything right now. If you need some time, you can have what you need. I'm not going anywhere."

Her eyes flitted back to me and her lips lifted upward marginally. "Thank you for understanding. There's a lot to process and I just need the space to do that."

I blinked. There it was again. That slight bump in the rhythm of her voice that let me know something was off. I wanted to demand she confess every single thought, big and small, that caused her hesitation. I wanted to insist that she spill it all so I can know precisely how to soothe those concerns, but if I did any of that then I'd be contradicting myself. If I said she didn't have to say anything right now then I had to stand on that.

Nodding, I lifted her hand and pressed a kiss to the inside of her wrist.

"No problem," I murmured with a confidence I didn't feel.

Chapter Twenty-Two

Jucee

The Talk

When I told Poppa that I needed some space after her pop-up at the gym and then our lunch date, I was really just buying time. As much as I loved that woman, love didn't mean shit if respect wasn't present. She'd sounded so earnest sitting across from me at the restaurant with the bill of her fitted at that forty-five-degree angle, but how could I trust that?

I was going to have to make a decision sooner than later, but until then I just tried to focus on other things. Amani was with his father this week, but Samir had called and explained that Sanai had a bad case of colic. While he and Morgan were doing everything they could, the kids were miserable with the crying baby in the house. Their solution was to relocate the bigger kids until the baby was better. LeeLee and Pooh had gone to their grandmother's house, but Amani said he wanted to come home. It was a perfect excuse for me to decline Poppa's texted offer to bring over dinner.

I just needed more time.

It was after nine when Samir showed up with my baby draped over his shoulder. Amani was already in his pajamas and passed out like a rag doll. He didn't stir, not once, as his father laid him in his bed and pulled the covers up over him. I stayed in the living room, waiting for Samir to come back out before heading for the door. On a normal day, we might kick it for a little bit before he headed out, but with Morgan home alone with Sanai, I didn't want to keep him longer than necessary.

We reached the door and I hugged Samir to my side before twisting the handle, but instead of releasing me so that I could open the door, Samir stared at me.

"What is it?" I asked, confused by his sudden silence.

"What's up with you and Cyn?"

Ah, hell. I should've known he was going to go there but because Samir didn't usually have anything to say about the people I dated, I thought I was in the clear. Blowing out a breath, I spun on my heel and stalked over to the couch, shoving my face in a cushion.

I heard the turn of the lock on the door before Samir plopped down next to me and pulled the cushion out of my hands.

"Cute, but that's not an answer."

"I don't want to talk about it," I whined.

He shrugged. "Tough."

Pouting, I folded my arms across my chest. "I forgot how mean you could be."

Chuckling, he shook his head. "And I forgot how big of a baby you could be when dealing with something you would rather avoid." He let off a low whistle. "I just know Cyn has her hands full with your spoiled ass."

Well, that was a jolt to my spine, making me sit ramrod straight as I glared at him. "I am not spoiled, but even if I was, it wouldn't have anything to do with her!"

"Hmm," he murmured. "That's a significantly different tone

than the one you were singing the last time we talking about her. What changed? Relax that tension in your shoulders and catch me up to speed."

I deflated, blowing out the indignant breath I'd sucked in. Samir was right—I hadn't told him the bad of me and Poppa, only the good, which was clearly a mistake on my part. So, I gave him the rundown of everything that had transpired. When I finished, his lips were pursed and he stared at me through narrowed eyes.

"But y'all talked, right?"

I nodded. "Yeah, a couple of days ago. We went to lunch." "Hmm."

Frowning, I cocked my head. "What?"

"What what?"

"You said 'hmm.' What was that about?"

He raised his hands up. "I'm just processing what you told me. That's it."

When he didn't elaborate, my frown deepened. "*Samir.*"

One of his eyebrows rose. "You sure you want to hear my thoughts? 'Cause you know I won't hold back."

I paused, considering his warning. It didn't take me long. "Lay it on me."

Nodding, he grabbed both of my hands in his and leveled me with knowing look.

"Cyn isn't your parents, JuJu. She's not gonna abandon you because you're not who she wants you to be."

My throat tightened. He didn't pull any punches, going straight for the jugular and hitting his mark with one swing.

"But she did!" I insisted. *At least...that's what it felt like.*

He squeezed my hand. "No, she didn't. Is what she said and how she was moving fucked up? Absolutely. But I don't think her dragging her feet to define what the two of you were doing, or flippantly calling you straight instead of bisexual, is on the same level as your dad putting you on the street when you were twelve because your mama caught you kissing a girl after soccer practice. And I *don't* think it warranted you excommunicating yourself from everyone she's related to."

I shook my head. He was wrong there.

"No, I had to. As soon as she told them what was going on with us, they were gonna pick a side. Why the hell would I wait for them to pick her and kick me to the curb when I could just leave before any of that happens?"

"Oof!" He cringed, ducking his head for a brief moment before returning his gaze to mine. It was so full of sympathy that it made my chest hurt. "Juju, them people weren't gonna throw you away. *They love you.*"

Again, I shook my head. "I mean, yeah, they love me, but that love only extends as long as I'm with Poppa."

"Do you really believe that?"

"I—" I paused, because, while my instinct was to immediately confirm, there was a second instinct, a less bold but equally sure instinct that said, "No." No, I didn't really believe that the love they had for me hinged on my relationship with Poppa, but I didn't know for sure, and the lack of conviction was enough for me.

I just… I couldn't risk it.

Seeing my internal battle, Samir shook his head.

"Let me ask you something else. Did you tell Cyn how you felt when y'all talked?"

Pressing my lips into a flat line, I gave him a blank stare. All he did was laugh.

"I take that as a no."

"I said we talked."

He ignored me. "Juju, I know firsthand how you'll retreat instead of saying what's going on inside your head. Expressing yourself could save you a lot of stress."

"Samir—"

He lifted his hands up as if he could hear my thoughts and wanted to protect himself against them. "Look, I'm not saying you have to forgive her—or even take her back. I'm just saying that you take things to the extreme when sometimes a softer hand is what's necessary."

Huffing a breath out through my nose, I stretched my legs out in front of me and leaned back against the sofa. There was a tiny, slight possibility that he had a point, but...

"You gotta be with someone first in order to take them back."

Samir snorted, the goofy sound pulling my eyes from the ceiling and over to him.

"Be for real," he laughed. "Y'all were so damn together that I already had my stepparent speech ready."

I slapped a hand over my mouth to muffle the shriek his words incited.

"You're a fucking nut, you know that?"

He nodded. "Yeah, and you're stubborn as hell, *and* water is wet." Tugging on my hand, he pulled me over to him and wrapped an arm around my shoulders when I dropped my head onto his chest. "I get it, JuJu. Cutting ties is how you protect yourself. You had to do that to survive and it's your nature now, but babe, hear me out. You're not in survival mode anymore."

My heart rate sped up and I felt those unshed tears gear up to make an appearance.

"It isn't you and your granny against the world anymore. You have community. Even if things with Cyn don't pan out, her family isn't your only family. You have me, and 'Mani, Morgan, Pooh, and LeeLee. And you already know how my family has been claiming you as their own since we well before we got together—that hasn't changed in three years and there's nothing you can do about it. Not only that, you also have your

Sanity fam. Mal, and Mercedes, and all of the girls up there. You have people, Juju. You aren't an island, never have been, and never will be."

Wrapping my fingers into his t-shirt, I buried my face in his chest and sobbed. Samir had peeled back all of my layers and I was raw and exposed, vulnerable in a way I hadn't allowed myself to be in a very long time. We'd known each other so long that I'd forgotten how well Samir knew me. In the blink of an eye, everything I'd known had been taken from me, and although my grandmother had swept in and saved me, I still went through life waiting for the other shoe to drop. The problem with that is I never allowed myself to fully enjoy anything because I was always waiting for the moment I lost it.

I was scared out of my mind, and he'd clocked that.

He didn't have to say it, but I know that the main reason he recognized it is because I did the same thing with him. Of course, I didn't realize it at the time, but after we split and I was able to examine what happened to us, and why we had to split, I saw my part in it. Just like Cyn had been trying to cushion herself because of past hurts, I'd been doing the same. It was wild that Samir had made that connection and I hadn't, but I understood.

He let me cry, rubbing my back and murmuring words of support as I soaked through the thin cotton he wore. When I finished, I sat up and reached for the box of tissue on the end table.

"How you feel?" he asked, elbows on his knees as he peered at me, somber-faced and eyes searching.

"Better," I answered honestly. That cry was long overdue and had unlocked a few things that I'd been holding on to when I should have let them go.

"Good." He tilted his chin toward the back. "Go splash some water on your face. You're looking a lil snotty and puffy."

"Rude ass," I laughed as I went to my room to do just that. I was gone less than two minutes, but as soon as I reentered the living room, there was a soft knock on the front door. Brows lifted, I glanced at Samir and shrugged before I went to the door. The moment I looked through the peephole, I gasped and stepped back from the door, my eyes immediately refilling with tears.

Poppa stood on the other side of the door, her hands in her pockets as she stared right into the tiny fishbowl window. I knew she couldn't see me but it felt like we'd made eye contact.

"What are you doing?" Samir questioned. I turned around to see him giving me a crazy look.

"It's Poppa."

Twisting his lips to the side, he dropped his neck forward. "Okay…" He trailed off, as if I wasn't making sense. "Are you gon' let her in or…"

I swallowed down the lump in my throat. "What is she doing here?!"

He blinked at me slowly. "I'm pretty sure you could ask her that if you…you know…opened the door."

Blowing out a breath, I shook my head.

"You do it."

To his credit, Samir didn't roll his eyes or call me a baby. Instead, he stood from the couch and walked over to the door. When he pulled it open, he slapped hands with Poppa and stepped back to let her into my apartment. All of the nerves that I'd been grappling with started beatboxing and breakdancing in my stomach and chest when I set eyes on her. I didn't know what to do, I didn't know how to feel, but I did know that seeing her made me happy. I didn't know why she was here, or what made her show up at this particular moment, but her presence made me happy. Even if I was still trying to cling to my anger, seeing her brought me a sense of peace and joy.

Her eyes swept over me, taking me in, eating me up, setting me on fire with the undeniable emotion I saw reflected there.

"What's up, Jucee?"

I dragged my tongue across my lip in an attempt to still my heart before offering a soft "Hey."

The single word was supposed to be nonchalant and easy, but if the amused look that Samir bounced between me and Poppa was any indication, it sounded as breathy as it had felt when I said it.

"Aight, that's my cue." The clap of his hands at the end of his words broke the stare-off that Poppa and I were engaging in.

It dawned on me that he was leaving, and that's when those nerves in my belly began to audition for the stage play adaptation of *Breakin'* 2. Turning to him, I started to ask if he could stay a little while longer. And because Samir knew me as well as he did, he cut me off before I could even begin. Stepping in front of me, he framed my face with his hands and peered down at me.

"I love you, Juleesa, and because I love you, I'm not going to stand by and watch you let something that is so right for you die without a fight. You have to talk to her—you have to tell her how this hurt you and what you need going forward for this work. What you have with Cyn is a good thing and it makes you happy. *She* makes you happy, and when you're happy, my son is ecstatic. That means I'm even more invested in this working out."

I laughed wetly. I couldn't even be mad at that logic.

"I love you too, 'Mir."

He smirked. "Of course you do. Now, talk to your woman so y'all can fix this." Releasing my face, he pecked my forehead and then turned to Cyn. They slapped hands and he pulled her into a hug. When she nodded, I realized he was saying something to her, but it was over quickly, and they separated and Samir was out the door in the blink of an eye.

And then it was just me and Poppa standing in my living room.

"Can I—"

"Do you—"

We both started speaking at the same time, and it was so stupid and awkwardly cliché that I cringed and then immediately busted out laughing. She joined in and thankfully moved from by the front door, coming closer to me.

"You go," I insisted, waving a hand at her.

She nodded and spread her arms. "Can I hug you?"

I bit my lip. My first instinct was to be upset that she felt she even had to ask, but that was silly. Poppa was only respecting the boundaries that I'd laid out two weeks ago. In lieu of speaking, I stepped into her arms and pressed my face into her shoulder. Wrapping her arms around my back, she squeezed me so tightly that I immediately teared up—not because it hurt. It didn't. But because of what she was saying with that embrace.

When her lips touched my temple, I lost it, full-on sobbing as if I hadn't already cried buckets with Samir just fifteen minutes prior. How I had any saline left was a wonder.

Poppa clung to me, kissing me and humming a melody I didn't recognize, but was soothed by nonetheless. We stood there, in the tri-state area where my foyer, living room, and kitchen met, hugging and rocking from side to side, and it was so pure and nourishing and *healing*. Without a word being exchanged between the two of us, I felt refreshed, renewed. And when we finally separated, Poppa met my eyes as she grabbed my hands and squeezed them.

"Yeah?" One word that translated into several questions. I heard each and every one of them.

So, I nodded. Because *yeah*.

I was okay. I was better than okay. Now, I could say the things that I'd been hiding inside of my heart without anxiety about what would come after. Now, I knew that even if I lost Poppa, I wouldn't lose everything; I might lose her, but if I had to pretend to be something I wasn't just to make her feel comfortable staying with me, then I would lose myself, and that was the one thing I couldn't afford to lose.

So, I nodded again. And then I pulled out of her grasp, and then her embrace. And then I took a couple of steps back, putting some space in between us, giving myself some breathing room to say what I needed to say. It wasn't much, but it was a lot.

"Poppa, I'm bisexual. I don't know why we never really discussed this before now, but it's not something I'm ashamed of, and it's not something that I hide. It is who I am and it is not going to change."

"I know—"

Shaking my head, I held up a hand. I couldn't let her interrupt me because then I would get wrapped up in her words and forget to finish sharing my own. This was important.

"Let me finish. I'm not going to waste my time defending myself to you because I'm worth more than that. You've known me for three years, and if you suddenly think that I am capable of deceit and abuse solely due to the fact that my most significant romantic relationship before you was with a man, then it is *you* who isn't worthy of *me*. I'm human, so I'm in no way perfect, but being bi is not and has never been one of my flaws."

So, get it right or get left!

I didn't say that last part out loud though, because as much as I believed in what I was saying, I didn't want Poppa to go. I loved her so damn much that if she chose to stop fuckin' with me because of this, it would crush me. It wouldn't end me, 'cause I'm a survivor, but I'd be down atrocious for a while.

I took a breath and blew it out through my nose. "I need you to respect me enough to not only acknowledge all parts of me, but to not treat me like shit out of habit because you're insecure. You let that girl kiki all in your face, hugging and kissing all on you in front of me when you didn't even want her, but you hugged and kissed on me in private, and acted like nothing had changed between us in front of everyone else. That was so disrespectful and it *hurt!*" My voice cracked on that last word and I squeezed my eyes shut to stave off the tears that threatened to crash the party. When I felt like I was safe from another crying spate, I reopened my eyes and met Poppa's gaze.

"Can I speak now?" she asked, her voice low.

Having said my piece, I nodded and wiped the sweat from my brow.

"*Baby,*" she began, and my knees went to trembling. She was playing dirty already because *why* did she have to use that tone? Why did she lead with *baby?*

"I'm sorry that I was too scared of change to lean into my feelings for you. I'm sorry I didn't shut things down with Jackie from the moment I realized that she couldn't make my heart skip several beats the way it did just from me looking at you. I'm sorry I allowed that fear to manifest as some hateful shit coming out of my mouth, instead of just owning up to how things had evolved for us.

"Part of me wishes I could go back and stop myself from saying that dumb shit, but another part of me knows that wouldn't change anything because, even though I didn't mean it the way it sounded, my thinking was still fucked up." She paused, dropping her eyes to the ground and shaking her head before lifting her gaze back to mine. The passion I saw in those dark brown depths stole the breath from my lungs.

"I see you for who you are and there isn't a damn thing about you that I would change—from the color of your toenail polish, to your sexuality, to the way you like your food to touch. All of that combined is part of what makes you, Juleesa Marie Jones, my best friend and the love of my life. You're my metronome—when shit feels off pitch and out of key, I know all I need is a few minutes in your presence to get my life back in rhythm. You're that exactly as you are right now, and I'm sorry that I made you feel like you have to defend yourself. I don't know what I have to do to make up for the way I hurt you, but I want you to know that I'm prepared to spend whatever time necessary trying to figure it out."

Though my heart swelled at the sincerity in her voice, my face fell at her last sentence. "That's not the type of life that I want, though."

Poppa's face scrunched and she tilted her head to the side. Confusion was written all over her. I hurried to finish my thought before she could jump to conclusions.

"We're talking about this right now because I don't want to spend the rest of my time with you rehashing this."

Her confusion melted away and was replaced with that undeniable emotion again.

Undeniable, not to be confused with unnamed.

Poppa loved me. Of that, I was never unsure. She told me with her words and showed me with her actions.

She closed the distance between us and linked her fingers with mine, holding our hands at our sides.

"Making sure that you're good, even if it's ten years from now, isn't rehashing. It's not stirring up old shit. What it is— what it *will be*—is me checking in. Just like you check to see if I ate, I want to check to make sure you're still comfortable and that I haven't unknowingly hurt you. That's the love I have for you." She lifted our hands up between us and stepped closer. "I never want you to think that I'm too comfortable to recalibrate."

A sob tore through me. I dropped my head, closing my eyes against the tears. Poppa placed my hands on her chest and pulled me even closer, letting my forehead rest against her shoulder, interlocking her fingers behind my back.

"I meant what I said at lunch the other day." Her words were soft but sure, spoken directly into my ear. "Unlearning the little shit hasn't been an overnight thing for me, but I'm committed to creating a safe space for you. I love who you are when you're free and happy, and I want you to be able to be that woman with me."

I inhaled and released a deep, shuddering breath. Poppa's fingers dug into me. I pulled back and met her gaze, allowing her to see into the depths of my soul as I spoke.

"I want to be that woman with you too."

Chapter Twenty-Three

Jucee

Real Lovey-Dovey Like

It was still dark outside when I opened my eyes. Stretching, I lifted my head and peered at the glowing blue numbers on the digital LED clock on the nightstand to my right.

Four fifteen in the morning.

Sighing, I rolled over onto my left, propping my head up on my elbow. This was my favorite time of day because, not only was the house still cool since the sun had yet to bust through the sheer curtains like the Kool-Aid man, but everyone was asleep and the house was still. When I was in college, this was the time when I'd do my homework, even though it had just been me and Granny. It was one of the many reasons why Samir thought exotic dancing was the right profession for me; I was a night owl to my core.

Lifting the covers, I peered over at Poppa. Face relaxed, hands pressed together as a resting place for her cheek, she looked so...perfect. Like she was exactly where she should be, here in my bed beside me. The soft slack in her face was so appealing. Like clay I could mold if I dug my thumbs in with the right amount of pressure. But even if she were clay, the only thing I'd create would be another one of her, because she was already everything. Literally everything. It was her. My Poppa. The woman I loved.

But this slumbering person in front of me was also Poppa in her rarest form. When her brows weren't pinched because she was deep in thought about the beat or melody or lyrics to a song. When her lips weren't twisted to the side as she fought to hold her tongue because somebody said something ignorant. Hell, even without her face being half-hidden by the shadow of the bill of a fitted cap.

She was just...being.

I saw so much more of her face this way. And, more importantly, I was able to stare at her as long as I wanted without her interrupting me with a heated look and a searing kiss. I loved those moments but sometimes I just needed to stare at her face in peace.

Cyndi Thomas. A product of Carissa and Marvin Thomas's love. A Mission Bend girl that tried to claim SWAT every now and then. The dopest producer this side of the Mississippi. My Poppa.

That was my baby and I loved her so much it should've been terrifying.

And yet...

Lifting the cover a bit more, I scooted closer, being careful to keep my movements light so as not to disturb her before I was ready. There was barely a foot of space between us, so in seconds her body heat was warming me, the first indicator that I'd breached her bubble. My lips curved up at the feeling. I was so head-over-heels about this woman that the mere sensation of being heated by her internal temperature had me a lil moist between the thighs.

And I wouldn't change a thing.

I continued moving until our knees touched and her cloth-covered titties brushed my own. Once I was as close as I could be without being on top of her, I lifted my chin and placed a feather-light kiss on the tip of her nose. Then I leaned back and waited.

Nothing happened. She didn't move a muscle outside of her chest slowly rising and falling. I repeated the action on her exposed cheek, the one not pressed into the pillow, and waited for her reaction, but there was none.

That wouldn't do.

Raising my leg, I eased it over her hip, bringing our bodies a few inches closer together.

"Poppa," I whispered as I leaned in and pressed a soft kiss at the corner of her mouth. "*Poppa*. Wake up, baby." I punctuated each word with another kiss.

By the time I was saying "baby," Poppa was stirring. Her eyelids fluttered for a moment before she cracked one open. The slit was so small that I couldn't even see the white around her pupil, and couldn't even be sure she was wholly looking at me.

Grinning, I pecked her lips. "Good morning."

She grumbled something low in her throat that sounded like "What are you doing?" and then she closed her eye again. Knowing that once she was awake she wouldn't immediately fall back to sleep, I waited once more.

With a yawn, she rolled onto her back and stretched. I started to retract my leg but she quickly dropped a palm onto my thigh, holding it in place. Instead of being at her hip, my inner thigh was now draped across the divot between her thighs where I prayed a furnace was slowly heating up.

Fully stretched, Poppa turned her body back toward me, sliding my thigh higher up on her hip and pulling me even closer. Our bodies were flush against each other and my heart rate was quickly spiking as the early-morning lovemaking I'd initiated became a reality. Then she leaned into me, her head fitting into the notch between my neck and shoulder. I blew out a breath through my nose and immediately sucked another one in, inhaling her scent greedily while I waited for the press of her lips to my skin. My mouth fell open in a gasp when she pulled her head back and dug her teeth into the skin at the base of my neck. I then immediately expelled that air when she gripped the gusset of my panties and a first then second thick finger briefly pressed against my lower lips before sliding between them, moving up and down through the wetness that had been there when I'd awakened.

"*Poppa*," I whined, sucking my bottom lip into my mouth as my eyelids lowered of their own accord. "I wanna eat your pussy."

"Mmm," she hummed. "You shoulda just did that shit. Now, I'm gonna fingerfuck you until you cum on my hand."

And then she breached me and my toes instantly curled at the delicious intrusion. I grabbed onto her shoulder with one hand and cupped one of my titties with the other, thumb and forefinger finding my already-stiffened nipple with ease. She pumped once, twice, three times before pulling out completely and returning with two fingers. I cried out; I couldn't help it. The intrusion felt so damn good.

Narrowed eyes met mine and Poppa smirked at me.

"You better not wake up my baby," she grumbled, her voice still rough with sleep.

Biting my lip, I nodded. I knew when I started this that the goal was to get to breakfast in bed before Amani woke up. It would fucking suck to rouse him ahead of time and not get my chance to moisturize my face with Poppa's pussy.

The kiss I'd been expecting before finally landed, Poppa's lips brushing over my collarbone before sweeping up my neck and along with my chin as she steadily fucked me. My breaths were coming in pants and pressure was building in my middle. A moan slipped from my lips. A little one though, nothing too crazy.

Her head popped up and our eyes met.

"Baby," I whispered pleadingly. Not sure that I was asking for anything more than for her to keep doing what she was doing because if she stopped I might spontaneously combust, and that would be sure to wake Amari.

And because she was first my friend and she knew me, Poppa heard the unspoken request in my single endearment.

Stretching my neck, I met her halfway as she kissed me, our tongues touching just as she pulled free of me and used her wet fingers to assault my clit with short, deliberate strokes. This time, she caught my cry on her tongue and swallowed it down, slipping her free hand underneath my head to grab the back of my neck. The kiss was sloppy and messy, our mouths open, tongues dancing. I breathed through my nose, filing her scent away with every inhalation, knowing that at some point later in the day I would want her, and the memory of her unique aroma would sate me until I could hold her in my arms again.

With Cyndi Thomas, I was a *goner.*

Unequivocally.

My head was a film reel of moments from the future. Flashes of us spending our lives together, growing in love, growing as women—as parents. There were family vacations to Disney World and Christmas pictures with matching pajamas, meals cooked together, restaurants tried together, award shows attended as dates, matching outfits and—*oh!*

The crest of the orgasm that had been steadily building inside of me surfaced and my back bowed. Breaking our kiss, I closed my eyes and tilted my head back.

"Hell naw," she murmured as she used her hand on my neck to bring me right back to her. "Bring those lips back here."

"Baby," I panted. My eyes watered. The pressure was mounting and I felt a sharp stab of panic that I might actually wake my son by screaming my head off.

"Juleesa Marie," Poppa gritted.

All I could do was blink at her. She hadn't stopped nor slowed her strokes and I was about to fucking cum and yet she was being so fucking *demanding.*

"Gimme. My. Mutha. Fuckin'. Kiss."

I surged forward, my teeth clacking against hers, our lips fusing together just in time. Tears fell from my eyes and my body shook as I came. Poppa held me, swallowing the sounds that would've surely roused my baby until they faded away and all that was left were hitched whimpers. Then she cuddled me, murmuring words of encouragement and praise. She kissed my lips and eased her hand from between us. I watched, eyes low and lids heavy, as she sucked my essence from each of her digits. And when she was finished, she tilted her chin up, just slightly.

It was an invitation, one I recognized and immediately accepted. The kiss was both salty and sweet. Unhurried, lazy like the dawn of the day easing upon us behind those sheer curtains. I sucked my own flavor off of those lips and tongue and then rolled her onto her back as I climbed on top of her. Her smirk was so fucking sexy; I couldn't wait to watch the way it morphed into something else.

Sliding down her body, I took her boyshort briefs with me, tugging them off and tossing them up near my abandoned side of the bed. Her legs fell apart and I dropped a kiss onto her inner thigh as a reward for her being so helpful. With a hand on either side of her pussy framing my favorite dish, I laid flat on my stomach and dived in, spreading her lower lips with my tongue and nosing her clit. She was already so wet, evidence of her arousal pooling at the base of her opening, calling out to me like the "Hot Now" light at Krispy Kreme. Curving my tongue, I scooped it out and swallowed it down, her flavor dancing along my tongue and making me ravenous.

The low twinkling of my phone's alarm ascended, letting me know that I only had about half an hour before my baby would come jumping into the bed with us. Slightly disappointed at having to trim my full-course meal down to a quick bite, I swiped my tongue up and down Poppa's sopping pussy before shoving my whole face in and sucking her clit into my mouth as if I'd been a Hoover in a past life. Ten fingers dug into my scalp, twisting up in my braids and tugging.

The slight sting turned me on something fierce and in return, I ate Poppa like she was a ripe mango freshly plucked from a tree. I slid my hands underneath her, digging my fingers into her plush ass as her juices dripped down my chin. When her thighs began to cosplay as earmuffs, I knew she was close. Retracting one hand, I pushed two fingers inside of her and curled up, beckoning her orgasm to me as I increased my suction.

"Shit," she panted, lifting her butt to press her pussy even closer to my face. I took it all, humming with pleasure, wanting every bit of the way she was losing control. Needing her to enjoy this just as much as I did.

Her pussy tightened on my fingers just as she started fucking my face, and I was in heaven. I might've been moaning louder than her. No. I absolutely was because Poppa had managed to keep her voice low this entire time, showing me how she felt with her body instead of verbally.

It was admirable and annoying all at once. I wanted to hear the desperation in her voice—wanted to hear her begging. But that just meant we'd have to run this back, and that was quite okay with me.

Poppa came with soft grunts, her back bowed as she pressed

my face into her and clamped down on my fingers. Seemingly boneless, she collapsed back against the bed and released me.

Crawling over her, I draped a thigh across her body, an echo of our positions just an hour earlier, and nuzzled her neck.

"Good morning," I whispered, completely sated and filled with love for her.

Chuckling, she lifted my chin and kissed me as if we had all of the time in the world.

"Good morning, baby," she cooed as she slowly pulled away before slapping a hand down onto my ass. "Now, get on up so we can shower real quick before baby boy comes in here."

Grinning, I did as she said, relishing in the sting of her touch, giggling like a schoolgirl as she climbed out of bed behind me, hands firmly planted on my hips as she followed me into the bathroom.

Chapter Twenty-Four

Cyn

Been Around the World

"Something is in the air, man. There seems to be more fine-ass women in here than usual."

Smirking, I shrugged at Cody's comment and leaned back in my chair. We were back at Sanity, waiting for Jucee to hit the stage and dance to a new, unreleased track of mine. A quick look around proved he was right though. Sanity was a safe space for the community, so it always attracted women, but today was different. The place was packed more than usual and I didn't know why.

Samir and Morgan had joined us tonight. Before everything, I would've been insecure about Samir being in the building, but I understood that he was important to Jucee. Their friendship meant a lot to her. He was a part of her village.

So was Morgan. And Mercedes. And Mal. And hell, even Cody's goofy ass.

And I was there too, pulling double duty in a way no one

else was privileged to. Holding on to fears from my past had me in such a chokehold that I'd almost lost out on that privilege.

Jucee killed her set. The song was more upbeat, made specifically to inspire ass-clapping, and she delivered in spades. I watched the room go bananas, people standing on chairs, folks bent over with their hands on their knees. They were loving it. Mission accomplished.

Once Jucee finished and disappeared through the curtains on the stage, the lights came up and so did chatter about the song. I just sat back in my seat and soaked it all in.

I could see Mal across the room making her rounds as usual. Most everyone knew she was the owner, but some folks just watched her move because she commanded attention. When she made her way over to our table, I stood and embraced her. Standing back, she greeted everyone at the table before turning back to me.

"Your girl killed it tonight." Pausing, Mal eyed me. "She is your girl, right?"

Grinning, I nodded. "Yeah, she is. And you're right, my girl did amazing."

* * * * *

Acknowledgments

Before anything else, I want to thank every single queer Black woman and femme who found some way to let me know what *D'Vaughn and Kris Plan a Wedding* meant to them. You told me that you felt seen, and you felt heard, and you felt cared for. The love you poured into me was the fuel I used to write this book. I'm eternally grateful. And to my support system, those who encouraged and those who inspired me: thank you. My babies forever and always. My day one, my ace boon, and my voice of reason, Sapphire, Jaquana, and Jasmyn. Thank you. Thank you, Tasha, for #20kIn5Days and for the Wordmakers community. And last, but never, ever least, thank you to Romancelandia.

Read on for an excerpt of Chencia C. Higgins's
D'Vaughn and Kris Plan a Wedding,
a Black sapphic romantic comedy where a fake reality show
engagement turns into very real feelings...

Do you have what it takes to say I Do?

All Genders Welcome!
Ages 25–40

Are you single?
Are you queer?
Are you good at lying?
Do you have six weeks to spare?

If you said yes to all of these things, then you should audition to be a contestant on Instant I Do, the reality show where strangers are paired together in a race to win 100K each! Send us a headshot and a video no longer than thirty minutes telling us why we should pick you!

See you at the altar!

Week One

Chapter One

D'Vaughn

The Real Deal

"Are you just going to stare at it?"

Blinking out of my reverie, I looked up from the hefty, legal-sized, manila envelope that had been delivered directly into my hands not even an hour earlier, and stared at my best friend, my lips turned down pitifully. Pushing an obviously annoyed breath out through her nose, Cinta stomped across the living room and snatched up the envelope from where I'd placed it on the coffee table. Spinning on her heels, she stomped back across the room and leaned against the round bistro table that made up the dining area of the tiny apartment that we shared. Shooting a quick glare at me, she ran her fingernail underneath the seam, opening the envelope and pulling out its contents.

My heart lurched in my chest at the thick stack of papers now in her hands. *That had to be a good sign, right?* They wouldn't send me a ton of paperwork just to tell me that I hadn't been selected...right? Instead of voicing my thoughts, I stared anxiously at the woman who knew me better than anyone, watching her eyes rove the first page.

"What does it say?"

Ignoring me, Cinta pulled the first page off of the stack and tucked it on bottom, continuing to read in silence.

"Cinta," I called, getting annoyed that she was reading on while I was still in the dark.

She continued reading, moving the second page to the bottom. That was the last straw for me, because there was no way in hell she'd read the second page that damn fast.

Cinta! I screeched, shooting onto my feet.

Brows lifted, she swung her gaze over to me. "Girl, why are you yelling?"

I just stared at her, my face scrunched into a pout. Taking pity on me, she giggled and waved the papers at me.

"If you wanted to know, you could just read them yourself."

I took a single step toward her, lifting my hand to reach for the papers before pausing and shaking my head.

"I can't, Cinta," I whined, fear causing my voice to tremble. "I'm scared. Just tell me if it says yes or no."

Pursing her lips, she shuffled the first page back on top of the stack. "Well…" she drawled, her lips drooping with remorse. "I'm sorry to say…but both of those words appear on the page."

Releasing an indignant shriek, I flew across the room and snatched the stack of papers out of her hand. As my eyes flew across the first paragraph, my heart skipped at least three beats and my brain felt a little fuzzy.

Congratulations, D'Vaughn! We received your audition and believe you would be a wonderful addition to season three of Instant I Do.

The papers shook as my hands began trembling and the words blurred as my eyes watered. I looked up to find Cinta beaming at me.

"You're in, boo!"

I was in?

I couldn't believe it and wasn't sure if I should jump for joy or crumble onto the couch and cry.

Auditioning to be a part of *Instant I Do* had been a long shot. I wasn't a particularly outgoing woman and, although I was attractive, it was no secret that reality shows tended to put a certain style and shape of woman in front of the camera. Petite, with flawless skin. Dazzling smiles and relaxed hair. Skin so fair it was almost translucent. So aggressively heterosexual they were willing to fight another woman over a man offering community dick that was mediocre at best. In the more than twenty years that I'd been watching reality TV, it was clear what was the norm, and I was none of those things.

Well, I did have a dazzling smile thanks to three awkward years of orthodontia in junior high, and I was known to rock a bone-straight wig every now and then. That's where the similarities between me and the "norm" ended. Beyond that, I didn't tick any of the other boxes.

Yet, I held papers in my hands that said they'd chosen me. Far too often, even the calls for queer representation tended to leave out people who looked like me, but not this time. They'd accepted me in all of my cocoa-brown-skinned, plus-sized, and lesbian glory, so I suppose they were doing something different for season three. Brushing away the warm trails of tears from my cheeks, I read on. The first page informed me that I was to be a contestant on the show and then listed the contract, non-disclosure agreement, filming schedule, and terms and conditions that made up the rest of the stack. There was also a party I was required to attend where I would meet the other contestants. Moving back over to the couch, I sat down and spent the next hour silently reading through every page.

When I finished, I turned to Cinta with a wide smile on my face.

"Is this really happening?" I asked in a dazed voice.

Nodding, Cinta grabbed my forearm. She'd read everything just as I had, and knew the minute details of what I'd been tasked with for the next six weeks.

"Not only is it really happening, Vaughn, it's happening right now!"

"I can't believe this."

"You'd *better* believe it. I told you that you'd be great for that show."

"Yeah, but I don't—"

"It's not about how you look, D'Vaughn, even though you're gorgeous. I have no doubt that you could go all the way with this thing because you *never* bring anyone home. *Instant I Do* is all about convincing your family that you're marrying a stranger, right? Well, you're perfect for that because your family has no idea what your type is, so they'll believe whatever you tell them."

I gave her a skeptical look. In theory, what Cinta was saying might be true, but she was forgetting one crucial detail.

"Except..."

Cinta waved me off. "That's a small detail."

Furrowing my brows, I gave her a disbelieving look, only to have her raise her eyebrows. After a moment we both burst out laughing. I shook my head.

"A small detail, huh?"

She held her index and thumb an inch apart. "I might've went a tad overboard, trying to downplay it."

Snorting, I shot her another glance before straightening the papers in my lap. I had to sign them all and then have them notarized. "You think?"

Cinta sighed and leaned back against the couch. "It's likely to be a shit show."

Pushing a heavy breath out of my nose, I nodded. My hands shook with nerves at the knowledge that my deepest struggle was coming to an abrupt end. Placing them on my bouncing thighs, I dug my fingers into the flesh, grounding myself as I swallowed that anxiety down. This was necessary. It was past time for my family to know everything about me so that I could lose the stress on my shoulders and breathe easier. I hadn't possessed the ability to do it on my own, and now I was getting the backing of an entire network.

"Yep. It's probably the main reason they selected me. I mentioned it in my audition and their eyes probably lit up when they heard that. It's guaranteed drama."

"And that's what makes up these shows."

"It's what gets them millions of viewers every week," I corrected. I wasn't naive enough to think that my particular situation didn't have a hand in securing my spot on the show. In fact, I'd used it as bait, knowing that my personality was otherwise too plain to be given a shot and that I needed a hook. It wasn't in any of my paperwork, but I was sure that it had worked like a charm.

It got me in; now I just needed to make sure that it didn't get me kicked off the show.

Party Time, Excellent

The party was at a mid-rise condo on the outskirts of downtown, within walking distance of both Minute Maid Park and BBVA Stadium. I parked on the street and used the code from my paperwork to get inside of the gated building. There were two men already on the elevator when I stepped on, probably coming up from the parking garage one level down, and after nodding their way, I moved into the back corner and fiddled with my phone as a distraction. Inside of the canvas bag hanging from my shoulder was the signed sheaf of papers. Per instructions, I'd had them notarized before sealing them in the tamper-evident envelope that was also included in the box. It was all incredibly official and very, *very* real.

My stomach rumbled with nerves and I hoped that the men couldn't hear it. I stepped off the elevator and onto the eighth floor, taking my time as I walked down the eerily quiet hallway until I reached the right door. I knocked twice and stood back, willing my knees to stop knocking and my heart to stop racing. When the door opened, the sound of music and laughter reached me, and my nerves escalated. While I preferred to avoid large gatherings of people I didn't know, I wasn't the most awkward person in social situations. I knew how to hold my own.

Dropping my head back, I stared up at the giant of a man who stood on the other side of the door. He smiled and moved back, gesturing for me to enter. Clad in boot-cut jeans and a clingy, scoop-necked shirt, he looked significantly more casual than I assumed everyone would be.

"Hi there. D'Vaughn, right?"

Nodding, I stepped inside of the posh apartment and promptly froze when I caught sight of the camera pointed right at me. A second man, this one dressed in soft khakis and a white shirt that blended in with the wall behind him, stood in the corner of the foyer holding the large piece of equipment on his shoulder and motioned for me to keep going. I'd been expecting this, of course—today's event had been at the top of the list on the film schedule—but it still caught me a little off guard. Releasing a breath, I dipped my chin once, shooting the man who'd opened the door a quick glance before I continued into the apartment and observed the bright, inviting decor in the foyer. There was a chandelier overhead that highlighted the art on the walls and the two large plants in attractive, glazed ceramic pots on stands.

"That's me," I confirmed with a close-lipped smile.

The man behind me closed the door. "Welcome, D'Vaughn.

We're glad you could make it. I'm Kevin Henderson, one of the executive producers of *Instant I Do*."

Relief gripped me. No wonder he was dressed down; he was staff. Turning around, I held out my hand which he shook with a firm grip. "Pleasure to meet you, Kevin."

Smiling, he nodded. "Did you bring your paperwork?"

I reached into my bag and pulled out the sealed envelope, handing it over. His smile widened.

"Ah, excellent!" After tucking the envelope under his arm, he showed me the closet where I could hang my coat and bag, and then pointed me straight ahead, down the short hall of the foyer. "You'll find everyone else in there. Go on in, grab a drink, and mingle."

Facing the direction from which the noise level came, I hesitated, causing Kevin to chuckle.

"I promise you that no one in there will bite you."

Lifting a brow, I turned to him with pursed lips. "How can you be so sure?"

"We ran extensive background checks on each of you," he informed me, a somber look on his face. "No one was a biter back in elementary school."

Throwing my head back, I busted out laughing and he shot me a wink. In five short minutes, Kevin had managed to eradicate more than half of the nerves plaguing me, and I suddenly felt more at ease than I had all day. It was almost enough for me to forget about the man standing seven feet away, capturing our entire exchange.

"Okay," I conceded with a nod of my head. "I'll take your word for it."

He nodded toward the hall and, without saying another word, I took a deep breath, smoothed my hands down the front of my dress, and headed toward the noise. The sound of laughter erupted just before I entered the living room of the condo and I was grateful that just about everyone's attention was focused on the teller of the joke instead of the doorway that I had walked through.

The great room of the condo was divided in half, with a sleek, chrome-filled kitchen to the left, and a sunken living room decorated with a stylish leather sectional on the right. Cameras on tripods sat beneath boxed lights in each corner of the room, and two people dressed in all black circled the space while carrying cameras with furry microphones mounted on top on their shoulders. In the living room were six people standing in a semicircle, deep in conversation. They stood against one side of the room, next to one of the three large windows that overlooked the busy streets below, with the lit baseball stadium towering over residential and commercial buildings just a few blocks away. Nearly everyone in the group held a glass in their hands, and I decided that that was a smart move. Holding a drink would not only occupy my hands, but it would give me a reason to speak as little as possible.

There was an island in the kitchen with an under-mount sink and an eye-catching graphite countertop that currently doubled as a wet bar. It was covered with a cluster of glassware, an assortment of alcohol, a bucket full of ice, and several mixers and accompaniments. Shooting a cursory glance at the group of people on my right, I noticed one of the cameras swing toward me and hooked a mean left, heading straight for the island, and filled a ten-ounce tumbler with Jameson, chilled ginger ale, and a couple cubes of ice. I forced myself not to look up.

"Remember to act natural," Cinta had reminded me as she helped me get ready for tonight. It was so much easier said than done.

Clutching the edge of the counter, I took a fortifying sip from my lowball glass, allowing the crisp bubbles from the soda to coat my throat before I deigned to face the other people in the room. According to the paperwork I'd received, there would be a total of five couples this season, so it was likely that one of the six people already present would be my fiancée for the next six weeks. It probably wouldn't do me any good for my first impression to be that of a wallflower. Taking a breath, I girded my loins and moved across the room, being careful when descending the short flight of stairs into the living room. The absolute last thing I needed was to face-plant onto the gorgeous cherrywood floors.

I approached the group at a snail's pace, feigning as if I didn't want to spill my drink, but stalling until the last possible second. With my eyes over the rim of my glass, I observed the group. All eyes seemed to be on one woman who looked to be thriving under the attention. She was tall, with long pink hair that looked like it grew out of her scalp as it framed her mahogany-toned face and hung down to her waist. Cinta would have drooled over a wig so beautiful. A white bodycon dress molded to her substantial curves, curves that put mine to shame and made my heart flutter with joy at the same time. I'd fully expected to be the biggest person on the show this year, but whoever this woman was blew that theory into the stratosphere. Seeing another undeniably fat woman warmed my soul and made me tip an invisible hat to this season's producers.

The woman tossed her hair over her shoulder and lifted the wine goblet she held into the air. "We need to toast to *Instant I Do finally gaying up the show!*"

The group burst out laughing, and everyone raised their drinks into the air, knocking their glasses against one another in a ripple of clinks. Lifting my glass to my mouth, I giggled softly. I agreed wholeheartedly with her sentiment, and had said as much in my audition video. To my surprise, her eyes flitted over to me and she pursed her artfully painted lips, a playful look in her brown eyes, which were framed by thick lashes.

"Oh, no, ma'am! There is no way you're going to hide your gorgeous self over there, honey." Breaking the circle, she crossed the living room, her six-inch heels clacking elegantly against the hardwood floors as she made a beeline for me. Wrapping a hand around my wrist, she tugged me over into the circle.

All eyes were on me, and I knew without looking that at least one camera was likely zooming in on my face which was quickly growing hot with embarrassment. The last thing I'd expected was to have the attention of everyone present. In fact, it was something I had planned to actively avoid.

"Everyone," the woman announced to the small crowd, "we have a new arrival."

Lifting my drink in lieu of waving, I smiled and offered a lame "Hi."

The pink-haired woman turned to me. "What's your name, honey?"

"D'Vaughn."

"Nice to meet you, D'Vaughn. I'm Diamond."

"Hi, Diamond," I responded, a smile creeping onto my face. Diamond's energy was so infectious that it seemed impossible to not smile when around her.

Glancing around the circle, I found nothing but friendly faces smiling back at me. I received waves and greetings in return, continuing the job of putting me at ease that Kevin's friendliness had started. By the time we were all introduced, I felt immensely more relaxed.

"Miss D'Vaughn," Diamond began, stepping back to eye me from head to toe. "I gotta say, you are wearing this mint-green dress, honey!"

Smiling, I dipped my head and murmured, "Thank you."

A couple of people chimed in to agree, and my face warmed all over again. The short-sleeved, A-line dress with sweetheart neckline cinched at my waist before flaring out down to my knees. Cinta had made it for me as a celebration gift after I submitted my audition video, and when I'd tried it on there hadn't been a doubt in either of our minds that it accentuated my best assets. I took a sip of my drink, trying to think of a way to shift the conversation away from me, but before I finished my thought, loud speaking interrupted me.

"Aye! Party over here!"

Following the shout, we all turned toward the entryway as two people appeared. As I laid eyes on them, I involuntarily sucked in a breath, swallowing liquid down the wrong hole. Of course, I began coughing, bringing everyone's attention right back to me. I could have melted into the floorboards.

"I'm fine," I wheezed, waving everyone off as I tottered back into the kitchen to grab a handful of napkins.

Turning my back on the rest of the room, I tried—and failed—to clear my throat as quietly as possible. I was wondering how much worse things could get when a hand came to my back just as a cold bottle of water was pressed against my left palm. Gratefully, I closed my eyes and sipped from the bottle, sighing with relief when my cough slowly ebbed away. When I felt like I could breathe without choking, I sighed and turned to the kind soul who'd helped me, thanks already forming on my lips. The words died, however, when I found the very person who'd caused me to start choking in the first place.

The finest person I'd seen in a stone's age stood directly at my elbow, with her hand on my back and her face mere inches from mine as she bent to get a good look at me. We were the same height, which meant she was just a few inches taller than my five-five when I wasn't wearing heels, with smooth tawny skin that was dusted with light brown freckles across her face. Her hair was a mass of dark brown locs that hung around her face in crinkly waves. Her arms and neck, exposed by the short-sleeved button-down that she wore, were covered in colorful tattoos, and I counted at least six piercings just on her face and ears.

"You alright, beautiful?"

Her voice was as rich and smooth as the Jameson I'd been sipping on, and my tongue felt heavy in my mouth. I tried to say something so that I wouldn't just be standing there, staring at her stupidly, but nothing came out. Defeated and even more embarrassed, I nodded.

Offering me a small smile that made my heart flutter a bit, she tilted her head to the side. "Are you sure?"

I nodded again, wondering why the previously loud room suddenly seemed so quiet.

"I won't believe you unless you say something," she teased, her eyes crinkling at the corners.

"I'm fine," I croaked before taking another sip from the bottle in my hand. It wasn't clear if the water was now for my throat or my thirst, but it got my eyes off of whoever she was, and I considered that a victory. In my peripheral I watched her subtly lean away from me and drag her warm, brown eyes down and up my frame. I couldn't tell if she liked what she saw, and I quickly averted my gaze when she brought her attention back up to my face.

"Alright, beautiful. I'mma get out of your face, then."

Allowing myself to look her way, my eyes immediately fell to her mouth and I saw her smile widen in real time before she stepped back, putting a few extra inches of space in between us. She shot a glance over her shoulder before turning back to me and nodding slowly.

"I'll see you around, yeah?"

Again unable to formulate a response, I nodded and watched her walk away. Once she was out of the kitchen, it was as if the volume in the room had been raised back to normal levels, and I turned around to see that conversations had continued on in my absence. After getting myself together, I rejoined the group just in time to witness another round of introductions go up for the benefit of the two new arrivals. Unsurprisingly, Diamond took the honors, pointing out everyone and giving a quirky little tidbit about the person based off of what she had observed over the night.

There was Margo, the pansexual princess who was a little uptight, but had a great ass; Kirk, the bisexual boy-next-door with thick black curls streaked with blond highlights and a megawatt smile; and Tanisha, the lesbian femme who only dated other femmes and was obsessed with matte lipstick. Beside Tanisha was Nicolas, an unassuming guy who had declared with a shrug that he had no preferences "as long as the hole is wet." Finally was Bryce, who looked like a graduate of the Diamond School of Fashion. He wore a shiny bandeau top and miniskirt combination that matched both the sky-high stiletto heels on his feet and his robin's-egg-blue razor-cut bob. His beat was a level of perfection that made me want to burst into tears, and the bag he carried was from a line that was famous for its limited pieces. It was clear from first glance that Bryce didn't follow the culture, he *was* the culture.

Diamond went person-to-person in the small circle until she made her way to me.

"This is D'Vaughn. She's adorable and likes to hide from the spotlight."

"OMG!" I gushed. "How did you know?"

"I have a sixth sense about these things, honey," she declared, winking at me before turning her attention to the newcomers, the cause of my coughing fit and the person whose words had caught my attention in the first place.

"Now," Diamond continued, "since I haven't had a chance to suss you out, why don't you two introduce yourself to the class," She pointed at the gorgeous butch. "How about you go first, handsome."

The tattooed woman chuckled. "Thanks for the compliment, beautiful." She winked at Diamond before continuing. "I'm Kris. I was born and raised in Spring, but I live in the Montrose area now." She tapped a finger against her chin as she looked up at the ceiling. "Hmm, what's something interesting about me?"

Diamond propped a hand on her hip. "This humility has got to be an act."

Kris chuckled and my heart did that fluttering thing again when her cheeks lifted. I shot a quick glance around the circle, certain that I couldn't be the only one affected by her.

"It's no act. I'm incredibly boring on most days. Oh! Here's something interesting about me. I auditioned for *Instant I Do* because I want to find the love of my life."

My eyes widened to saucers, as did almost everyone else's. The group fell silent with varying looks of disbelief on our faces. After taking a look around, Kris laughed and nodded.

"I guess I don't have to ask if anyone thinks that's crazy. Come on, y'all, it's a love show."

"It's a marriage show," Margo corrected.

"Right," agreed Nicolas. "Love and marriage are not mutually inclusive."

Kris shrugged. "In my opinion, they should be."

Nodding, I observed her for a moment before adding, "It's a popular sentiment."

Kris met my eyes. "Indeed it is, beautiful. And it's probably what got me selected this season."

"Aside from the pure perfection that is your face, I'm almost certain that's the case, honey," Diamond mused, before moving on to the other person who'd arrived at the same time as Kris. They were a burly individual who towered over everyone else, wearing boot-cut jeans and a plaid button-down that was rolled up at the sleeves. Their face was beat with a crisp cat-eye liner, and an eyeshadow and blush that matched their shirt. They introduced themselves as "Jerri with an *i*," and instructed us to use they and them pronouns when referring to them.

After introductions, the conversation shifted to expectations for the upcoming season. A few people wanted to hear more about Kris's quest for love, but I needed to avoid her for my sanity's sake. It was bad enough that I almost choked to death at the sight of her, I didn't need to add "perpetually struck mute whenever she's around" to my contestant profile on the sea-son opener. Somehow, I was dragged into a conversation with Kirk and Jerri, but quickly begged off to refill my drink. To my dismay, they followed me, grabbing drinks of their own as they talked over my head about gender roles and what was expected of us during the season. Since I hadn't been familiar with the show prior to auditioning, I was genuinely curious, but had nothing to add to the conversation so I kept quiet. The tenth contestant arrived, and with them came a final round of introductions. This one was quick and dirty, with Diamond calling out names and folks waving from wherever they were in the room.

About an hour into the night, my feet started to protest my upright position. Although the dark green platform heels were usually comfortable, that was mostly when I was mov-ing around. Standing in one place and allowing my weight to settle made the shoes near torturous. Fully capable of appear-ing to be engaged in the conversation while sitting, I made my way over to the couch and eased down on the end, leaning my knees to the right and crossing my feet at the ankles. Almost immediately after I sat down, three other people joined me on the sectional, with Tanisha sitting next to me.

"Hey, Dee!" she chirped, pleasantly.

Dee wasn't a nickname that I went by, but I figured I'd let it slide for the night. If Tanisha ended up being my fiancée for the next six weeks, I'd correct her when we discussed strategy.

As if she had heard my thoughts, Tanisha sighed and leaned into me.

"You know, you are exactly my type."

My brows rose and an uncontrollable smile lit my face.

"Really?"

She nodded, brushing her microbraids over her shoulder and twisting in her seat until she was facing me. Her ombré lips pursed as she eyed me from head to toe, the undeniable interest in her eyes warming me from the inside and making me blush.

"Yep. To a T." She gestured at me. "All this pretty brown skin and those dimples? I love it. Then, to top it off, you're thick *and* know how to dress? Perfection."

Bringing a hand to my face, I covered my eyes, my cheeks hurting from how hard I was grinning. "Please stop."

Tanisha grabbed my hand and lowered it from my face. "Don't do that. Don't cover up that gorgeous face."

Dropping my eyes to my lap, I stared at the glass in my hand. I was on my second and final drink of the night, but I might be tempted to have another if Tanisha didn't let up.

Scooting closer to me so that our thighs pressed together, Tanisha bent her head to look at my face. "You're either not used to being complimented, or you're shy as hell and my attention is embarrassing you. Which is it?"

Lifting my eyes to her face, I tried to suppress my smile. "You are embarrassing the hell out of me right now."

With a nod, she scooted away from me just enough so that we were no longer flush against each other. "Alright. I'll ease up; but you should know that if you were my fiancée, I wouldn't."

"Well," I began, lifting one of my shoulders, "it's a possibility."

She shook her head. "Making you my fiancée would be too easy. When I said you're my type, I meant that you're the kind of girl I could fall in love with. This show is about convincing our family and friends that we are doing something unbelievable. Nothing about me and you together would be unbelievable."

I stared at her, lips parted, as I took in what she'd said. Tanisha's words made my heart beat a little faster. I could see her point, though. Although I didn't have a "type" in the traditional sense, my dating history tended to trend toward women who looked like Tanisha. With her caramel skin, pouty lips, and curvy shape, it wouldn't be hard to convince those who truly knew me that we were a thing, and from the attraction I felt toward her, and her flirtatious nature, I wouldn't even have to pretend that I was into her. But truthfully, my aim wasn't to convince my loved ones I was into a stranger—not exactly. I was here to do something that I'd been unable to do, but was wholly necessary. It mattered not if my match didn't make sense.

After I agreed with her, we moved on to a different topic, and she did as she said she would, easing up off of me. Able to breathe, I was in the middle of listening to Tanisha describe her perfect date, when I felt someone tap on my shoulder. Looking up, I saw a dark-skinned woman with a pixie cut smiling down at me.

"Hi, D'Vaughn. I'm Bethàny, one of the executive producers for the show. Can you come with me?"

Nodding, I stood from the couch and sat my empty glass on the coffee table atop a coaster, before smoothing my hands down my dress and following Bethany across the living room. When we reached the foyer, she made a right down a hall of closed doors before stopping at the last one on the right. She turned to me, a bright smile on her impish face, and spread her arms on either side of her.

"Are you ready?"

Cringing, I hesitated. "Uh...ready for what?"

Sensing my unease, Bethany shook her head and touched my arm. "No worries, D'Vaughn. It's just a little chat."

"Um, okay then. Let's go."

Bethany pushed open the door, entering the room first. I followed behind her, stepping inside of the bedroom and casting an assessing glance around. There was a full-sized bed bracketed by two nightstands against one wall, and a round, plush rug in the center of the floor. In the space between the bed and the door was a chair with one of those professional light umbrellas trained on it and a microphone dangling above it. A few feet in front of the chair was a huge camera mounted on a tripod. The lens of the camera was aimed at the chair.

Bethany gestured for me to have a seat and I did so gingerly, pressing my knees together and crossing my ankles demurely as I eased down into the chair, my palms sweating more than a little bit. It was a bit nerve-wracking sitting directly in front of a camera, but it was something I was going to have to get used to, at least for the next six weeks. Standing off to the side of the camera, Bethany smiled at me.

"Thanks for giving me a moment, D'Vaughn. This won't take long."

I nodded, curious about what I'd be doing. "No problem," I offered as if I'd really had a choice.

"This little setup here——" she waved at the camera and microphone "——is for what we at *Instant I Do* like to call the Jitter Cam."

That didn't sound promising. "Jitter? Like...wedding jitters?"

Nodding, her smile widened as she winked at me. "Exactly like that! And just like wedding jitters are a natural and normal part of the wedding process, we want your interactions with the Jitter Cam to be as natural as possible. You'll see different variations of this setup over the next six weeks. At random intervals each week, you'll take fifteen to thirty minutes to talk about what's going on, how the wedding planning is progressing, how you feel about your fiancée, et cetera, et cetera. Sometimes it will just be you and the camera, and you'll have the opportunity to speak your mind. Other times, it'll be interview style, with your executive producer asking you questions off camera."

"I'll be doing this several times a week?" That didn't sound too bad. I'd grown up watching *The Real World*, so the concept of a "confessional" was something I was familiar with.

"Generally, you'll only do one Jitter Cam per week, but it isn't unheard of to be pulled into a second or even third session after completing certain tasks during the week."

I nodded. "That sounds pretty painless. What's the catch?"

Tossing her head back, Bethany let off a short bark of laughter. "There isn't a catch. I promise."

Narrowing my eyes, I tilted my head to the side. "Well, we just met, so I have no idea if that promise is worth anything."

Still laughing, she shook her head. "You have a point. The good news is that you can talk about that as soon as I'm out of the room."

My eyes widened. "Wait, like...right now?"

Grinning, Bethany nodded. "Yep. There's no time like the present."

I pursed my lips. "That's the catch."

Her shoulders shook as she laughed again. "Nope. Still not a catch. We need to capture your reaction to the party."

"But the party isn't over."

"Which means everything is fresh. Don't think about it too hard; just give your initial reaction to what you've experienced thus far, and your first impressions of everyone. When the timer goes off, you can come on out."

I nodded and watched as she left the room, then I turned my attention to the camera in front of me. Taking a deep breath, I squared my shoulders and folded my hands in my lap.

Here goes nothing.

Jitter Cam 01-D'Vaughn

Um. This isn't awkward at all. Let's see. Well, so far things seem cool. The party is a nice way for everyone to get to know each other, but I guess I don't really see the point of it, since I won't see eight of those people after today. Speaking of those people, Diamond is a trip. She's hilarious and the complete life of the party. Whoever ends up as her fiancé had better be someone who won't fold under her dynamic personality. I know it won't be me, since she's a straight, trans woman. She's gorgeous though, and I hope she makes it all the way.

Um...Kirk is pretty funny. I think him and Jerri have hit it off. Actually, you know what? Kirk is a huge flirt and was up in Margo's face as well. Margo is...a lot. I mean that in the nicest way possible. She's very...severe...for lack of a better word. She reminds me of the stereotypical schoolmarm from a boarding school. Just unyielding and hard to please. Yikes. That sounds terrible. If you see this, Margo, I apologize. Anyway, um...I wonder what made her audition for the show, but I guess I don't have to wonder why she was selected. It would be a miracle if she can convince people that she is in love with someone, let alone getting married.

Oh, and Jerri is freaking hilarious. Whenever I'm around them, I laugh until my ribs hurt. Kris is...fine as hell. That's it. Just sexy as all get-out for no damn reason. Like...good luck to whoever is paired up with her, because you're going to need the strength of the gods to keep from drooling whenever you look at her. Matter of fact; let me say a prayer right now.

Lord, keep your hand on Kris's fiancée. They need you now more than ever because they won't be able to convince people they're marrying her if they're staring at her dumbly at every turn. Gird their loins and strengthen their poker face. Cross my heart and hope to die, stick a needle in my eye. Amen.

My mama would kill me if she heard me joke like that while praying. Lord, forgive me. Mama, if you see this, forgive me too.

Hosea seems cool, but something about him feels...disingenuous. Like...he's cisgender and *Very Manly*. He presents as heterosexual, but I wonder if he isn't hiding behind that facade. Now that I think about it, he strikes me as the type of person who isn't out to their family. As a fellow mothball, I recognize that in him and I'll be saying a prayer for him tonight. If he *is* closeted and is using this show as the vehicle to come out to his family—like *I'm* doing—I hope that the people he loves, love him enough to accept that being gay is a part of who he is and always has been.

Let's see. Who am I missing? I haven't really had a chance to talk to Bryce or Nicolas but I can't lie. Bryce is flamboyant and seems to have his eyes set on Hosea, which would be great television if they actually got paired together. Nicolas seems cool, if a little gross. He doesn't seem to be leaning toward any one person though. I'm still squicked out by that 'wet hole' comment. Why are men like this? Honest question.

Last but not least, there's Tanisha. Um...I...like her? I don't know why I said that like a question. I'm not unsure about it. I *like* her. It's weird to say that about someone I literally just met, but it's true. I like her energy. She's gorgeous and she smells so *good*, and she isn't stingy with compliments. I don't really have a type but if I did, it'd be her. Of course, I didn't say that to her, but I didn't have to, since she told me straight up that I was *her* type. That, um...that was nice to hear. She was pretty adamant that we wouldn't get paired, but maybe she'll be wrong. Who knows?

Welp, those are my initial thoughts about everyone. Here's to the next six weeks. Hopefully I'm not knocked out before we even make it to the weekend. I was gonna come out to my mama eventually...one day, maybe, but it would be so much easier to do with a camera around, since she'd rather die than present anything other than a solid family unit in front of others.

Ah, well. Wish me luck.

Will fake turn into forever? Pick up
D'Vaughn and Kris Plan a Wedding to find out,
available now wherever books are sold.

Copyright © 2022 by Chencia C. Higgins